MW00928729

ETERNITY

KAREN ANN HOPKINS

© 2017 Karen Ann Hopkins
All rights reserved.

ISBN: 1976235901
ISBN 13: 9781976235900

Praise for Embers and Gaia

"An impending apocalypse provides a compelling backdrop for romance in this page-turning first installment of a new YA series. Hopkins (*Lamb to the Slaughter*, 2014, etc.) expertly weaves her plotlines together in this compulsively readable teen romance story..." Kirkus Reviews

"*Embers* is the start of an action-packed paranormal YA series." InD'Tale Magazine

"*Embers* is an incredibly unique paranormal book!" Loose Time Reading

"*Embers* is an amazing paranormal, action, romance book!" Bookalicious

"Loved this book! *Embers* gives you an amazing account of the children that descended from the angels. I loved how the author gave the reader a scripture passage before each chapter. I give this book 5 stars!" Curling Up With a Good Book

"If you are a fan of paranormal or angel stories, I advise you to read *Embers*. You will love this story and will want more when the book ends." Gen Gen's Book Reviews

"This was a very entertaining and compelling read. I could not put it down or get enough and the world building is phenomenal." Bookish Escape

"*Embers* is without a doubt one of the most exquisite, breathtaking and romantic novels I have ever read. Totally epic! A must read! 5 stars!" Bittersweet Enchantment

"*Embers* is an amazing story that I highly recommend to those paranormal, angel book lovers. I was glued to the very end. 5 stars!" Sassy Book Lovers

"*Embers* was a brilliant Young Adult paranormal novel based on angels. I thoroughly enjoyed how fast paced and detailed it was." Nay's Pink Bookshelf

"Hopkins' refreshingly original idea is what makes this read truly worthwhile. Her world building is dark, bold and interesting and her characters are far from being black and white…" The Nocturnal Library

"Finally, a supernatural story to immerse myself into and thoroughly enjoy! Karen Ann Hopkins has come up with some very unique characters – angels and demons, like no other!" Bumbles & Fairy-Tales

"I would definitely recommend Embers to paranormal/supernatural romance fans." Books in the Spotlight

"This is a sexy and action packed paranormal that everybody is looking for, with supernatural characters that are completely unique and distinct. I absolutely recommend this to everyone!" Her Book Thoughts

"*Gaia* was an explosive read full of action and suspense." A Bookish Escape

"*Embers* and *Gaia's* stories match the true beauty of their covers and I absolutely cannot wait for more of this epic series." Such a Novel Idea

"This series is on my favorite angel-themed series of all time. This world is phenomenal." Pause Time Book Blog

"The plot was unique and riveting…I was hooked from the first few words of the books and didn't stop reading until I had finished the entire novel." A Dream Within a Dream

"Hopkins has written another brilliant page turner, with twists and turns, vivid details and captivating characters." Sassy Book Lovers

"*Gaia* is an explosion!" Her Book Thoughts

"This series by Karen Ann Hopkins is truly amazing!" So Bookalicious

"The Wings of War series is quickly becoming one of my favorite series!" Don't Fold the Page

Books by Karen Ann Hopkins

Serenity's Plain Secrets
in reading order
LAMB TO THE SLAUGHTER
WHISPERS FROM THE DEAD
SECRETS IN THE GRAVE
HIDDEN IN PLAIN SIGHT
PAPER ROSES

Wings of War
in reading order
EMBERS
GAIA
TEMPEST
ETERNITY

The Temptation Novels
in reading order
TEMPTATION
BELONGING
FOREVER
DEPCEPTION

This one is for my fans. Without your love of Ember's world, this book would never have been written. Thank you for the steady stream of encouragement. Your enthusiasm inspires me and keeps me writing

ACKNOWLEDGMENTS

Many thanks to Grace Bell, my editor and friend; Jenny Zemanek of Seedlings Design Studio, my amazing cover designer; and Heather Miller for her proofreading skills. The Wings of War is a success because of all of you!

I'm always grateful for love, encouragement and support on the home front. Thank you, Jay, Luke, Cole, Lily, Owen, Cora, and Mom, for everything you do!

Revelation 6:1-8

Now I saw when the Lamb opened one of the seals; and I heard one of the four living creatures saying with a voice like thunder, "Come and see."

And I looked, and behold, a white horse. And he who sat on it had a bow; and a crown was given to him, and he went out conquering and to conquer.

When He opened the second seal, I heard the second living creature saying, "Come and see."

And another horse, fiery red, went out. And it was granted to the one who sat on it to take peace from the earth, and that people should kill one another; and there was given to him a great sword.

When He opened the third seal, I heard the third living creature say, "Come and see."

And I looked, and behold, a black horse, and he who sat on it had a pair of scales in his hand.

And I heard a voice in the midst of the four living creatures saying, "A quart of wheat for a denarius, and three quarts of barley for a denarius; and do not harm the oil and the wine."

When He opened the fourth seal, I heard the voice of the fourth living creature saying, "Come and see."

And I looked, and behold, a pale horse. And the name of him who sat on it was Death, and Hades followed with him. And power was given to them over a fourth of the earth, to kill with sword, with hunger, with death, and by the beasts of the earth.

CHAPTER 1

SAWYER

Fires raged everywhere, almost too hot for my skin, which felt as if it was peeling off. I glanced down, unfurling my hand and turning it over. Angry red boils bubbled and I looked away. My ruined flesh didn't bother me as much as the incessant heat scratching at my skin and the acidic air filling my lungs. The constant drone of soldiers marching along the packed dirt roadway below made my head throb. The occasional shout of orders from a dark Angel interrupted the demonic procession, rousing me from my ominous thoughts.

My gaze followed the line of Samael's soldiers that stretched for miles and miles, until their malformed bodies blurred in the distance, blending in with the fiery hills where the pass went straight through the Gates of Hell. Before I'd been transformed, I would have shivered at the sight, but now, I merely sighed, wishing it would all end.

"You're even quieter than usual, Demon. What's on your mind?"

The voice was smooth and accented, sounding very civilized and polite. But the air around us chilled with his words, and I forced myself not to shake away the sickening tremor that consumed me. The Lord of Darkness was all charm and friendliness at first glance, until something upset him and the façade would drop away, revealing evil incarnate.

I turned to my commander, seeing his unfurled wings first. They were such a deep coal-black color that with flashes of light from the flames, some of the feathers appeared almost greenish. And when those wings were spread wide, it meant that Samael was in an especially foul mood.

Before I could answer, he tossed some of his long black tresses back with an angry shake of his head. His eyes narrowed and he licked his red lips. "Heaven's Angels are imbeciles. Brother Gab dropped his horn and some little man picked it up and blew it."

"The Horses of the—" I didn't get any more words out. Samael waved his hand and walked past me, stepping up to the edge of the plateau that jutted out above the roadway.

"Yes, yes, those horses." He took a deep breath, cupping his chin and tapping his mouth with his finger.

I willed my legs to work and stepped up beside Samael, only glancing his way long enough to see his focus was on the steady stream of his army moving from Hell into Purgatory.

Confusion clouded my mind. "I would think such news would make you happier…" I trailed off.

Samael tilted his head my way. His eyes were the darkest shade of blue, like pools of midnight. He lowered his voice, causing me to go on high alert. He was trying hard to stay patient with me. It was times like this I wondered why the commander talked to me at all. He was Satan, and the Apocalypse had begun. Didn't he have better things to do than hang around making small talk with me?

"I've grown quite bored of the shadow and fire that dominate Hell's landscape. Purgatory is incredibly dull. While Heaven has its perks, Earth is the real prize." Samael closed his eyes and pursed his lips, letting out a wistful sigh. "So many pleasures, so much pain."

His eyes popped open and he looked straight through me. "It's the humans that add such dimension to the place." Thrusting his arms into the air, his voice gained volume. "And my damn brothers are going to ruin everything!"

I hesitated, but now my own curiosity was raised. "So you don't want to the rapture to take place?"

Samael's wings folded neatly behind him with a *swish* and his shoulders slumped slightly. "It's all about timing, Demon. It's a game—a twisted game we play with the Angels and Father himself. I must tread carefully if I'm to win." His eyes shifted my way, his brow lifting. "I won't make the same mistake I made last time. Even though Father has been absent of late, He definitely isn't gone. I learned the hard way that He's much more powerful than I am."

"Then how do you hope to defeat Him?" I dared to ask.

His head rocked back and he giggled, the sound being both mesmerizing and terribly frightening at the same time. When he calmed, he took a quick breath. "Oh, I won't attempt to beat Him with strength this time." He grinned from ear to ear. "I'll usurp the Almighty with cleverness—beating Him at His own game. I think I understand what He really wants of mankind." His smile deepened and his eyes fastened on me. I couldn't help swallowing, but I didn't drop my gaze. "And I'm going to use that against Him."

"And what of the four horses arriving and heralding in the end of times? Does that interfere with your plans?"

The corner of Samael's mouth lifted. "That's why I like you, Demon. You get right to the point, and you talk to me with the authority of an Angel. But you're no Angel. Just a Demon." His smirk tightened and his voice came out in a firm whisper. "Don't ever forget who I am."

His change of mood was like a gust of wind, making me lean back, and clenching my dead heart. The air around us darkened considerably. Flames licked up my legs, spreading to the ledge.

"No, sir. I won't ever forget." I held my breath, waiting to be reduced to ash. The movement of the soldiers resounded in my ears. When nothing happened, I risked a glance at Samael. He was watching me with the sharpness of a hungry raptor.

I didn't know if I'd have the opportunity to speak to the Supreme Commander again, so I took a chance. "But what of them?" I gestured toward the troops, who were moving steadily in the direction of the place where I assumed they'd finally breach the fiery wall of Purgatory to enter the land of men. "If you plan to defeat God with your wit, what's all the fanfare for?"

The tenseness on his face melted away, and he suddenly brightened. "My physical battle is with the Celestial Host. My brothers aren't going destroy the one thing worth ruling around here. I won't let that happen. Earth will be mine. The men and women that inhabit it will bow down before *me*. They will provide me with a millennia of entertainment—and the only thing in my way are the Angels."

He took a step closer, spreading a wing out. A talon brushed my cheek, and it took everything I had in me to keep from being reduced to a mindless beast, falling at Samael's feet and begging for my life. That's what the Demons, Growlers, and all living creatures did when they faced the Supreme Commander; they lost their minds.

The talon scraped along my jaw and down my neck, and I felt blood bubble to the surface of my skin. I didn't attempt to wipe the drops away. I was a statue, waiting for the sharp claw to rip into me.

Those deep blue pools swirled before me and I couldn't look away. The beauty of Samael's face was unrivaled. And that made him even more intimidating.

"Tell me, was it the Watcher girl who gave you this strength to stand before me with such confidence?"

Watcher girl? I blinked. "Who?"

Samael dropped his wing and his irritation returned. "I must know for sure that you're mine, Demon. That no one else has sway over you or your heart. That is imperative to my plan—and my ultimate success."

"What do I have to do to show you that you're the only one who commands me?" I said through gritted teeth. I wanted Samael to trust me—to show favor to me.

"Never fear, Demon. You will have plenty of chances to prove your worthiness. The time is near."

A ruckus below wrenched Samael's attention away from me. I followed him to the edge of the plateau. A spider-like creature was eating the head of a Growler. The whip of a Dark Angel cracked into the monster's back, but it didn't stop ravaging its fellow soldier. The bloodlust was up and several more creatures jumped on the body of the fallen Growler. Their faces and torsos were human-like, but their legs bent in grotesque angles as they scurried around the body, trying to avoid the Angel's whip.

Samael winked at me. "Mustn't have that kind of thing going on in my army."

With a powerful thrust of giant wings that knocked me backwards onto the hard, flaming ground, Samael swooped off of the ledge, diving into the melee. I scrambled to the precipice to watch the scene below.

Samael didn't need a sword, ax, or gun. His hands were enough. He passed through the scrambling defilers like a black torpedo, and in his wake he left a swath of body parts and puddles of blood. Not only were the original instigators killed, but a dozen others as well. Growlers, Demons, and strange creatures littered the ground.

Samael flapped his wings and surged upward, leaving his destruction behind as he aimed for the front of the line. A few more

Dark Angels arrived swiftly, cracking their whips and spurring the soldiers to move on again.

A gust of wind at my back made me whirl around. Another Dark Angel stood, waiting. His skin was pale and his features bland. A few gray feathers from his outstretched wings fell into the flames crawling along the ground. They sparked and then sizzled, filling the hazy air with a burnt-hair scent that caused my nose to wrinkle.

"You're coming with me," he said plainly.

I nodded. I was ready to get on with it. I belonged to Samael, and proving myself was in the forefront of my mind. There were tickles of other things swirling around in my head, but the thoughts were only random bursts of confusion.

Whoever I was before Samael brought me here was gone.

I was Demon now.

CHAPTER 2

EMBER

The terrain around us was dry and the dirt path we followed meandered between bushes and pockets of small trees. A bird whistled and the smell of pine needles filled my nose. I stretched my legs to keep up with Eae's long strides, feeling Insepth's presence close behind me. Death and Conquest were taking up the rear, and I only caught the occasional word from their quiet conversation. It seemed hiking in the California hills was a fascinating side trip for the young-looking, platinum-haired Horseman, while Death, the older, stoic Horseman, was unimpressed.

Hot sunshine beat down on my head, and when we turned a corner around a prickly shrub, stepping into a grass-covered clearing, I shielded my eyes with my hand and looked up. At first, I saw only blue sky with a few wispy clouds, but after several blinks, a gleaming white structure began to materialize. The single tower didn't cover much ground, but it stretched straight up into the sky, narrowing to a point at a distance so far away, I had to strain my eyes to make out the top of it.

"How marvelous!" Insepth exclaimed. Pausing beside me, he craned his neck and shaded his own eyes as he gazed upward.

"It is the Tower of Angels." Eae sounded proud as he went on, "It was built nearly eight thousand years ago and has been moved a dozen times since then."

I dropped my hand and stared at the wingless Angel. "You actually move *that*—" I pointed at the monolith "—thing around?"

A small smile tugged at Eae's lips. He was definitely enjoying my incredulity.

"It isn't an easy task, but for Angels a doable one," he replied smugly.

"Why move it at all?" I retorted, regretting my harsh tone when my guardian Angel's brows shot up.

"The tower was created for us to monitor mankind. As humans multiplied and spread over the earth, we moved with them." He shifted his sharp gaze to the wide valley and the sprawling city there. In the distance, there were more of the dry, scrub-covered hills, and below our vantage point, not very far away, was the world-famous Hollywood sign.

Eae continued. "A few hundred years ago, we saw the expansion leading to this area, and with the convergence of ocean and mountains, decided it was a suitable place for our watch tower. It has always been an oddity to my brothers that the humans who came here first, without ever spying our Angelic tower, named their city, Los Angeles—The Angels." He rubbed his chin thoughtfully.

"And you use the same shielding magic we do to keep the humans none-the-wiser of its existence," Insepth said. His voice dripped with admiring approval.

Eae snorted. "Angel magic is far superior to that of the Watchers." His face scrunched. "But in theory, your statement is accurate."

Insepth winked at me before he took a swig of water from the bottle he had pulled from his pack. He offered it out to me and I stared at the bottle, my dry lips pressed tightly together.

"Go on, Ember. Take a drink. You need your strength." He wiggled the bottle in front of me. "This fast you've forced on yourself helps no one."

I swallowed the dry knot in my throat and turned away, staring at the smooth, glimmering surface of the tower. There were no doors or windows that I could see. Normally that would have made me ask a bunch of questions, but I didn't have the energy for curiosity anymore.

I closed my eyes and tried to *feel* Sawyer, but there was nothing— only a hole where our connection used to be. He was my friend, my guardian, and my one-time lover. He was also a Demon, and he'd done the unthinkable when he'd made a bargain with the Devil, saving me, but in so doing, damning himself to serve the Fallen Angel.

The image of Samael's wings wrapping around Sawyer, and them shooting into the sky was still vivid in my mind. I shivered. Everything was real. Demons, Growlers, Watchers, Angels, dragons, and even the Devil—they all existed. The end of the world was upon us. Despite that, all I could think about was the sadness in Sawyer's eyes when he walked past me to his doom.

From the beginning, I'd been inexplicably drawn to him, and after he'd become my guardian through Ila's magic ceremony, our bond had deepened. My mentor trusted Sawyer enough to bind me to him, but I'd always had my doubts. Not about his feelings. No, that was never in question. I knew he would do anything to save me, and he had proven it countless times by murdering my enemies. When he sucked the life out of Marshall, I'd silently rejoiced, but the apprehension of knowing that he would stop at nothing to aid me had been unnerving. Perhaps it was that I worried all along that his unfailing loyalty would be his undoing, or maybe it was his evil past that had kept me up at night. He'd been a Demon for over a hundred years before he'd even met me. I'd seen the horrible acts he'd committed during our bonding ritual. I wasn't surprised that the Devil had come for him. But it still hurt like hell that Sawyer was gone.

I wanted to go after him, to somehow save him from his torturous fate, but the others wouldn't let me. They'd explained how foolhardy it would be, and that even if I did by some miracle manage to pull it off, Sawyer wouldn't be the same. The taint of the Devil was real. Eae had told me about it in great detail.

So I was here in Los Angeles with my guardian Angel, a Watcher—who had been my mentor, enemy and maybe something more—and two Horses of the Apocalypse, waiting for the Angels to arrive. It was beyond belief, but I'd gotten used to insanity.

It didn't really matter anyway. The stabbing pain in my heart for Sawyer would soon disappear—along with everything else in the world.

I opened my eyes to the wary looks of four beings. Without meeting Insepth's gaze, I took the bottle of water and drank deeply. He was right. What good would it do if I fainted in front of the Angels? After everything I'd already been though, I wasn't about to wimp out now.

Insepth handed me a granola bar and I didn't argue. I forced it into my mouth and took a bite. The crooked smile the earth Watcher gave me settled my nerves. As long as Insepth had his humor, I could at least pretend everything was all right.

"Why are they keeping us waiting?" Death stepped forward, frowning. He was a tall, straight-backed man with gray hair and a hard face. Occasionally, he'd shake his head or make a long snorting noise that made me remember that his true form was a mighty black horse, whose sole purpose was to bring death to all humans on earth.

"It seems patience would be something your kind would be used to," Eae said with a tilt of his head in the Horseman's direction.

Death laughed and it sounded like a low whinny. "Before, we were in a different plane of existence, where time had no relevance." He threw up his hands. "Now, with the sun coming up and going down in our very presence, a sense of urgency fills us."

Conquest nodded, his eyes wide.

"Which plane of existence exactly are you talking about?" Insepth's voice was friendly interest, but I knew him better. He was always working an angle.

Eae clucked his tongue before Death or Conquest could answer the question. "That is of no importance at the moment, and certainly not something a Watcher needs to know."

I finished chewing the last of the snack and swallowed. "If we're all going to die, why does it matter?" I blurted out.

Insepth chuckled, but Eae was not amused. The Angel rolled his eyes in a very human-like gesture. "Until the time when God chooses to end it all, we will operate as usual."

"Won't it be a little late to have our questions answered then?" I said, my cheeks warming.

Eae's mouth thinned and he shook his head. "You don't have to know everything. That's one of the problems with humans, their insatiable curiosity."

Death cleared his throat. "The girl speaks the truth. The horn has been blown and my fellows and I have jobs to do. The mere fact that we're here signals the end of times is now."

The beating of wings filled my ears and I looked up. Sun glared behind two approaching forms. I caught a flash of red hair and I relaxed, pushing out a breath.

The wind from their pumping wings lifted my ponytail and I braced my feet more solidly to keep from toppling over. Uriel stepped to the ground, his long, fiery hair gleaming in the sunlight. He folded his crimson wings behind his back, making room for Raphael to land beside him. The brown-winged warrior had a boyish face, leaving him looking younger than Uriel. And where my descendant, Uriel's woolen tunic was woven of threads of red and tan, Raphael's was golden-colored. They were both tall, chiseled, and beautiful to behold.

"You made it here quicker than I thought," Uriel commented, his piercing blue eyes boring into me.

I shrugged. "I wasn't in as big a hurry as that one was." I gestured at Death, who raised his chin further.

Uriel continued to stare at me, making me squirm inside. "I trust no problems arose in the Watcher's eastern valley?"

My lips parted. Why can't the arch Angel just say Ila's name—or even the proper location of her valley in the Smoky Mountains of Tennessee? I got the impression that the arrogant Angel didn't want to acknowledge that Watchers had names or that places were named by humans.

"No one liked the arrangements. Horas and Ivan were especially irritated with being left behind," I answered truthfully.

Uriel's voice lowered to a threatening pitch. "It is not up to Demons and Growlers to make plans involving Angel business."

I shrugged. Uriel had saved me a few times, but that was only because he'd had sex with an ancient ancestor of mine, impregnating her, and creating a line of humans with blood ties to him. If I wasn't his long lost relative, he wouldn't have shown me the time of day, or worse yet, he probably would have already struck me down for being a Watcher. The only thing that Uriel held in more contempt than humans, was the offspring of Angels and mortal women, who then had magical elemental powers.

Everyone was quiet. Except for the birds chirping and the bushes scraping together in the breeze, the hillside was silent. I stared at

Uriel. His lips stayed pressed together for an uncomfortable moment before they softened and he blinked.

His voice was quieter when he leaned in. "Are your emotions in check and your mind clear?"

My cheeks burned. Uriel was referring to what happened to Sawyer. He was probably worried that my guardian being ripped away from me by the Devil was going to reduce me into a sniveling, emotional mess.

"I'm fine," I said tightly.

The Angel's brow lifted and his mouth opened to say more, but Raphael cut him off.

"Such talk can be left for later. The child has her wits. I told you not to worry so." Raphael acknowledged me with a short nod and then stepped aside, motioning me to pass with an outstretched arm.

When I hesitated, glancing at Insepth, Death took the lead, brushing by me. Conquest offered me an apologetic shrug as he joined Death, walking toward the tower. The scent of horse hair filled my nose and I inhaled the pleasant smell. I probably would have been more intimidated by the Horsemen of the Apocalypse if I wasn't such a horse lover. Mostly I was just in awe of them.

Insepth flashed a look of firm determination, but waited for me to take the lead. Eae forced an encouraging smile, but I wasn't fooled. He was as nervous about the Angel meeting as I was.

I searched inward until I felt the hot fervor of Fire, the solid strength of Earth, and the emotional caress of Water. Air was hiding, but I knew it was there, too. The elements gave me the confidence I needed to step forward and in between the two warrior Angels. Now that my guardian was gone, I would have to rely even more on my Watcher abilities.

But as I tilted my head to look up at the windowless tower, a chill passed over me. And even my Fire couldn't chase the feeling away.

Now that I was close to the tower, I could see flecks of blue, green, silver, and gold peppering the glazed white marble. I reached out to place my palm to what I imagined was cold smoothness, when Raphael snatched my wrist in the air. His cool hand gripped me tightly and all my elements flooded me at once.

His usual smile turned into a hard leer and I realized that for all of Raphael's boyish charms, he was just as deadly as the rest of the Angels. "Only Angels may touch these walls with their hands." He lifted his chin in Insepth's direction. "We have lifted our magic to give the two of you passage in this holy place. Do not become arrogant in your standing among us. You are only Watchers. You have no rights here—and even God has forsaken your kind." When my eyes narrowed, Raphael leaned in close. Tingling energy emitted off of him, thrumming my heart faster. I held my breath when he whispered, "I am trying to help you. Don't be fooled into complacency. You have no friends here. Uriel, Eae, and I are the only ones who will not strike you down in a heartbeat."

His tone was so serious, I nodded back, unable to tear my gaze away. Raphael's brown eyes seemed to sear a hole right into my very soul. Abruptly, he stepped back and nodded to Uriel, who placed his palm against the stone the same way I had been about to do.

Angelic writing and strange markings appeared, and then there was the sound of crunching rock. A doorway-shaped slab appeared and dropped back, leaving an opening in its wake. A cool breeze blew out from the darkness, extinguishing the warm California air. Uriel stepped inside, with Death and Conquest close on his heels. Raphael waited with hands laced in front him.

I glanced at Insepth, who looked equally as worried about stepping into an Angel warded building as I was, where the only doorway we knew about would probably disappear behind us once we entered.

"I suppose they've had ample opportunity to kill us already and they haven't done so," Insepth said with a slight smile before he advanced through the doorway.

Eae inclined his head. "You readily plunged on a dragon's back into Purgatory, but you hesitate on the threshold of Angel domain. I don't understand."

"She's afraid of Angels. Who can blame her?" Raphael said in a level tone.

"This Watcher girl is afraid of nothing," Eae retorted.

I held up my hands. "You're both wrong." I looked at Raphael. "I'm not afraid of Angels, just wary of them." I turned to Eae. "And I'm always afraid—afraid of losing the people I love, like I lost my parents, Piper, Ila, and Sawyer. I never want to feel that hurt again."

Every fiber of my being buzzed with adrenaline as I stepped into the dimly lit interior of the tower. It took a moment for my eyes to adjust, and then my mouth dropped open. The inside of the tower was completely vacant, just the same marble walls, curving into the floor with no visible seams, almost as if the entire building was carved out of a single slab of stone. The only light illuminating the inside of the structure were faint sun beams, streaming through the openings at the highest peak of the tower. I could barely make out the golden shine of a platform of sorts suspended in midair close to the very top.

"What purpose does a hollow building serve?" I asked no one in particular.

"Things aren't always what they seem, child," Raphael said. He pointed to the floor. "The same length of tower that soars above the ground, is drilled into the earth beneath. That's where the more mundane activities occur."

"I gather the meeting is up there?" Insepth flicked his hand skyward.

"Of course. Shall we proceed?" Raphael unfurled his wings, spreading them wide. A few brown feathers fluttered to the floor. It was then that I noticed other feathers of every color littering the expanse of the giant room.

"Seriously?" I asked, noticing Insepth's pinched expression.

"We don't need stairs or elevator devices in this place. Only our wings." Uriel turned around and motioned for me to step forward.

I'd ridden on a dragon's back. Catching a ride from an Angel couldn't be that bad.

The burst of colors at my side startled me. Death was suddenly a black horse, but not an ordinary horse. He reared up, jumping into the air, and as he surged upward, a cloudy mist rolled out beneath him. His shrill whinny seemed to shake the walls as he took flight. Another burst of colors, like an explosion of autumn leaves, erupted, and a snow white horse joined the black one in the air.

I watched Death and Conquest, engulfed in the clouds they created, carried to the top of the tower. Their hooves striking stone sounded loudly, *clip-clop, clip-clop*, when they landed on the platform. The power and magic of the Horsemen left me so breathless, I hadn't noticed the newest arrival until the Angel was beside Eae, talking quietly to him.

The Angel's wings were ebony, matching his skin. The tunic he wore had silver threads that gleamed even in the low light at the bottom of the tower. Eae nodded, and the Angel's wings circled around him. A second later, they were ascending, the gust from their departure snapping my face.

The image brought back the memory of the Devil taking Sawyer away. I swallowed and quickly shook the vision from my mind. Without looking at Insepth, I stepped up to Uriel. His arms encircled me, and then his wings. The force of our bodies rocketing away made me press against the Angel, grabbing at his muscled sides with my hands. It was over before I had much time to think about it. He deposited me beside Inseph, who looked equally unstable when Raphael released him.

I blinked several times, seeing spots, and swallowed down the hot juices that rose in my throat.

"I apologize for the speed. We don't really have a slow motion take off," Uriel said.

I nodded and Inseph reached out to steady me. When I could finally focus on my surroundings, a warm breeze brushed my face, and streaks of sunlight painted the marble beneath our feet. I couldn't raise my chin to see the Angels who stood in the center of the dais. The brightness they were emitting made it as painful to look directly at them as it was to stare at the sun.

"We have guests. Surely you will allow them to gaze on your magnificent faces?" Raphael called out. There was a hint of mocking in his voice that made me wonder about him all the more.

The room dimmed and I raised my face. There were a dozen of them, but my eyes were quickly drawn to Michael. He was the tallest of them all, and his silver armor shimmered with a light all its own. His hair fell long and blond on his shoulders, and his hand rested on the hilt of the enormous sword at his hip.

I licked my lips, remembering how he had turned tail and run away when Samael had arrived with his army of Fallen Angels. For all Michael's mighty glory, even he had known he was no match for the others. My attention slid from Michael's scowling face to the black-haired Angel at his side. My heart beat harder in my chest as I grasped for my elements. But they were trapped deep inside of me by the Angel's warding.

"That one—" the Angel bellowed, pointing at me "—is mine!" His knee bent and then he was pummeling toward me, like a missile.

It happened too quickly to move a single muscle. His talon scratched my face, and I closed my eyes, ready to be obliterated, when a voice shouted, "Gabriel!"

My eyes popped open just as Gabriel was yanked backward, a glistening golden rope looped around his waist. On the other end of the rope was an Angel I hadn't seen before. He wasn't as tall as Michael, or even Uriel, but his shoulders were broad and his muscles bulged. His azure wings matched his tunic, and his trimmed beard was dark and curly. He looked like a heavy weight wrestler, and when he jerked the rope, Gabriel fell, cracking the stone floor when he landed.

"You will not pass judgment on this girl. That is our decision to make together, and she has come here at my invitation," the stout Angel's voice boomed. I covered my ears, trying to block out some of the sound.

As Gabriel climbed to his feet, his eyes never left me. "Her fate belongs to me, Raguel. We are equals, and I will not stand down."

Michael stepped forward. His white wings shook and his eyes flashed. "I feel your same frustration, Gab, but Raguel is right. He was chosen by our Lord to uphold justice, and his decision trumps your desire for vengeance." Michael lowered his voice. "Once the immediate threats are dealt with and order is restored, I'm sure Raguel will give you leave to punish the Watcher for interfering with your captive in the way you see fit."

"Don't offer promises on my behalf, Michael," Raguel said in a threatening voice.

Uriel and Raphael stepped up on either side of me. I felt dwarfed between their tall, muscular bodies, but ever so thankful they were there, as I recognized the pure loathing directed at me from Gabriel's dark eyes. Death and Conquest had returned to their human forms. Death looked bored, but Conquest's eyes were round with curiosity.

I didn't think either one of them would interfere to help me, but Conquest appeared more interested in what was going on. Insepth was a few steps behind me. I couldn't see him, but somehow, even without my Gaia, I felt his presence.

Gabriel's glare finally shifted, landing on Raguel. His eyes narrowed, and then a smile twitched at the corner of his mouth. There was a tension-filled moment of silence before he walked over to the gleaming wall and leaned back against it in a leisurely way as if nothing had happened. His glare returned to me and I looked away.

Another Angel stepped forward and cleared his throat. He was fair haired, tall, and slender. He moved like a cat. His wide-spaced golden eyes regarded me, but only fleetingly, as he surveyed the room. The marble walls were lined with Angels, and I wasn't sure when they'd arrived. A shudder passed through me. I was in the lion's den and I was totally and completely powerless.

The newcomer flicked his finger and Insepth moved forward, sliding in between me and Raphael. The Angel raised his hands, moving a finger within inches of each of our foreheads. Insepth flinched away, but I held my ground. I remembered when Azriel and Eae had said their goodbyes by placing hands on the other's foreheads when we were in Purgatory. If the Angels wanted us dead, they would have allowed Gabriel to have his way. We had no choice at this point but to go along with whatever the Angels had in mind.

His touch was feather light and crisply cool. I felt his invasion into my mind like the puff of a winter breeze. It was over quickly and the Angel's hands dropped to his sides again. He tilted his head.

"We welcome you. I am Phanuel, the seventh of the supreme Angels." He glanced at Gabriel, who still sulked against the wall. "You have nothing to fear while you are here. We simply want to talk with you."

"I thought this meeting was about our presence in this land?" Death came forward. His long face was tight with irritation. "Why waste time on these two?"

Phanuel glanced between Michael and Uriel. It was Michael who answered him. "Strange, unprecedented things have been happening, and most of them involve these Watchers." He gestured his hand at me and Insepth. "Her lover arranged for Samael and his followers to breach the barrier between the planes—something that should have been impossible. They were in Purgatory when the dam broke, and they were both at the site where two dragons were freed from their Angelic bondage." His eyes shifted to Uriel and he hesitated before saying, "I believe it's in our best interest that they're kept here with us, under lock and key, for the time being."

Gabriel's hoot sounded very uncharacteristic for an Angel, but I didn't look his way. Uriel's frown held my attention.

"This was not discussed with me, Raguel," Uriel said quietly.

"Because of your blood connection to the girl, it didn't seem sensible to tell you our plans of incarcerating her in advance," Raguel answered in a level voice. "But it was also not our intention for her to be killed by Gabriel in our presence, either."

"This is not right!" Eae said loudly, but I held up my hand to quiet him.

Silence fell on the platform as the sun dropped lower in the sky, causing long shadows to spread across the floor. I was tired—so very tired. For several months my entire life had been chaos. From the night I fled Ohio with Angus and Cricket to escape my aunt's abusive husband, my world had been turned upside down. There was a short time of bizarre normalcy when Ila taught me about Watchers and my powers, and when I went to the high school in the Smoky Mountains. I even attended a homecoming football game in Oldport. Not long after, the Demons killed my friend Hannah, and I'd felt the need for justice and revenge. The day I'd entered the compound to destroy the Demons seemed like an eternity ago, but not even a full season had passed. In the end, it had been Ila who had done most of the damage, coming to my rescue and finishing the monsters off for good. But since that day, I'd been constantly on the run, fighting Demons, Watchers, and Angels. I'd inadvertently brought destruction to an Amish community, and my best friend had been murdered because of her connection to me. Even a dragon had lost his life helping me.

And then there was Sawyer. My first and only love. He too had paid the ultimate price for following and protecting me. Death and chaos plagued me wherever I went. Maybe the Angels were right. I'd been fighting a war, for what? To stop an event that was foretold thousands of years ago—something that God wanted to happen?

I was being punished for my arrogance.

I stepped forward, swallowed the tightness in my throat, and raised my face to Michael's. My heart was so heavy. "You're right to keep me here." His head bent and his brows arched. "I wish I didn't even have these powers. I wish I wasn't a Watcher at all. I have been a menace—" I glanced at Uriel, who had his arms crossed "—and you must stop me."

"No, no, Ember—don't say that—" Insepth began, but I interrupted him.

"I will stay here willingly, but you must let Insepth go. He hasn't done anything wrong. Let him go, so he can spend what little time he has left with friends and the nature he loves so much." Michael's smirk made me angry, and I couldn't stop my voice from rising as I took the steps needed to stand directly in front of the arch Angel. "Why would you care about a single Watcher returning to his life, when that life is about to end anyway? Everybody is going to die, and then you and your friends will have a world without humans and part-humans. That's what you want isn't it—what you all want?"

A shadow passed over his eyes. It was indecision. My heart thumped wildly as Michael considered me.

Everyone on the platform seemed to be holding their breath. I didn't dare move a muscle. I was afraid Eae or Insepth would do something idiotic to rescue me. Maybe even Uriel. And that couldn't happen.

Looks passed between Michael, Raguel, and Phanuel. I heard Uriel sigh at my side. There seemed to some kind of non-verbal communication transpiring between the Angels. When Raguel finally spoke, I wasn't surprised.

"So be it, then. You will be confined here, and the other Watcher shall be released."

"This doesn't seem fair."

I turned in amazement. It was Death who had spoken. A kind of powdery mist emitted from him and I thought he was about to change form.

"It's none of your concern, Horseman. This is Angel business," Michael said with coolness.

Conquest snorted and everyone looked his way. Up until that moment, the fair-haired Horseman had seemed kind of tame to me, but now, his eyes sparked with raw energy.

"We came to this time and place because of your foolishness, Angel." His voice rose as he strode across the floor and stopped beside me. "Where is the order? Why have we not heard the voice of our Lord?"

My heart skipped and I wanted to tell Conquest to shut up, but my mouth wouldn't move. Insepth looked hopeful, and Uriel's face had brightened considerably.

Angels shuffled on their feet, glancing around.

"I admit that we have not heard from Him in a while, but we know His wishes and since the barriers are crumbling, we will prepare for the end as is stated in the Scriptures," Michael said.

"The time of man has come to an end! Get on with your work, Horsemen!" Gabriel pushed away from the wall, facing Conquest with black wings stretched wide.

Conquest didn't shrink back. He inclined his head and smiled.

Death joined Conquest, reminding me that they were a herd. His lined face twitched when he said, "We do not take orders from Angels, only our Lord and Savior. The horn was blown and we came. We now must learn where the Almighty One is, but your ignorance tells us we've come to the wrong place."

Gabriel snarled before he pulled his long sword from its scabbard with a scraping sound. The metal shone brightly in the waning daylight.

"Not this way, brother," Michael growled. He grabbed Gabriel's arm when it swung downward, catching it just in time before the blade struck Conquest's head. There was an explosion of colors and a gust of wind that knocked me into Insepth.

Before I could protest, Eae's hands were on my sides and I was being lifted into the air. I landed on Conquest's white-haired back, and I instinctively held onto his mane. I didn't really want to go with him, but everything was happening so fast. Out of the corner of my eye, I saw Raphael hoist Insepth onto Death's back. The brown-winged Angel drew a spear from the sheath on his back, and Uriel's sword was already clashing with one of the Angels who had swooped forward in Gabriel's defense.

My eyes widened at the sight. Angels were battling each other. Conquest's muscled back gathered beneath me as he pranced in place, sparks flying from his hooves when they struck the marble floor. I wrapped my fingers deeper into his mane, squeezing my thighs for balance.

Raguel's voice shouted above the commotion, and Michael slashed the air with his sword, causing a rush of wind that reminded me of the force he'd released to destroy Insepth's Biltmore replica, flattening the mansion in a few seconds. Everyone stopped fighting and struggled for footing. Except the Horsemen, who seemed impervious to the Angel's destructive blast.

"You will lower your weapons! I command you!" Raguel stood beside Michael in the eye of the storm.

As weapons were lowered, the wind lessened. A new Angel strode up and I recognized the black-cloaked figure with the round, tattooed face. The Angel of Death had arrived.

"Azriel, help us restore order here," Raguel demanded.

This was the same Angel who had slaughtered all the first born of Egypt, and we'd already met briefly in Purgatory. His eyes were a dead gray color and he moved across the floor in a floating manner. His mere presence had subdued everyone in attendance, even the flighty horses, who were still bowed up tight, but had ceased stamping their hooves.

"What insanity is this?" Azriel's voice was melodic and soothing. I wondered if he used the same voice when he killed all those Egyptian children.

"Simply a difference of opinion as to how we should proceed," Michael said, casting a hard look around the dais.

"We have more pressing matters." Azriel gripped his golden scythe. "The barrier beneath this city is crumbling."

"What! It's too soon," Raguel stepped up to Azriel.

"I have seen it with my own eyes." Azriel raised a slender eyebrow. "What will be our response, brothers?"

Before anyone could answer, there was a deep rolling rumble, and then the tower began shaking. The horses whinnied wildly as the marble beneath their feet shifted. A flock of birds burst upward beyond the window openings, and the sky dimmed to the grayish haze of twilight.

Conquest was about to bolt, but he paused, canting his head to listen to the Angels.

"We must seal the breach, and stop those that will enter from the underworld!" Uriel shouted, unfurling his wings to take flight.

"No! This is meant to happen—it's the beginning of the end and we mustn't interfere," Gabriel raised his sword, pointing it at Uriel.

I saw the same hesitation pass over Michael's and Raguel's faces.

"Our Father has not sanctioned this—and you all know it," Raphael said. "We must protect the humans, until we are directed otherwise."

Michael nodded, and Raguel lifted his arms, calling out, "Go to the breach and stop the evil ones from entering this sacred place. Uriel and Raphael are right. No orders have been given from our Father to begin the rapture. Something is amiss, and until we know for sure, we'll uphold our vow to care for mankind."

Chunks of marble the size of sofas began falling, and Angels swooped out of the way to avoid being hit. But when some tried to leave through the giant, glass-free windows, Gabriel beat them there, extending his wings to block the openings.

"Who are we to stop the Will of God? And surely it is His Will that this is happening!" The tower continued to shake and crumble, but Gabriel obstructed the way.

"Brother, do not defy us. We must wait for a sign from our Father. And you cannot stand alone," Michael shouted up at him.

"He isn't alone." Phanuel took flight, along with two dozen other Angels. "We are done helping the humans. Let them suffer Samael's wrath!"

I heard Eae gasp, but the sound was muffled by the power of the earth cracking. A section of the floor fell away, dropping the hundreds of feet to the bottom with a crash and a billowing cloud of dust. Wings flapped and feathers drifted in the sooty air. When the walls began breaking apart the Angel warding disappeared.

For the first time since we'd arrived in Los Angeles, Insepth spoke in my mind. *"This is the best we could have hoped for, Ember. We'll stay with the Horsemen for as long as we can!"*

Raphael grabbed Eae before he plummeted when the last piece of the platform fell away. He pumped his wings, aiming toward the southern wall that was now gone, leaving a view of a pinkish-red sky and a cloud of dust rising from the falling debris.

Conquest whirled in the air as he spoke in my mind. *"Hold on!"* He reared upwards, dodging a slab of descending stone. A cyclone gathered around him and a jolt of electricity tingled through me when he darted after Raphael. Uriel and Death were on either side of us. The rushing clouds that the Horsemen created blew away everything behind us. I clung to Conquest's neck, burying my face in his mane. He gathered his muscles and I saw his eyes were blazing red when he turned his head. His shrill whinny, joined by the same noise erupting from Death's mouth, rose above the deafening sound of the toppling building. The rush of clouds built around them until we were the cloud. We passed Raphael and Uriel, and shot upwards into the sky.

I opened my eyes for only a second and saw that Death was next to us. Insepth offered me a rigid smile as he grasped the black horse's neck, unable to even mind speak in our mad dash to escape the crumbling tower and the spiteful Angels.

The explosion behind us hurt my ears and knocked Conquest and Death forward, causing them to stumble for imaginary footing within the clouds. The sting of the concussion was like little needle pricks on the side of my face, making my eyes water as we streaked though the dust of what was left of the magnificent tower.

I forced my eyes open. We rode into clearer air and I finally looked down. The fissure was massive, spanning the width of a football field and going on for as far as I could see. Angels whisked in and out of the gaping hole in the earth. Where the tower had stood was only smoke and rubble. I gasped when I saw the first of the beings erupting from the crater. They were the same creatures from my nightmares when I had dreamt of the compound. Red-eyed beasts with monster heads on top of human bodies. They bounded to the surface, only to be struck down by Angels. Michael and Raguel were there, and so was Uriel. I didn't see Raphael and my heart leaped into my throat. Where was Eae?

I tried to pull back on Conquest's mane. "Stop! We have to go back!"

"Human girl, we are finished with Angels. We must find God and our own destiny."

His voice in my mind was unyielding and I knew there was no persuading him. And I couldn't just jump off and go back.

I looked over my shoulder as the tumultuous scene disappeared beneath us, quickly growing smaller and smaller.

"Just think of it, Ember—we might actually meet God," Insepth's voice was a wispy breath in my mind.

I was about to argue whether that was really a good thing when a war cry shook the air.

I heard Death say, *"No, Conquest. It's not our battle or our concern."*

Conquest's muscles tightened and he shook his head. *"Stay brave little one. Your spirit might just keep you alive. But you must harden your heart."*

I was contemplating his strange advice when something struck my side. There was no way to stay on Conquest's back. I rolled away from him, clawing at the air futilely. The mighty white horse continued on, not slowing or even bothering to look back.

"Ember!" Insepth's scream pierced my mind as he went airborne. *"You must call on the Air to save us. It's the only way!"*

He was almost close enough to touch, and I reached out for him. He did the same, and our fingers brushed. We were falling through the sky at such an incredible speed that everything below was just a blur "I don't know what to do!" I yelled into the wind, unable to focus enough to mind speak.

Inseph grasped my hands and pulled me closer. His face was only inches from mine. "My dear, Ember. If this is our end, please grant me one thing."

Before I could say a thing, his lips were on mine and my Gaia jumped to life inside of me. Inseph's mouth was warm and firm for a second, and then he was yanked out of the sky in a flurry of pumping wings.

"Ember!"

I swiped for him, but he was gone.

Gabriel appeared. He dove at me, his sword at the ready.

My Fire reared to life. I thrust my hands forward and flames shot out through the space between us. But the moment they hit the Angel, they immediately dissipated. My insides trembled and I called on my elements to save me, fearing that it was hopeless. I couldn't beat an Angel, especially while I was distracted by plummeting to my death. An hour ago, I wanted to be their prisoner. Now I was disgusted by my own weakness. Sawyer wouldn't want me to give up and submit to the Angels. He certainly wouldn't want me to die. If that happened, his sacrifice was for nothing.

Harden your heart. I remembered Conquest's words and closed my eyes. Gabriel's long, powerful sword slashed at me, and I felt the cold touch of steel slice my cheek. I gulped for air, sensing the ground rising up to smash me to bits. I could call on my Gaia in an attempt to have the earth catch me in some softer way, but when I opened my eyes, Gabriel's sword was raised high again. *There wasn't time.*

Anger burned my insides. Then something unfurled, like a small blossom at first, expanding without thought. Just as Gabriel's sword fell, a gust caught me, twisting me out of harm's way. The storm gathered strength. A stream of energy moved me through the air, pushing me away from the Angel at a rate that he struggled to keep up with. My skin pushed back and my head pounded. I couldn't breathe.

And then I was falling, dropping out of the sky once again.

Gabriel's scream filled my ears before I landed with a splash. Cold water filled my mouth and wrapped around me.

The impact was too much. Darkness clouded my mind and bubbles pelted me.

Before the blackness was complete, I called out with my mind, *"Help me."*

CHAPTER 3

MADDIE

The sky over the football field was shades of pink as the last remnants of the golden sunset faded beyond the hills that surrounded Oldport. The heavens dimmed, taking on a grayish hue that made me shiver. I zipped up my hoodie and exhaled, feeling a heaviness in my gut that I had never felt before.

"It'll be all right. Ember will stop it from happening."

I stared at Preston. His unruly blond hair blew into his face from the stiff breeze, and he didn't even bother to push it aside. We'd been friends since first grade, but lately our bond had grown significantly. We'd witnessed real Angels battling our friend, Ember, who we now knew was a descendant of Angels. We'd even met Satan and the four Horsemen of the Apocalypse. As if all that wasn't enough to give a girl a nervous breakdown, we had also been informed that we were the newest Scribes of God, and we had been given the task of recording the end of the world.

I rubbed the side of my temple, squeezing my eyes shut. Preston and I had come down from the mountain the night before, and after tossing and turning in bed for several hours, I'd finally fallen into an exhausted, dreamless sleep. When I awoke that morning, I tried to convince myself that I'd imagined the entire thing—that I probably just needed medication of some kind, or at the very least, a lot of therapy.

But Preston had dashed my attempt at delusion by showing up at my house before the sun had even risen. He wanted to talk about it, make plans about what we were going to do. I couldn't deny the insane truth when someone else had experienced it alongside me. No, Preston wouldn't let me pretend it hadn't happened, even though the sounds of people hooting and hollering at our high school's soccer game rang out around me, and the scent of roasting hot dogs and hamburgers filled the evening air. He was stoically preparing for the Apocalypse, the same as my grandpa, who was a pastor in the local Baptist church.

I opened my eyes, and Preston was regarding me with a slight frown.

"I need to speak with Grandpa. He'll believe us and know what to do," I implored with a dry mouth and trembling heart.

"We might not have time." The crowd stood in the stadium, applauding a goal by our team. Preston turned to the field and began to clap, but quickly, his hands dropped to his sides. He lowered his voice and glanced at me. "Soon, this is all going to be gone—"

"Don't say that," I snapped. "It might not come about so fast. Ember said she was going to try and stop it." I placed my hands on my hips. "She has an arch Angel and some other magical friends on her side. She might succeed."

"But you argued with her about it yesterday, saying if it was God's will, she shouldn't interfere." He ran his fingers over his mouth, shaking his head. "You said something to the effect that you're ready to meet the Lord and weren't afraid of what was coming."

The timer on the score board counted down as our team lead by a point. Tension filled the crowd as the ball dropped and was kicked back toward our goal. People called out encouragements on both sides of the field, and the bright field lights made the transition from day to evening hardly even noticeable.

I lived for these moments at the field on soccer nights. I cheered at the football games, and being captain of the cheerleading squad meant a lot of hard work and responsibility during those games. But when I came to support the soccer players, I was able to relax and actually enjoy the game with friends. I hadn't felt any resentment that it was all going to end until I'd reached the stadium. I tried to control my selfishness, but sadness squeezed my insides when I realized that there would be no more bundling up to join the community in support of the hometown team. There also wouldn't be any more late night movies with Lindsey or make out sessions with Randy. I wouldn't even graduate from high school.

Seeing Randy and Lindsey pressing through the crowd with hot dogs in hand, I sniffed. "I've changed my mind," I whispered.

Preston squeezed my shoulder, but didn't say anything.

"Did you see Colby get that goal?" Lindsey exclaimed, sidling up against me as the wind grew colder and dry leaves danced across the grass.

Lindsay was my best friend and had been since kindergarten. Her blonde hair was pulled back in a ponytail, but long strands had escaped and were slapping around her face. Her bright blue eyes twinkled with excitement. Colby was her boyfriend and she was beaming like a proud mamma hen.

I couldn't help it. I swallowed a gulp and grabbed Lindsay into a tight hug. At first she was a little stiff, but I didn't care. When her arms slipped around me, she asked, "What's wrong, Maddie? Did you get bad news from someone?"

I clung to her for a few more long seconds and then abruptly pulled back, wiping my eyes. "No, no. Nothing like that." Lindsay's eyes were wide with worry. "I just want you to know you've been the best friend ever—" I swallowed back my tears "—and I love you like a sister."

Lindsay's brows rose and she threw her arm protectively around my side. She glared at Preston. "What did you say to her?" Then her gaze landed on Randy. "Or was it you who upset her?"

Randy threw up his hands. "I didn't do anything." My sweetheart took my hand and said, "We're about to win, Maddie. That should put you in a good mood. I'll treat for ice cream after the game."

He smiled, pressing his fingers into my hand. For Randy, everything was about sports and ice cream. I laughed and both Randy and Lindsey leaned back a little with round eyes. The sound bubbled out from deep inside of me. I embraced the joyful feeling, reveling in it.

But Preston's hard glare brought me back to my senses. I wouldn't let him ruin the short time we had left. I pressed my lips onto Randy's. He didn't hesitate in wrapping his arms around me and opening his mouth to the kiss. The stadium erupted in cheers and Lindsey squealed. I knew our team had won.

The kiss deepened and I saw an image of a wedding by the river, and then one of several children running around a yard. The last picture in my mind was of Randy and me, gray haired and old, sitting on a porch swing and holding hands.

There was the sound of an explosion, followed by screams and gasps.

"What the hell?" Randy clutched my arm, tugging me backward toward the parking lot.

Lindsey was already on the field and I saw her turn, looking at the place where the goal post had stood a moment before. Dust choked the air, and bright orange flames flared up in several places. The players and coaches from both teams were running across the field, and people bumped into us from all sides.

Another blast rocked the stadium, and I blinked, trying to find Lindsey and Colby, but smoke filled my eyes. A girl from my English class fell beside us, and Preston reached down, pulling her up with a frantic tug. The girl yelped and ran by us as the crowd from the bleachers spilled out. Kids jumped from the higher seats, crying out when they hit the ground. The cool autumn wind that had blown only moments before was replaced with the hot breath of fire.

"My God, what's happening?" Randy shouted, shielding me from the fleeing bodies.

"Come on. We have to get out of here!" Preston grabbed us, pushing us sideways.

But it was too late. Inhuman shrieks reached my ears, and I glanced over my shoulder. *Things* were emerging from the flames. Red eyes and long teeth flashed, and then they were on top of the people, slashing and biting. The screams seared my ears. Kids I'd grown up with were dying right in front of us. Teachers and parents I knew were cut down like stalks of grass. Wherever there was fire, the Hell beasts appeared through the smoke. They were huge and didn't carry weapons. They didn't need them. Their claws and jagged teeth were enough.

But it wasn't the monsters that held my attention the most. It was the line of Angels that spread out behind them. They didn't have shimmering skin like Uriel or Michael had. Their faces were shadowed and their wings were torn and drab looking. They were like dark statues with their wings folded behind them, just watching the murderous scene unfold.

I strained to see. A lone man walked forward from the Angels. His eyes glowed blood red and his dark hair whipped about his face in the wind. His face was familiar, and I remembered him with a slap to my mind that left my insides weak.

"No, no...not this..." I cried into Randy's arm.

Randy dragged me after Preston, and I forced my legs to work faster. The barking stopped us, even though a group of teenagers sprinted ahead into the plume of smoke. Something hit the boy running alongside me, knocking him to the ground, and when I grabbed for him, I saw the severed leg near his head. I screamed and bile rose in my throat.

Preston kicked it aside and pulled me back. The creatures surrounded us, their snarling faces splattered with blood. I heard the sounds of a baby crying and a woman shouting. Gun shots rang out and I guessed the police had arrived, or some of the inhabitants of Oldport were fighting back. Either way, it didn't matter. Monsters poured out from holes in the earth, spreading fire in their wake. This was it. Ember must have failed.

A scaly hand swiped at me from the gaseous fog, and Preston struck at it with his fist. Randy shoved me behind him and spread his arms wide. At least Preston and I understood what was happening, poor Randy and everyone else were taken by surprise—their worst nightmares had come to life.

I heard a snarl behind me. When I turned, a giant dog's head lunged forward, snatching Randy. I screamed, but didn't let go of his arm. We were shook from side to side like rag dolls, and then there was a sickening crunch. Warm wetness poured onto my face.

Tears flooded my eyes and my heart froze. "Randy!" I cried out.

An eye the size of a dinner plate glinted above me, and gore dripped from the beast's mouth. Another giant dog head sliced through the smoke, and then one more.

"Lord, please save us," I mumbled the prayer, pressing into the grass as the twin heads inched closer.

Putrid breath pushed my hair back and made my stomach churn as their jaws gnashed at me. I squeezed my eyes shut and begged, *"Please, Lord!"*

Something came shooting out of the sky, fast as a bullet. The dog monster was knocked away. A hand like cold steel encircled my arm, and then I was jerked into the air. Another pair of wings flapped nearby and I spotted a glimpse of blond, bushy hair. I knew Preston was also being carried away.

Oldport was burning. Smoke and flames spread out in all directions below us, ending only where the valley reached the foothills of the Smoky Mountains, where the land was unspoiled. Another explosion shook the air and sirens wailed. I began to sob as I repeated the Lord's Prayer over and over in my head. *Our Father, Who art in Heaven...*

Preston and I were set down on a ledge overlooking the town. The night was crisp and cold, untouched by the destruction below. I remembered the red haired Angel. He was Uriel, Ember's ancestor and protector. He scowled at the newcomer, a powerfully built Angel with wings the color of the Caribbean Sea.

"Why here—why now, Raguel?" Uriel demanded, gesturing wildly at the scene of carnage below.

"I do not know," Raguel replied tiredly. "None of this is unfolding the way it was foretold. Why would a simple mountain town be of any importance to Samael?"

Preston knelt on the ground, gripping his sides and taking deep breaths. Randy's blood soaked his clothing, as it did mine, and tears streaked his face too.

I turned on shaky legs toward the Angels. Grandpa had taught me about the Bible and God. I'd attended church every Sunday since I was an infant, and I'd read the book of Revelation several times. I was a true believer and my faith gave me strength.

My hands balled into fists. "I saw *him* down there."

"Who?" Uriel came closer with cocked eyes.

"Ember's boyfriend—Sawyer—the one who was taken away by the Devil."

Uriel and Raguel exchanged glances. Their faces were like unforgiving stone.

"Then this foray is an attack on Ember? A lowly Watcher, caught up in the end of times?" Uriel spat the words out angrily.

"Perhaps. But you fool yourself if you think that is what your spawn is. In only one meeting with the girl, I sensed her power, and uniqueness. There is something special about her, and Samael has surely recognized her potential as well." Raguel rubbed his chin in a human-like gesture, giving his resting wings a little shake.

A few feathers floated away on the breeze, drawing my gaze back to Oldport. I could see the edge of the subdivision where I lived was on fire. My parents were there and they might be dying. I gasped, fresh tears filling my eyes. Preston rose and put his arm around me. I leaned my head against his chest, wishing I could wake up from this nightmare.

"Samael might have been testing the loyalty of his new subject, or maybe he picked this place because two of the Scribes are here. Nonetheless, I can't deny it any longer. It has begun," Uriel said grimly.

"I don't feel right about this, brother. Something is amiss. But if it be the truth, I pray our Father shows us guidance." Raguel's departure was abrupt. With a single pump of his blue wings, he leaped into the dark sky, disappearing into the clouds.

"You're not leaving us?" I pulled away from Preston, staring up at Uriel. His red hair was pulled back, and instead of the woolen tunic I saw him wearing before, copper-colored chain mail covered his chest. Strange, indecipherable writing decorated the armor.

Uriel gave me a serious look. "You must record what you saw here this night. Your memories will carry on for thousands of years."

"But what's the point if mankind isn't going to be around to read about it?" Preston asked, and I swiveled around, waiting for Uriel's answer.

Uriel tilted his head, his brow raised. "What has been written has gotten us to this place in time, and we have been instructed to protect the Scribes so they may complete their task. It is not my place to question the logic of it—" He paused, looking at the stars that still shone down, even though the world was ending. "But sometimes I have questions, and I am baffled about the events occurring around us. I can only hope that we'll get the answers we need to proceed to the next phase, whatever that might be."

The fiery Angel's voice was low and humming, calming my raw nerves. The pain and shock from losing everyone dear to me had left a void where my heart had been. But my mind was still clear, and a thought came to me.

"Where's Ember?" I dared to ask.

Preston looked up, a hopeful glint in his eye.

But Uriel's suddenly tight muscles and deep frown dashed my hopes.

"Forces beyond my control took her from me. I tried to find her, but she is gone. I do not feel her presence any longer."

CHAPTER 4

CRICKET

The scent of lush grass filled my nose and I inhaled deeply. The sun was setting, bringing with it crisper air that felt good on my bare arms. I nearly bumped into War when he stopped abruptly. The creamy-pink sky seemed to have his attention. I followed his gaze, glancing up at the scalloped clouds.

"It's pretty, huh?" My voice sounded dry and forced. I still hadn't gotten used to human talk. It took a long time to form thoughts and push them out my mouth. The Horsemen didn't seem to have the same problem, though.

"It's magnificent!" War smiled back at me broadly and my chest constricted. "I don't remember the lands of men being so striking."

"You've been here before?" I asked.

War leaned against the rock wall. He removed a long blade of grass from his mouth, twirling it between his fingers. His hair was short cropped and chestnut colored, along with his beard. His tanned skin fascinated me, as it was very similar to the color of hair that covered his body when he was in equine form.

"It's been thousands of years ago now, and not this new world. My brothers and I were created for a single purpose—the annihilation of mankind at the time of God's choosing. He showed us many things, and gave us instructions." He shrugged. "But I never had the leisure time to explore on my own." He dropped his head back and extended his arms. "Just the feel of an evening breeze on my face is new to me."

"And you like it?" I had so many questions for War. I was afraid there wouldn't be enough time to have them all answered.

"Oh, yes. I like it very much. But having your company greatly improves my enjoyment."

His smile became crooked and my cheeks heated uncomfortably, something that never happened to me while I was in my true form.

War's eyes lingered on my face until I looked away, trying to hide my embarrassment from him. I couldn't stop my heart from madly fluttering. I shook my head.

"What is the Creator like?" I tried to change the subject to safer territory.

War laughed loudly, and the sound rumbled through the quiet countryside. The trees bent lazily in the light wind, and leaves fluttered down. Ila's valley was the nicest place I'd ever lived. And after traveling to Adria's murky underwater world and fighting giant sharks in the shallows, I never wanted to leave this beautiful place ever again.

He wagged his finger at me. "You are a clever one, young mare." His smile softened. "His voice is quite pleasant. It vibrates in your mind, with patience and also authority."

"Have you seen Him?"

War's eyes widened and he said, "No, no. I'm not sure if anyone has ever *seen* Him, even the Angels."

"So how do you know who's talking to you, then?" I kicked at the grass with a boot that squeezed my foot uncomfortably.

War smoothed down his beard in a sharp tug. "I never thought of that. At the time, I absolutely believed it was Him, so there wasn't a doubt in my mind."

"Why is He doing this?" I narrowed my gaze at him. Colors were sharper with human eyes, and sometimes it was too bright in the sunshine. I was most at ease at this time of day, when the daylight had left and the moon emerged. "I want to run in the fields, eat good grass, and roll in the dirt. Why is He destroying all this goodness?" I couldn't keep the shrill of resentment from my voice. First, I was forced into human form, and now I knew the world was going to be destroyed. I wished for the carefree days when I'd hang my head over the fence, spending time with my friend, Rhondo. He was somewhere many miles north of these mountains, and I wondered if he sensed the end was near. Was he afraid?

War came away from the wall, closing the distance between us. He stopped a few feet away, giving me space enough to not feel threatened. "You have more questions than I can answer." His face dropped and his warm brown eyes became moist. I stood up straighter and swayed toward him. "When the time comes to cut down humanity, it will not be a pretty sight. My brothers and I will unleash war, famine, plague, and death. Human life will be wiped out. But the land and sea will also suffer, and so will the animals. Afterward, there might be a time of regrowth, when the birds, reptiles, fish, and land animals flourish, but there was no mention of such a thing to any of us. The time *after* the final battle is a mystery to us all."

I took another step, bringing me close enough to War that I could smell his hot, smoky scent. His eyes continued to search my face and his lips parted. I understood why the old woman, Ila, had instructed Ember to change my form. It was for War and his arrival. Somehow Ila had foreseen this moment in time—a moment when I might make a difference.

"But it's up to you, isn't it? Everything can't be destroyed without you." I brushed my lips on his, letting our breaths gloriously mingle. "If you and your brothers say no, it can't happen."

War's fingers braced the back of my head, and he pulled me against his muscled chest. I was tall, but he was still several inches above me. And even though a part of me wanted to kick out at the Horseman and run across the field, throwing my head sideways in defiance, the human part wouldn't allow it. My knees were weak and my heart hammered.

His tongue was in my mouth. I sighed and he made a groaning noise that made me press even harder into him.

I was lost and pure instincts took over. His hands travelled the length of my back and up to my short black hair. I began to tug his tunic over his head when he pulled away with a hard grunt.

He closed his eyes and opened them again. "When the time comes, I have to listen. I have no choice. It's a compulsion of sorts—the same kind that made me come here when the horn was blown."

"I thought we all have a choice," I said, crossing my arms in front of me. Now that War's heat was gone, I was chilled to the bone.

"Humans, Angels, and even animals, yes. But I am none of those. I was created for one purpose only. And I must fulfill the oath I took that day so long ago on the mount."

"Then you will make the biggest mistake of your life, before you have even had a moment to live," I scolded him.

War closed the gap again and reached for me, but I stepped away. He looked forlorn when he stared back. "Since I've arrived, I haven't heard Him. Death and Conquest are looking for Him now. I pray when they find Him, they will discover He has changed His mind."

"What about the meeting? Is Ember still with them?" The hair on my neck pricked and my quivering gut told me bad things were happening.

War confirmed my fears with a frown and slouched shoulders. "She is no longer with my brothers. There was an Angel uprising, and a breach in the wall between this land and Hell."

I smacked War's chest, and he grasped my shoulders, holding me firmly. I struggled, but found it was no use. His strength was far superior to mine. I went limp in his arms, and was opening my mouth to demand answers when a boom sounded from far away.

Another one quickly followed and I looked up at War. His eyes were wide and his skin instantly paled. "It has begun." He pointed to the east and I saw a glow radiating in sky, on the other side of the hilltop.

I pulled away from him, staring. "It can't be…"

With a swirl of wind and colors, War was a magnificent chestnut stallion. He turned his head and nickered to me.

The *change* wasn't horrible, but it wasn't pleasant, either. I didn't hesitate. War was part of my herd now. I opened up to my true essence and let it flood in. There was a moment of queasy itchiness, and an explosion of colorful dots.

Then I was racing alongside the Horseman of War in the direction of the little cabin in the woods.

CHAPTER 5

IVAN

The thundering roar in the distance made me stop and turn. My heart raced and I pushed my ball cap back. "It can't be—"

"Oh, but it is," Famine replied.

The Horseman stood between Sir Austin and Youmi. They were all staring at the glowing sky just beyond the hilltop. Oldport.

"Are you sure? It may be some other kind of explosion—perhaps a gas leak." Sir Austin's Scottish accent was thick and strained.

Famine shook his head. "Sorry, chap. The barriers are breaking and Hell's creatures are coming forth. I can *feel* it."

"We must stop it, then!" Sir Austin's power as an air Watcher stirred the wind into gusts around the cabin. Debris from the previous battle took flight, and I had to duck when a piece of fallen metal from the barn roof nearly struck me. "The villagers are under attack."

"What can two Watchers and a Horseman do?" Youmi said, backing away. "It is their doom. We will all have to face the evil soon enough."

Sir Austin turned to his friend, frowning. "What would you have us do, then—run away—ignore what is happening?"

Youmi bowed his head and his ponytail swished on his back. His bright red kimono looked very out of place in the mountains of Tennessee. He was also far away from any large bodies of water, which diminished his water Watcher abilities greatly.

"We can't stop the end from coming. Ember and Insepth are wrong to even attempt it." He raised his head and his eyes were like dark pools. "Let us spend our remaining days with family and friends—let us leave this place."

Sir Austin's mouth thinned, but he remained quiet. Another explosion shook the ground, and the light above the town brightened into a red cloud. Lutz roared, and I sank my hand into his dense fur. The Growler rarely left bear form, but I knew what he wanted to do. He wanted to fight. The crimes he had committed when he'd worked for the Demons, protecting their compound, had left a heavy guilt on his shoulders. Helping the villagers, even if he died in the process, was a way to atone for his sins—something constantly on his mind now that the end was near.

"We can't just leave. People are dying down there. Some of them are my friends." I glanced between the Watchers and the Horseman.

Famine sniggered. "That is noble of you, pup, but your sacrifice would be like trying to stop a flood with a single grain of sand. Now that it has begun, they will come—monsters and Angels—humankind is lost. Best you think of yourself and your pack."

"My pack is scattered. Ember and Insepth are with the Angels. Horas is scouting. And Sawyer is…gone."

Famine's brows shot up and he bent his head. A few blond locks fell into his face and he didn't bother to push them aside. "They are your pack? Watchers and Demons?"

I nodded, looking away. The disbelief on Famine's face was sincere. He didn't understand.

A shrieking whinny turned all our heads. A red horse and a black one charged up the hill, their manes flying and their hooves pounding. They skidded in front of us with an explosion of colors. War emerged from the cloud first, closely followed by Cricket. It was still strange to see Ember's mare in human form.

"Death and Conquest are seeking the Creator," War told Famine. "They will discover what we are to do."

Famine shrugged. "This valley is no longer safe. The rank of Watchers, Growlers, and Angels is heavy here. Those scents will attract the creatures from Hell."

War's eyes shifted to Cricket, who came to stand beside me. "Then we will destroy them. We have the power to do so."

"Normally, I'd agree with you, brother. But it isn't only the corrupt ones we must be wary of. Conquest has informed me that the Angels are at war with each other. Some joined Gabriel and Phanuel, others are holding true to the Old Order, backing Michael, Azriel, and Raguel. Uriel and Raphael seem to have gone rogue, more concerned with the humans than their own brothers. If a group of Angels comes against us, the scales will not be balanced. Who knows what that outcome would be?"

Sir Austin's wind continued to surge, carrying with it the scent of acidy smoke.

I grasped Cricket's hand, searching her eyes for an ally. "We should help the villagers. Ember would want us to."

Before Cricket could respond, Horas streaked into the clearing. He doubled over and gulped for air.

Cricket ran to him, placing her hand on his shoulder. He straightened, wild eyed. "We can't…help…them." He threw his head back and panted. "The streets are overrun with all manner of Hell beasts. Even the hounds are there, snatching up anyone in their paths. Oldport is destroyed. It's a complete bloodbath."

"My God!" Sir Austin gasped.

Horas' mouth twisted. "It gets worse." His gaze landed on me and my heart sank. "There's a contingent of Fallen Angels there, although they aren't partaking in the killing. And Sawyer is the one leading them all."

I blinked back hot tears. "That can't be." I shook my head. "He would never do such a thing."

Horas' voice was firm. "He's not the same man we knew, Ivan. He follows the Dark One. His eyes were blood red and cruel. His humanity is lost."

"Samael would use this man against you. He will revel in it," War confirmed.

Cricket looked at War and swallowed. "He wasn't a man. He was a Demon, and our friend."

"He is no longer your friend." War lifted his head and sniffed the air. "He is coming for all of you."

My only friends in the compound had been Lutz and Sawyer. Lutz taught me the Growler ways, but Sawyer took care of me, driving me back and forth to the village to attend the school. At first I'd been leery of the Demon, but I soon sensed there was something different about him. He had a kind nature, and he was appalled by the actions of the other Demons and ashamed by his own behavior. He'd saved me on more than one occasion, and he'd fallen in love with Ember, becoming her guardian and mate. That he was now murdering people in Oldport was too terrible to think about. Would he really kill us?

But I smelled it too. Fire and death were barreling this way.

Angus barked and nipped my hand. He knew what was coming, and he wanted to escape.

A goat bleated on the other side of the fence and one of the cats rubbed up against Lutz's legs. Rabbits and chickens peppered

KAREN ANN HOPKINS

the yard. These were Ila's pets. When she'd died, she'd left them in Ember's care, and we'd all been helping her to keep them safe

"Youmi and I will create a loophole to get us away. We don't have the same abilities as Insepth or Ember, and only enough strength to create one in a short period of time. But we can at least get us far away from here." Sir Austin looked determined.

"But where should we go?" Youmi asked.

"We can't leave without talking to Ember! She won't know how to find us," I clutched my head when another explosion rent the air in the distance.

"Trust me, she has ways to find you. You'll be reunited again. But if you stay, she'll only find your bones and ashes when she returns," Sir Austin said emphatically.

I looked at Horas, and he nodded. "I believe him. Ember has powers she hasn't even touched on yet. She'll come for us, no matter where we are."

Angus nudged my hand and I gazed out at Ila's valley. An evening mist had settled over the grass and autumn colors blazed along the tree line. The log cabin was nestled into the hemlocks and flowers still bloomed on each side of the path leading to the front door. This had been our oasis, our sanctuary, the only real safe place in the world. And now Sawyer was bringing Hell to it.

I squeezed my eyes closed and listened. A family of coyotes was yipping, warning the other forest animals to abandon their homes and flee. Their frantic calls helped make up my mind.

"We leave now," I said.

"But where?" Sir Austin asked.

It seemed strange to me that a powerful Watcher was relying on my decision in a crisis. Even Horas was staring at me, which made my pulse quicken.

"We go back to Romania. The Growlers are still gathered there, and now that the Watchers of Light are defeated, we don't have to worry about that threat anymore."

Sir Austin nodded his head slowly. "It's a good location. Youmi can make his way to the sea from there, and I won't be so far from my home, either."

A gust of wind that wasn't from the Watcher belted our faces. The scent of smoke was becoming heavy on the air and my eyes watered. The forest was burning, the glow spreading over the mountain. I could see the first licks of flames across the valley, and with them, came the stench of Hell hounds.

"We have to gather the animals!" I shouted above the gale as a torrent of dry leaves came pelting down from the trees.

"There's no time." Sir Austin knelt to the ground beside Youmi. They were weaving their elements, creating the loophole. "Our opening will last mere seconds. We'll barely get through ourselves."

"I will stay with Ila's pets!" Cricket exclaimed, calling out to the goats. They began leaping the rock wall, until all fourteen of them were gathered around her.

"No. We have other places to journey to," War said firmly. "They must fend for themselves, like all other living creatures."

Cricket's eyes narrowed. "You are not my master."

"They're coming!" Famine yelled, pointing at the bottom of the meadow, and the poplar grove that was now engulfed. "The Watcher's warding has been broken!"

A giant dog's head appeared from the flames, followed by another snapping one. Their howls brought the hairs up on my neck, and I resisted the urge to change into a wolf. In Purgatory, we had only one of these three-headed monsters to deal with. Now I could see a dozen heads poking out from the burning foliage. There were other red-eyed, pale creatures among them that walked on two legs and had the distorted faces of animals.

A figure stepped out from the trees, and an icy grip seized my chest. His eyes were ablaze and his legs carried him swiftly. It was Sawyer.

Lutz was in my mind. *"I will take the little critters far from here. You go to your kind, pup. Try to live before death claims you. Perhaps we'll meet again."* He bumped his bear head into my stomach and turned, roaring loudly.

The goats were the first to reach him, falling in alongside him as he gathered his muscles and leaped into the forest in the opposite direction of where the beasts were coming. Cats darted off the porch to join him, and the rabbits pumped their little legs, dashing into the bushes to follow. Even the chickens joined the chase in a flurry of flapping wings and squawking.

Sadness twisted my insides as Lutz disappeared with his strange company into the forest. There wasn't time to grieve his departure or worry about what would happen if the hounds caught up to him. Lutz was a giant bear, but he was no match for a dozen Hell hounds.

"Come on!" I grabbed Cricket's hand, but she jerked it from me.

"They are my herd now." She lifted her chin toward War and Famine. "Horas will be with you and Angus." A tear slipped down Cricket's cheek.

I could feel the heat from the spreading fire, and sweat dripped from beneath my ball cap. Sawyer was almost upon us.

Cricket leaned in and whispered fiercely, "Ember made me into this wretched human for a purpose. I must stay with the Horsemen." The Horsemen had already changed into their equine forms and were waiting for her to join them. She winked at me and jumped onto War's back. "We'll hold them off, give you time to escape!" she shouted.

The great chestnut horse reared, screaming and tossing his head. Clouds exploded from his hooves and he surged into the sky, galloping over them as if they were solid ground. Famine took flight right behind him, his pale golden tail trailing behind him. The rush of clouds they created collided with the flames. Hounds bellowed and unnamed creatures shrieked.

The beating of wings was suddenly in my ears and I looked skyward. Dark Angels jetted from out of nowhere, their war cries ringing in the air as they sped toward the Horsemen and Cricket.

Horas grabbed my arm, shoving me into the portal that Sir Austin and Youmi had just opened. Angus jumped through in front of us, and then the Watchers let the loop go.

I looked over my shoulder. The hounds crashed through the rock wall and the barn had ignited. Trees crashed down and lightning streaked across the sky where the Fallen Angels pursued the horses.

I had one last glimpse of Ila's valley. Sawyer raced toward us, his eyes gleaming red, blood dripping from his mouth. His shriek pierced the thousands of miles that separated us. And just as the hole blinked out, a shot of flames slammed into me, searing my hair and shirt. Tendrils of smoke wicked into the crisp air, floating upward through the starry sky above my head.

I hit the ground with a sickening jolt, and fell back into dewy grass.

I couldn't stop the tears from rolling through the smudges on my cheeks.

Ila's valley burned. And the rest of the world would soon follow.

CHAPTER 6

EMBER

Waves. I heard the crashing of waves and felt warm sunshine on my face. I tried to lift my head, but my neck was sore and I dropped it back onto the soft surface and groaned.

"That's enough sleep for you, don' you think?"

The voice registered in my mind and I forced myself to sit up, pressing my hands down onto a rubbery substance. At first I could only squint, the light was so blinding, but I kept blinking and slowly I got used to the brightness.

"Is that you, Adria?" The words sputtered out of my dry mouth. I could taste salt on my tongue and I grimaced.

"Yes, your friend Adria is here. Mind you, I did not expect to be called on for help so soon." She shrugged. "But I am in your debt for rescuing my beloved Vorago."

The sound of splashing was followed by a loud humming noise. I swiveled and opened my eyes fully. The blurriness cleared and I could finally see clearly. My jaw dropped and I crawled to the edge, peering into the watery depths. My *ride* sliced through the waves and several dolphins dove alongside us. They jumped playfully, but

I hardly paid attention to them. I was more interested in what I was sitting on—a whale.

I reached out with my Tempest and my Gaia, touching the enormous water beast. It was a blue whale, and she was beautiful. Her nearly adult-sized calf was streaming beside her and another whale swam below us. The trios' hums filled my head in such a soothing way, I wanted to close my eyes and go back to sleep.

"I'm riding on a whale—a real whale." I spread my fingers wide on her skin.

"Yes, and you are lucky she was close by, or you might not be gushing like an awestruck child."

"I don't understand. I never called you for help."

Adria's dark skin glistened in the sunshine and shells and seaweed leaves kept her from being naked. A long braid fell down her shoulder, and small conchs decorated her hair. She threw back her head and barked out a laugh. The whale mimicked the dolphin woman by blowing a squirt of water from her spout. It was like being sprayed by a hose and I squealed when the cold water struck me.

"You don' even know your own talents. Still as ignorant as when you arrived on my shore, searching for a way to change your hooved friend into a human. Hah!" She eyed me with a broad grin. Your Tempest is what called me here. It's a part of you, and when it feared your death, it sent a shock of power through the ocean." She rubbed the whale. "This girl came to your aid, lifting you to the surface. I arrived soon after, but with the Angels in the sky, I didn't dare show my true form."

"Gabriel was trying to kill me…"

"That one is no good. He is stubborn and merciless. His grudges never die." Adria sighed. "He would have succeeded, too, if the ocean hadn't risen up to protect you." She leaned over. "That angry Angel dove into my world and the waves tumbled him over and over.

Schools of fish pelted him and orcas rammed into him. He fled the watery depths, joining a battle in the sky that was beyond comprehension. I never thought I would see the day when Angels would battle Angels. An' I'm not talking about the fallen ones. These were the Celestial Host striking swords at each other."

Memories came flooding back. "Insepth?" I whispered.

"What? That arrogant one? I never saw him."

I scanned the horizon and as far as I could see was water. My heart stuttered and I dropped my head.

"Now don' go getting all lovesick on me. This isn't the time for such things."

Anger brought my head up. "I'm not lovesick. He's my teacher and my friend."

She hooted and slapped the whale's back. "Your lies don' work on me, child. I am the water. I know your emotions and your heart. You have feelings for that Watcher, but you fight them. I don' know why. He would be a fine mate. Better than the brooding Demon."

Her words echoed in my head and then the tears were falling. I pulled my knees up below my chin and covered my eyes with my hands. "Sawyer was taken away by Samael—the Devil," I choked out.

"Nooo! Oh, poor child." Her muscled arms slipped around me. "That is a fate I would only wish on my worst enemies."

Adria hugged me and I clung to her, sobbing. Sawyer was gone and all my friends were far away. I'd probably never see my brother again or even meet my niece or nephew. Angels were trying to kill me and I couldn't stop the world from ending. I pressed my head harder into Adria's shoulder. I just wanted it to stop—I wanted the world to be normal again. I'd give anything to wake up in Ila's cabin to the smells of her cooking breakfast, or go back even further still to my old bedroom in Ohio, when Mom and Dad were alive.

The water queen pulled back and gave me a gentle shake. "Now, stop it! You must be strong."

I sniffed and rubbed my wet eyes. "Why? We're all going to die anyway. It was shown to me. There will be fire and monsters and torture. I thought I could stop it. But I know now that I can't—no one can."

Adria pursed her lips and snorted. "I don' know about all that, but I do know the Angels will make your lover suffer. And you might be able to save him from that.

"Insepth isn't my lover. It's Sawyer I want to save," I said.

She shook her head and scowled. "There's no saving that one. The Dark One was able to take him because he was soulless. From the moment he was turned Demon, it was his destiny to travel the path of evil.

"No. I won't accept that. I *can* save him. I must!" I argued, standing on unsteady sea legs.

Adria followed me. "Then you will be throwing away not only your life, but the lives of your friends and family. You will fall, and all will perish." She poked my chest with a long finger. "You were born Ila's descendant, with all four elements coursing through your veins for a reason—and it wasn't to save a Demon."

I shook my head. "The Angels' warding prevents me from using my powers. And even when I can draw on the elements, I'm weak compared to them."

"You are stronger than you think." Adria abruptly turned and spread her arms wide. "Look around you. If the Angels have their way, this will be gone. My home and all my friends will be gone." Her eyes sparked when she looked back at me. "You must fight to the end, like Ila would have wanted."

The thought of Ila made me stand straighter. What would she have wanted me to do? Deep down, I knew the answer.

And I know what Gabriel and the other Angels would do to Insepth. I couldn't leave him to that fate.

"Do you really think I can save Insepth?"

Adria nodded. "And together you can save the world." Her voice lowered. "But they'll be waiting for you. Your Watcher friend is the bait."

"Then how can I possibly hope to succeed?"

"Sometimes you just have to take a leap of faith." She grinned.

Insepth had basically said the same thing to me more than once. And no matter what impossible jam we were in, we always pulled through. I took Adria's words as a good sign.

"But where do I begin to look for him?"

Adria glanced up and I followed her gaze. And then I saw them.

"Angels. You'll need Angels to show you the way."

CHAPTER 7

CRICKET

I lifted my head from the grass and watched the yearlings gallop across the pasture. A bright bay bucked and kicked out at another that tried to pass him. They both threw their heads and whinnied. They didn't stop until they reached the herd of other youngsters. There was some rearing and bucking before they settled down to graze once again.

It is a joy to see them frolic under the stars. War spoke in my mind. He reached out and nuzzled my neck. I trembled beneath his touch.

How did you know of this place? I looked past War to see Famine grazing along the creek. The palomino seemed quite content to relax among the real horses.

War eyed me. *This region is known for its horses. There are many here. Most are bred for racing, but some serve other purposes. It is a place I always wanted to visit. And while we wait for Death and Conquest to learn our fates, why not?*

It's called Kentucky. I was foaled here. I remembered my dam's bristly muzzle cleaning my wet hair while I laid in the tall grass. "*Those months were far too fleeting.*"

What a glorious thing to be raised in this place. It's what I imagine an equine heaven to be like. War pranced forward, nipping a few bites of grass.

I followed him to the creek, glancing around, expecting monsters and fire to arrive at any moment. Seeing Ila's valley burning and being overrun by evil creatures had been too much to bear. I only hoped the charging clouds gave Ivan, Horas, and Angus enough time to escape. The wolf and the Demon had good hearts and they were my friends. I feared the bear and the little animals didn't make it. The entire mountain had been aflame.

I shivered. It was only a matter of time before that happened here too. The yearlings would be so afraid.

I focused hard on the woman's body that was a part of me now, and for once, I welcomed the change. I waited for War to follow suit. He hesitated and stomped his hoof.

"It's hard for me to mind speak when talking about human things," I admitted, swatting at a bee that buzzed near my ear.

I didn't like the small, weak feeling in the woman's body, but it was easier to have a conversation, and that's what we needed right now.

Seeing that War was being stubborn, I walked away. A moment later, he jogged up to me on human legs. There was a glint in his eyes.

"Damn, mare, you're a stubborn one."

"As much as I want to graze on the thick grass and have a good roll, there's more important things on my mind."

War snatched up my hand, pulling me to a stop. "I cannot relieve your worries. My hope is when the time comes, our Creator will allow me to take you with us."

"To live imprisoned in a stable made of rocks somewhere in the clouds?" I pulled away and crossed my arms. "I don't want to live like that—and neither should you."

War tossed his hands up. "I do not make the rules. I follow orders."

"But no orders have been given." I stepped closer, lifting my neck and hoping War caught my scent on the breeze. "Why can't we help Ember?"

"What—and disobey the Creator? Do you know what might happen to us then? We'll be as bad as the Angels who've rebelled."

"No one's been punished yet."

"Are all females so frustrating or is it just the human ones?" The corner of War's lips twitched.

"I have read that it is a common theme among females. They tend to be difficult by nature," Famine said, leaning against a tree trunk, having changed silently into man form. I stared at him with narrowed eyes, and he returned my look with a furrowed brow. "You saw the beasts and the fire, the Fallen Angels, and their Demon leader. Now that the barriers are broken, more will flood into this land. Even we cannot stop it from happening."

The starry sky darkened with clouds and the sudden wind bent the trees down. This was no ordinary storm and I looked up, waiting for something bad to happen. I was close to changing form when I spotted the black horse galloping across the sky. A white horse jumped to the lead and charged downward, bringing with him a gust so strong, branches snapped from the nearest trees.

There was a brilliant display of exploding colors, and Conquest and Death were striding in our direction. The hurricane died down by the time they reached us, and the moon peeked out once again.

"I see you've both fared well while we were battling Angels and scouring earth and Heaven, looking for our Creator." Death's face was harder than usual.

Conquest grasped War's arm and murmured greetings before he did the same with Famine, and then he smiled at me. "I'm glad the exquisite mare is still with us." His grin broadened. "You are a very welcome sight for tired eyes."

I blushed and looked away.

"You were supposed to talk sense into this one," Death jerked his thumb at War as he glared at Famine.

"The mare is one of us. I see no harm in her company," Famine replied with a shrug.

"Agreed," Conquest said, slapping the palomino on the back.

Death shook his head. "That is a discussion left for another day. We have work to do."

War's muscles tightened and he raised his head. I could smell his alertness.

"Did you find Him?" War's voice was steady, but quiet.

Death's mouth thinned and he turned away. "No, but we didn't expect His greetings when we returned, either. The horn has sounded, and we must complete our task. Perhaps when it is over, we'll find some peace."

"You'll kill everyone, including the horses of this world!" I said.

Death turned back. He hesitated before his face softened, along with his tone. "Terrible things are already unraveling. The chaos will cause more suffering to the inhabitants of this realm, than our destruction of it. The balance has been thrown off. Angels are behaving irrationally." His volume rose. "They are at war with each other. Beasts break free from their bonds in Hell. We are the only ones who can restore order to this forsaken world."

I faced Death. I could see the yearlings in the upper pasture, and beyond them were the pregnant mares with their tall foals still by their sides. Pristine white barns dotted the landscape. Their cupolas pointed toward Heaven. Somewhere north of here, I envisioned Rhondo lying beneath the old oak tree, enjoying the cooler evening air. I would not let these horses destroy it all. Somewhere was Ember and she needed me.

In a burst of colors, I was a black horse once again. I tossed my head, and dug my hooves into the dirt. Death had only an instant to change before I struck out at him. I crashed into his larger, hardened body, and bit at his neck. He whirled and kicked out at me, but I cut to the side, avoiding his striking hooves.

Stop this madness or I will kill you! Death shouted into my mind.

He knocked into me, sending me to the ground. I rolled into a standing position and charged at him with teeth bared and neck arched.

I will not allow you to kill this mare, Death. War's voice rattled in my mind. All I saw was a flash of his chestnut coat in the moonlight as he shoved me aside. He rose on his hind legs and came down on Death. Sparks flew and their screams were answered by concerned nickers from across the pasture.

Death got a hold of the crest of War's neck and bit down, causing blood to spurt. But War didn't show any pain, turning and planting both his hind hooves into Death's side. The kick separated the stallions and gave Conquest and Famine the space to plunge in between the two in their horse forms. Conquest pushed against War, while Famine turned his rump to Death, trying to get the black horse to stand down.

A blinding explosion of colors and all the horses were men again. I followed suit, and ran over to War, who had a gash running down the back of his neck.

"Are you all bloody insane?" Death growled. Famine stayed in front of him, not allowing the older man to pass.

"You bit me!" War thundered.

I felt around War's neck for a gaping wound, but there was none. I could only guess that since they were immortal beings, the wound healed quickly, but the blood remained.

Conquest hold up his hands. "Calm yourselves, brothers. We will not fight among ourselves the way the humans and Angels do. We are the first herd. Don't ever forget it!"

Death tilted his head and exhaled. "I wouldn't have bitten you if you hadn't attacked me.

"You threatened my mare!"

Conquest's brows lifted, and my cheeks burned.

"That's because she was attacking me as well." Death grunted and strode forward.

Conquest remained firmly in front of War, but he allowed Death to lean in and place his forehead close to War's. In man form the gesture looked strange, but if they'd been horses, it would have been easily understood as a sign of submission. Death didn't want to fight War.

War leaned over and inhaled deeply, a low sound erupting from his lips. When the three men stepped back, the tension was gone from the group. I was still very angry, though.

"Please don't do it," I pleaded.

"And what is the alternative if we don't?" Death asked, sounding worn out. "Let Samael rule this land? It would be far worse."

War looked at the other Horsemen, and then at me. "Until we hear directly from the Creator, we fight. We fight anyone who desires to destroy this" —he spread his hands wide, motioning to the surrounding fields filled with horses— "beautiful land for their own selfish desires."

Conquest nodded first, followed by Famine, and finally Death.

I slipped my arms around War and hugged him. He kissed the top of my head and whispered, "All will be well."

I didn't really believe him. But it didn't matter. I'd bought Ember some more time, and gained four new allies for the war to come.

CHAPTER 8

HORAS

Angus nipped my hand and I pushed up into a sitting position. Dim light spread on the horizon, casting long shadows down the mountainside. It was early morning in Romania. The terrain and forest were similar to the Smokies, but even wilder. I'd spent some time in this land in my early Demon days. They weren't bad memories.

A groan drew my gaze from the snow-capped mountain scenery to Sir Austin and Youmi, who were both stretched out on the damp grass. The air was cold and still.

"Opening loopholes was always Insepth's specialty. He could do it with very little effort." Sir Austin clutched his head and rolled to his knees. "Even with us combining powers, it wasn't easy."

"No, it was not easy." Youmi rose in a more graceful way than Sir Austin, but his movements were slow. As he stood, he stretched his arms skyward and looked around.

Angus barked in my face, startling me. The dog usually ignored me, but he wanted my attention. I stood and followed the German Shepherd into the trees. Ivan sat on a fallen log. His hands clutching his face.

I sprinted over and placed a hand on his shoulder and squeezed. "I saw him. Sawyer," he said quietly.

I rubbed the side of my head and sat down beside him. Angus whined and stretched out in front of us. The dog probably missed Ember and was confused by the sudden departure from Ila's valley. I was glad Ember's pet had come with us. I feared if he had stayed with Lutz, he would have died. The thought of the giant bear being overtaken by flames and Hell beasts was heavy on my mind. I hoped I was wrong. But Sawyer had been unique among Demons—loyal and brave, not easily swayed. The quality I admired in him the most was his ability to control his Demon compulsions. I knew firsthand how difficult it was. I'd struggled for a thousand years to retain some of my humanity. Sawyer was the only other Demon I'd met who had worked as hard as I did to do the right thing. More often than not, he had succeeded.

The image of this Demon, whom I had greatly respected and considered my closest friend, going rogue was more than a little difficult to swallow. But for Ivan, the poor pup, it must be even harder.

"Do not forget, he joined Samael to save Ember and the rest of us. If he hadn't made that bargain, we would have all died days ago when the Angels came to the valley." My voice sounded distant to my ears. It was a well-rehearsed line—one I'd told myself a hundred times.

Ivan lifted his chin and his eyes glistened. "It was him, but it wasn't him."

I nodded. I understood.

Ivan swallowed, reaching down to scratch Angus' head. "I was never afraid of Sawyer, or you. My instincts told me you were both good inside. That you had honor." He shivered. "But this time, I was terrified of Sawyer. I sensed the evil clinging to him, and he was coming for us. He would have struck us down with no remorse." He swiveled on the log and stared at me with wild eyes. "What could have happened to him to make him change like that?"

The sky brightened and birds began to wake, chirping to each other from the treetops. A mist gathered above the wet grass, and squirrels scurried along the branches above our heads. The forest was coming alive with the new day. The death and destruction we'd, just left was still far, far away. This place was protected by its ignorance. But soon enough, fire would rampage these hills. If what the Bible foretold came to pass, the rivers would turn to blood, disease and starvation would befall every living creature, and the world would burn.

But Ivan, with his innocent and youthful mind, wasn't thinking about any of that. He was overwhelmed with sadness and confusion about the loss of his friend. A part of me wanted to shake the pup hard, shouting at him to face the reality that was upon us. Sawyer carrying out Samael's evil orders was only the beginning. It was going to get much worse.

As I stared back at Ivan, seeing his moist and fearful eyes, I couldn't bring myself to do it. More than any of us, he didn't deserve this pain.

I licked my lips, forcing gentleness into my voice. "Sawyer is a soulless Demon. But he still loved and was loved. He made the ultimate sacrifice for us. When Samael took him away from us, Sawyer lost his connection to what was left of his human nature. Once that was removed, he embraced his true nature. It was a matter of survival and instinct for him. He couldn't stop the change, even if he had wanted to."

"Will that happen to you?" Ivan's words rushed out of his mouth.

I peered into the forest. The loss of my own humanity hadn't really occurred to me until now. Memories flitted across my mind. Days splashing in the waves, bread and wine with friends, and the feel of a beautiful lover in my arms. What if they were all lost to me? Would I leave this world as a monster?

"I don't know, Ivan. I hope not, but Sawyer was strong. If he fell, that might be my fate as well." I dropped my head, suddenly feeling exhausted.

Ivan flung his arm around my shoulder. "If that time comes, I hope I'm already dead."

I met his level gaze. "Me too."

His eyes glistened. "I haven't given up on Ember yet. She might succeed in stopping it."

I sighed. My own faith in the beautiful Watcher had been strong since the day I'd carried her to safety when she attacked the compound. I'd recognized her power straight away. There was something else about the young Watcher that made me believe in her, something I couldn't quite grasp. A sort of destiny connected to her. Now, I wasn't so sure.

"It's already begun. You saw what came into the valley. Samael's army is on the move. Most of the population of Oldport was killed by Hell's monsters. How can the world go back to normal after something like that?"

Ivan frowned, but his eyes remained bright, even hopeful. "I don't know if things will ever be normal again, but I do believe in Ember. She'll find a way to save us all."

I chuckled and forced a smile at the pup. I would love to have his faith. "I hope you're right."

Sir Austin pushed aside the branches. "We have company."

I exchanged a worried look with Ivan before we joined the gray-haired Watcher on the knoll. Youmi was already waiting, standing like a statue with his hands on his hips.

"There are too many to count," Youmi said.

I spied down the tree line with Demon eyes, not seeing a thing. I was about to question the water Watcher further when the howls erupted, sending a shiver down my spine.

The sounds rose, gathering more voices, but I still couldn't see any wolves.

"Where are they?" I whispered.

"They're coming," Ivan replied, a hint of excitement in his words. He pointed. "See, there!"

Angus growled, but Ivan placed his hand on the dog's head to quiet him.

Out of the trees came a lone black wolf, then others appeared. Dozens trotted out from the cover of the timber; browns, grays, and snowy white ones padded up the hillside toward us. A sunbeam sprayed down through the clouds, chasing the chill from the air. There were hundreds, perhaps a thousand of wolves arriving. They moved as one across the meadow like a massive shadow. I had seen many spectacles over the centuries, but never a sight like this.

"Who are they?" I asked, unable to keep the awe from my voice.

"It is the great gathering. Wolves from nearly every pack in the world are here," Ivan replied with pride coating his words.

"They are all *here*?" I asked, dumbfounded.

The gray and the black at the front were taller and more muscular than the others. They each had the confident look of leadership. Several smaller females fanned out behind them. The gray male and a tannish-colored female came forward, close enough to touch. When Ivan looked back at me, his eyes were round. His smile spread from ear to ear.

Ivan gestured to the wolves closest to us. "May I introduce you to my parents, Panoosh and Hilda."

CHAPTER 9

EAE

I slashed with the sword Raphael had given me. Black goo splattered my face as the Hell beast dropped to the ground, writhing and shrieking. Another monster appeared, and my sword stabbed again and again. I paused to wipe the sweat from my brow. Fires raged along the ridge and the heat was unbearable. Angry-looking blisters bubbled from my skin, but there was no time to think about the pain. The beasts kept coming.

Pounding wings above me snapped my head up. I recognized Azriel, but the two brown-winged Angels at his side were not known to me. They swooped into the jagged opening in the ground where Hell's creatures were emerging.

My heart leaped with joy when I heard the explosions and felt the ground shifting beneath me. The Angels shot from the chasm, and Azriel paused above it, spreading his arms wide. His chants carried the weight of God's authority and a blue light flashed from his fingertips, meeting the rocks below. The earth gave another heaving groan, and then all was silent. The brown-winged Angels dodged over the pockets of fire, extinguishing them with the draft from their powerful wings. Dust kicked up, spraying me in the face with sharp pebbles and debris, and I had to wipe my eyes with the back of my hand to see clearly.

I barely had time to turn around when I heard the screeching at my back. The beast was almost upon me and I lifted my sword, blinking away the dirt and sweat. It was close enough that I could smell the foul stench of rotten meat from its mouth. It moved with the speed of a mountain lion, and I knew without proper sight, I was at a serious disadvantage.

Its claw struck my thigh, and then it fell away, tumbling down the rocks below me.

I raised my head in amazement. Azriel faced me with his wings folded behind him. There was a strange look on his tattooed face.

"Thank you, brother. That one had nearly gotten me." I nodded at my superior.

Azriel pushed back his hood. His short-cropped hair was black and his skin pale. The contrast was striking in the sunshine. "You confound me, Eae." The Angel flapped his wings once in a show of irritation. "Your wings were taken by the same creatures you fight Hell beasts to protect."

I lowered my head. Sometimes I forgot my wings were gone. I'd gather my shoulder muscles to take flight and then I'd realize I was no longer an Angel—or at least a true one. When the Watchers took my wings, they took my powers and my connection to my Father. With the slice of a sword blade, they'd taken everything from me.

"That is true. But Watchers are not the same as humans. I will help where I can."

"You could have been killed by any of those beasts," Azriel admonished.

"I am diminished, but I am not helpless. I can still carry out my duties," I told him.

"What are your duties, then? You were called as a guardian over the youngWatcher, but that was no fault of your own. She has disappeared, so that task is forgotten."

My muscles tensed and I found it difficult to breathe. As an Angel, my emotions had been clouded with duty and loyalty. I'd watched over the girl, Ember, from the time she was a babe. I'd hide in the bodies of those closest to her, keeping an eye on her development. I'd known what she was from the beginning—a blasphemous consequence of a lustful Angel. It wasn't until later that I discovered she was an heir to the great arch Angel, Uriel. He had instructed me to not only watch the child grow, but to assist her in times of need. I was torn by my duties. On one hand, I had orders to obey, but on the other, I was disturbed as I witnessed the child become a young woman of great power. I soon saw the wrathfulness in Ember's soul. Her temper alarmed me. Yet over the years another feeling had developed for her—love. It wasn't until the day I was severed from the host I'd occupied for much of Ember's life—the spirited young Piper—that I knew true sadness. The human girl had died from the rendering, and it had ultimately been my fault. I was so intent on protecting Ember, I'd failed another one of God's children. If I'd only left her body before the Watchers had her, sacrificing my disguise to the ones who would kill me, the girl would probably still be alive today. Sorrow and guilt had been my companions ever since.

I looked up at Azriel, who waited patiently for me to speak. "I have a sin I must atone. Guarding Ember and helping any humans I can, moves me toward that goal."

The arch Angel shook his head. "The end is near. The others may bicker about how it will be brought about, but there's no question that sooner, rather than later, mankind will be wiped from this earth." He pointed where the cavernous gap in the earth had been a few moments before. "There are not enough Angels in the world to seal every crack. We waste our time."

I cocked my head. "Why, then, do you still labor at it?"

The corners of his mouth lifted and he raised his face to the breeze. "I will carry out my duties until I am instructed to stop. I am loyal only to our Father and the tasks he gave me so long ago." His smile faded and he arched a brow at me. "But what you are doing is different, Eae. Our Father did not give you instructions to destroy Hell beasts when they crossed into the land of men." He wagged a long finger at me. "That is your choice."

"Being with the girl and her friends has affected me, I admit. It seems wrong to stand by and watch them suffer."

"The suffering will come—you alone cannot save them, especially without your wings." His voice lowered and he leaned in. "Let me take you to the pinnacle. You can rest and recover there. Perhaps time in the great library or with the Book of Records will distract you from the goings-on here in this chaotic place."

Azriel was trying to help me. I understood why. He pitied me. An Angel without wings was something altogether strange. The casualty of such a gift from our Father was the ultimate loss.

"I am no longer an Angel. I will stay on the ground and face whatever happens beside the humans."

Azriel shook his head. "It is up to you, brother. I will not argue with you in these dire times of confusion. I pray our Father is merciful to you in the end." He placed his hand on my forehead. "The Lord be with you."

"And also with you," I replied.

With a mighty flap of his wings, he jetted into the sky. I shielded my eyes from the sun and watched him streak into the clouds.

When I dropped my gaze, loneliness touched my heart. The bodies of the Hell beasts I had killed littered the ground, bushes still smoldered, and smoke and dust choked my lungs. I strained to listen and could hear screaming and sirens in the distance. The city of Los Angeles was falling. Azriel was right. There weren't enough Angels to seal all the cracks. Very soon, the entire barrier would come crumbling down.

My head felt heavy. I wanted to be with Ember when that day came. I was her guardian Angel, and even without wings, I could ease her suffering in this world.

"Help us." The words were a quiet whisper on the wind.

I looked around, not seeing who had spoken.

The gurgle of crying met my ears, and I followed the noise around a scorched patch of trees. My eyes widened when they settled on the crouched figures. A boy, maybe ten or eleven years old, huddled with his arms around two smaller girls. Their dirty faces were streaked with tears and blood. A few paces behind them was a camper and a picnic table. The coals still burned in the grill and bowls of food were turned over on the red and white table cloth. The bodies of a woman and man were sprawled in the dirt, their bodies hacked up to pieces. Flies were already buzzing around them.

"Help us." It was the smallest girl who spoke. Her lips trembled and she whimpered.

I remembered Azriel's lecture. Why did I care what happened to the humans? I couldn't change fate. Even if I had wings, there was nothing I could do to save them all. It was a hopeless situation.

Ember's face entered my thoughts. Almost everything had been taken from her—parents, friends, and even her lover. And yet, she still had faith. She continued to fight, no matter what stood in her way. I inhaled deeply, feeling the warmth of the sun on my back. This world still had goodness in it. And as long as it did, I would fight on. Our Father hadn't spoken to me in some time, but my heart told me it's what He would want me to do.

And Ember needed me.

The children's wide eyes were glued on me. I lifted my hand and they scurried to me as fast as their small legs would carry them. The girls' arms encircled my legs, and the boy stood close.

I inclined my head toward the vehicle parked nearby, and eyed the boy. "Can you operate it?"

The boy's eyes grew and his mouth dropped open. He looked from the vehicle then back to me. "I can try."

"Good," I said, disengaging the girls and gently shoving them into the backseat. "I am Eae. You must be brave. We have a long journey ahead of us."

The boy climbed into the driver's seat and I walked around to passenger side. I was really too tall for the human machine, but without wings, I had no choice. I sat down, scrunching my legs up in front of me. The cross dangling from the mirror was a sign that I was on the right path.

"Where are we going?" the boy asked as he fumbled with the keys.

The engine roared to life and I smiled. Such an archaic thing, and yet so useful at the moment.

"First, we will go to the mountains of Tennessee, and if Ember isn't there, we'll travel northward to Ohio."

"Who's Ember?" one of the girls asked, pressing her head in between the front seats and gazing up at me with teary eyes.

I smiled at the child. "Hopefully, with a little help from our Lord, she'll be our salvation.

CHAPTER 10

EMBER

Uriel's red hair whipped around his face in the wind. That face looked even more serious than usual. His blue eyes drifted to Adria, who held her ground, and then to Raphael, whose mouth tipped up crookedly.

"Really, brother. How can anything this child does surprise you?" Raphael's hair was tied in a ponytail and his face was smudged from smoke. His tunic was torn at the side, but I couldn't see any injuries on him. But of course, Angels were better versions of Watchers. I'd expect them to heal from their wounds very quickly.

"Why must the one who carries my blood be so rebellious?" Uriel asked with a huff. He fondled his sword, glaring at me.

"Oh, I don' know. It might be because you're a belligerent Angel," Adria said, smirking.

I swallowed and moved closer to her. I was surprised that when the Angels showed up she didn't jump into the sea in a burst of colors, transforming into a dolphin. She'd recognized Uriel and Raphael and hadn't been afraid. Adria felt comfortable taunting the red headed Angel, and even seemed to be enjoying it.

Uriel's gaze shifted to Adria. "This child should forget the earth Watcher. If he has been captured by Gabriel, then he is a lost soul."

"Just like Sawyer," I whispered, turning away from the trio.

Adria's arm went around me. She squeezed, but didn't say anything. The whale had dropped us off on a small, rocky island earlier. There were several other islands about the same size nearby, and I could see a misty shoreline in the distance. I hadn't bothered to ask our specific location, but I guessed we were off the coast of Oregon or Washington.

Waves crashed on the moss-covered boulders we stood on, spraying my tennis shoes and rumbling in my ears. A few seagulls soared in the cloudy sky, screeching before they'd dive into the ocean. My travels over the past few months had brought me to some pretty exotic places, but all I really wanted to do was be in Ila's valley, or maybe visit Timmy and Chloe in Ohio. My brother and sister-in-law were expecting a baby. My chest tightened at the thought of bringing a child into the world just as it was ending. How unfair it was.

When I faced Uriel, I felt a surge of strength. I had to do whatever I could to save my little niece or nephew. If I failed and we all died, at least I would have tried.

"I couldn't save Sawyer. I understand that. But Insepth isn't lost to us. With your help, we can rescue him."

Uriel threw his head back and snorted. "That is precisely what Gabriel wants. He'll be waiting for us, and he won't be alone. A large contingent is supporting him, including Phanuel. The rest of the hosts are taking orders from Raguel, simply trying to bide time until the Horsemen usher in the end of days."

I ignored Uriel's narrowed eyes. He stood like a seven-foot-tall statue, his wings resting behind him but still vibrating from the cool breeze. For all his fierceness, I'd witnessed his softer side. Buried under the serious-looking, authoritative Angel was a rebel, like me, wanting to break free.

Raphael was also tall and muscular, with the same perfect features and shiny skin as Uriel, but he lacked the intensity. Even now, the corner of his lips twitched. He appeared to be amused with the conversation. He half-spread his brown wings, letting them flutter in the wind as he returned my stare.

"What do you think, Raphael? Is it possible for us to save Inseph from Gabriel and the other Angels?" I asked.

Uriel growled and Raphael eyed him. "Brother, let me speak. Your crimson hair and wings, and your scowling face makes you intimidating, for sure. But don't forget, we are equals."

Uriel's brow lifted, then he nodded.

Raphael turned back to me. "Uriel underestimates our combined power. A successful rescue is possible, but unlikely, given our small numbers. It's foolhardy at best." He tilted his head. "But the important question is, why should we even make the attempt? What purpose does it serve any of us to free a Watcher who has been hostile to Angels, and is powerful enough in his own right to cause mischief and headaches for us all? Tell me, Ember, why?"

My mouth went dry. Raphael, an arch Angel, had addressed me by name. Even Uriel, who was related to me, wasn't able to bring himself to refer to me as anything but "child" and "Watcher." I straightened, pulling away from Adria.

"Because he is my friend. He's helped me out of more than one jam. And that's enough for me." I swallowed, gathering the words in my mind. "But for you and Uriel it's all about doing God's will, right?"

Raphael pursed his lips and nodded once.

"Do you think God wants Gabriel to kidnap another Watcher, just like he did Adria's lover, Vorago?" I glanced anxiously between the two Angels. They looked thoughtful, considering my words. "Gabriel has gone rogue. He's not much different than Samael. He's doing what he wants, and he's even gathered other Angels to his cause." Uriel's brows arched and I hurried on. "He's dangerous, and if the Angels, the ones trying to follow God's instructions, let him get away with it, won't you all be going against God?"

"Ember makes a compelling argument, brother," Raphael said.

Uriel groaned, shaking his head. "What she talks about is war between the Angels. How can we possible sanction such a thing while Samael leads his forces from Hell into this realm? The end is near, we should be working together to carry out the prophecy."

Adria cleared her throat and we all turned to her. "Who knows what the prophecy is anymore. Things haven't gone the way they should have, and the order of events are all wrong. The mindless way you're all floundering shows you have no guidance from Him. He isn't speaking to you, which is curious, making me think He wants you to decide on your own."

"That's ridiculous! We are guided by our Heavenly Father in everything we do," Uriel insisted.

"Not as of late," Raphael said quietly.

Uriel turned his wrath on the other Angel. "Don't tell me you're seriously contemplating helping this little Watcher rescue another Watcher that has been nothing but a nuisance to us."

A smile touched Raphael's lips and I suddenly liked him a lot. "There is no place written in the Scriptures about Gabriel's uprising or Hell being unleashed before the Horsemen ride. The questions these Watchers raise are legitimate. I care not about this earth Watcher who Gabriel holds captive, but the fact that our brother felt justified in taking him, and defying the rest of us, is a problem. One that will only get worse after the rapture." He flapped his wings and shrugged. "Besides, I am bored. A battle with the disobedient ones will be an entertaining diversion from the tedium of the Apocalypse."

"No war should be waged for boredom, Raphael. Your rhetoric worries me," Uriel said in a defeated voice.

"So you'll help me?" I asked Raphael, taking an excited step forward.

"Gabriel and Phanuel cannot be allowed to defy our laws. You're right. They are not so different from Samael in their arrogance. A long time ago, we declared war on our kind at our Father's urging, but this time it will be our own choice. We will present our case to Raguel, Michael, and Azriel. If our brothers agree, we'll take up arms once again." He held me in a steady gaze. His brown eyes were filled with warning. "It is not our place to rescue Watchers or interfere with the end of days. Our battle is with the Angels. It will be up to you to rescue your friend."

Before I had the chance to respond, he jetted upward and disappeared in the clouds. The gust from his departure nearly knocked me down, and I had to spread my legs wide to regain balance.

Uriel sighed. "It seems you got your way again."

His wings unfurled and I rushed forward, grabbing his arm. It was hard as stone beneath my fingers, and even though his eyes snapped angrily at my hand, I didn't let go, fearing he'd bolt into the sky the same way Raphael had.

"But we don't even know where Insepth is being held," I exclaimed.

Uriel's mouth thinned. "I've known all along."

"Then why didn't you tell me in the first place?"

He shook his head and graced me with a gentler look. "Because I didn't want you to go and get yourself killed, that's why. I've worked deliberately to keep you alive. I'm not sure of the reasons for my own actions. It may be the affection I felt for the woman who was your ancestor, and who you remind me of. Or perhaps our Father is prodding me along the way. I realize now that I can't stop your foolishness." He leaned down and the energy around him was so great, I swayed backward. "If you succeed in rescuing the Watcher, which I doubt will be the case, you may be tempted to divert what was written in Scripture. Your interference will not be tolerated by the Angels. I will not be able to protect you if you go down that path."

I began to open my mouth, but snapped it shut. *One battle at a time, Ember.*

"You will find the Watcher in the place of Armageddon, where it is prophesied that a battle between Angels, during the end of times, will take place. We always assumed the war would be with Samael and the Fallen Angels, but now I'm not so sure."

I swallowed. "Where do I find Armageddon?"

"Tel Megiddo is a town near the Sea of Galilee in Israel. If a battle is to be had, it will be there. And that's where you will find the Watcher." He brought his lips to my ears and the sudden closeness made my knees weak. "If Raphael fails to rally the others, you will be alone. And you're no match for Gabriel, especially with Phanuel at his side. Tread carefully. You are not immortal like the Angels, and you are not human, either. When the Judgement comes, it's your soul you should be concerned about."

He pulled back and beat his wings. Uriel's departure wasn't as swift as Raphael's. He hovered in the sky, looking down at me for a moment. "I wish you God's speed!" he called out, and then he was gone.

The clouds parted, letting rays of sunshine through. The sounds of the waves were once again in my ears and the smell of seaweed and salt water filled my nose. I breathed it in deeply and exhaled. My elements were quiet, and I almost felt like a normal girl. I smiled. All I longed for was the boredom that Raphael hated. A few days leisurely hacking through the woods on Cricket was nothing but a dream now. My horse was human, and soon there wouldn't be any more trails to enjoy.

"Everything happens for a reason—even the small things. Your heart will guide you to your destiny."

I felt Adria's water power soothing my emotions, making me calm when I should have been a nervous wreck.

"You aren't coming with me, are you?" I already knew the answer.

"No, I am selfish. I've missed too many years with my lover. I want to spend what time I have left with Vorago. And when the sea boils, I'll need to comfort the creatures that live there. If I can ease their suffering, then I will. I will be with you in spirit though, dear Ember. I hope you get Insepth back, and that Gabriel finally faces justice for his crimes."

"I'll do my best."

"A loophole to the other side of the world will be easy for you. What you face once you arrive will be more of a challenge. But I have faith in you and call you sister."

Adria pulled me into a tight hug and the shells in her hair scraped against the side of my face. "Someday, we will meet again, and it will be a fine day."

She released me and dove from the rock into the sea. I followed her to the edge and looked over. At first, I didn't see anything, but then a shrill whistle erupted and I followed the sound. A dolphin breached the surface, jumping high into the air. It splashed into the water and a second later it jumped again, only this time another dolphin was beside it. Their joyful whistles filled the air and my insides warmed.

Would I meet Adria again? It didn't really matter. Seeing the pair of dolphins joyously playing in the waves was enough. At least Adria and Vorago had some time together.

I turned away from the glorious ocean and reached for my elements. Insepth had taught me how to weave the loophole, and with the combination of my elements, the task went quickly.

The opening I created looked like an egg-shaped, hazy window. A warm, dry breeze blew from it, and I could see palm trees and mounds covered with ancient looking ruins. There were square plots of croplands checkering the distance, and just beyond the opening were rock stairs that rose up between broken pillars.

I sucked in one last breath of sea air and stepped through the hole.

For the first time in many months, I was completely alone. And I was honestly glad for it.

Time was running out and I was afraid this was going to be my last battle.

CHAPTER 11

INSEPTH

The flapping of wings and the wind in my face pushed me backward. The room calmed and there were footsteps. My eyes were swollen, making my vision minimal at best. I focused on my sense of hearing, counting two Angels. I didn't have to guess for long who they were.

"How does your head feel, Watcher?" Gabriel kneeled in front of me, turning his gaze sideways to peer at me.

My legs were secured with an iron chain that was draped over a stone archway and suspended between the pillars in a pit at the center of the ruins. A few shards of sunlight squeezed through the slits above, telling me it was still daytime. The cool, dank air and the heavy covering of dust made me think that the buried structure hadn't been used in a long while.

Crimson-colored Angel wardings covered the smooth ceiling. They were newly painted on a swath of replaced stone. The rest of the structure was crumbling, but this small area had been updated because of me, I assumed. The Angels weren't taking any chances.

My head did ache. Hanging upside down for more than a day wasn't a pleasant ordeal. But I sure as hell wasn't going to give the damn Angels any satisfaction.

I spit out some blood from my cut lip and drew in a shaky breath. "Actually, it's a fine form of meditation—one I suggest you try, Gabriel."

The punch came swiftly, connecting with my stomach and causing me to swing wildly back and forth. I tried to draw into a fetal position, but the bonds that held my wrists and my exhausted limbs kept me from doing so. The pain that shot through me was numbed from dizziness quickly enough.

"Really, brother. Is it necessary to goad him so?" Phanuel reached out, grabbing my side, forcing my movement to stop. "He isn't worth your energy, I should think."

Gabriel chuckled. "Oh, so wrong you are. This one" —he poked me, sending me swinging again— "is very valuable to us. The female Watcher, Uriel's spawn, will come for him. Mark my words."

Phanuel exhaled. "Why are you obsessed with that one? She's young and weak—another being not worth your attention. Don't you think we have more pressing matters to attend to?"

"You have trouble seeing past that long nose of yours, eh, brother? Uriel will not let the girl fall. He may have no interest in Watchers or even humans, but this offspring of his is different. He has feelings for her, and we can use that to our advantage."

"How so?" Phanuel paced the room. "Your impetuousness is likely to bring the entire Celestial Host down on us. We have numbers, but an all-out war isn't sustainable for long. I agreed that the hastening of the prophecy in Revelation is a good move, but making enemies fighting with our own kind to accomplish our goal is suicide."

"Ha!" Gabriel barked. "With Uriel on our side, we near equal strength to the other arches, and combine that with these Watchers' powers, we'll be indestructible."

The blood settled in my head making it difficult to think, let alone talk, but I couldn't hold my tongue. "Ember and I will never join our power to yours, Angel. We'll die before that'll happen."

Gabriel slid back to his knees, grasping my face between his hands. "We have no intention of having your corrupt elements touch ours." He came closer and his power shone off him, forcing me to squeeze my eyes shut. "We have ways to extract your powers, and when we do, we'll have a formidable weapon at our disposal. But of course, once the elements have been sucked from your bodies, there will be nothing left of you except skin and bones."

"That's impossible," I whispered, afraid it was true.

"We're Angels. We've been reaping souls for millennia. Your *soul* is your element. It's not a pretty thing to strip a Watcher of their element—being akin to the severing of an Angel's wings—which I've heard you've had personal experience with. We've done it before, and it worked marvelously."

Fear pricked my insides. If it was my destiny to be destroyed in such a way, so be it. But not Ember—glorious Ember. She was the first of our kind to possess all the elements. Her Watcher abilities are unrivaled, except by the Angels themselves. Even with the world crumbling, her mere existence hinted at her greatness.

I remembered the feel of her lips on mine when I'd kissed her. From the first time I'd seen her and felt her Gaia, I'd been drawn to her. But my relation to her was first mentor, and then adversary. There was no time to explore the feelings I knew I had for her.

And then there was Sawyer. Her bond to the Demon was not just a passing fancy. Being a product of the earth myself, I was well aware that their love was real. After the mistake I'd made when rendering the Angel Eae from her friend and accidentally causing the girl's death, I had been compelled by guilt to let Ember have her Demon. I had even worked to protect him, knowing how hurt she'd have been if anything had befallen him. I had buried my own irrational emotions toward the girl, trying to do the noble thing, even though I knew from personal experience that being honorable usually left one dead or miserable—or both.

Then out of the blue, Sawyer did the unthinkable, binding himself to the Devil. He did it to save Ember, but it destroyed his connection to her, freeing her from him forever. When I'd stolen that kiss, it was because I believed death was imminent, but then Phanuel plucked me from the skies, and I helplessly watched Gabriel careening toward Ember. They crashed into the ocean, and then something happened that I hadn't anticipated. The ocean drove him away, as if repulsed by Gabriel. The last glimpse I caught of my student was on the back of an enormous whale as it crested the surface and carried her away. Hopefully to safety.

Even through the torture I'd endured from Gabriel, that kiss had taken up most of my thoughts. I was alive and so was Ember—and she'd kissed me back. My Earth had twirled with her Gaia for enough seconds to spark a connection I'd never felt before. Was it protectiveness or possessiveness, or something much deeper? I wasn't sure. After hundreds of years and the same number of lovers, I'd never experienced such a moment of joy.

Now more than ever, I wanted to feel it again. Only Ember could awaken my heart. But as much as I wanted her in my arms, she mustn't come here to save me. It would mean her death.

My chested constricted and my head throbbed. For the first time in my life, I'd fallen in love.

It was just my luck there would be no world to enjoy it in.

CHAPTER 12

IVAN

My mother pushed her long, gray hair back from her face, fighting the wind to hold it in place. Her gaze would occasionally settle on me and she'd smile, but it was forced. I wasn't sure if her ill mood was because she had to take human form for the meeting, or that the end of the world was upon us. When I was a pup, she had been an attentive mother, but she became distant during the years after my first change. She had refused to remain in human form, preferring the woods to town life, and sent me away to live with my grandparents. Father was a leader of wolves, and I understood his inability to leave the pack for even a few years, but mother's refusal to stay with her pup had seriously altered our relationship. We were almost strangers now.

"How can you be so sure they will come for us in our animal forms?" my father asked.

Lord Quintus was tall and lean, and even resting against the thick tree trunk, his muscles were strung tight. He ran his fingers through his cropped beard before he answered. "We have a spirit leader among our pack. She has interpreted the Scriptures for our kind, and says the same calamity to befall the humans will strike down every beast, both land and sea bound. There will be no escape for us." He leaned back. "We have two choices. We can hide in the woods or we can fight with the humans."

"We are Growlers, not the furless ones' puppets. I will not fight beside them," Hilda hissed out the words with a snarl.

I cringed at my mother's rudeness. She was not the leader of any pack, and should not have spoken for father. I understood her hatred of the humans. Hunters had murdered her family for their pelts when she had been a pup. She'd barely escaped with her life, and when my grandparents found her, she'd been out of her mind. Father later told me she was like a lost soul when he first met her. His gentle love healed her tattered spirit only partially. And now, she was falling apart once again.

I avoided my mother's angry eyes as my interest drifted to Tamira, Lord Quintus' daughter. She had changed to human form for the great gathering, and was sitting cross-legged beside her mother on the far side of the fire pit. She was as delicate looking as a young woman as she had been in wolf form. Smooth, black tresses framed her oval face. Her eyes were almond colored and widely spaced, and they'd occasionally rise to meet mine, only to dart away. Her cheeks would redden every time we made eye contact, and she kept turning into her woolen jacket to hide her face from me.

I was confused by her shyness. We'd run together through the woods to help Ember and Insepth defeat the Watchers of Light. Our voices had melded together to distract our enemies, and we'd barely escaped the collapsing mountain. Now the girl wouldn't even look at me.

She was so different from Piper. Memories of the human girl I had loved still reverberated in my mind. We'd shared a few kisses and I'd thought there would be many more to come. But her life had been stolen away. I stared at the flames, wondering if Piper would be angry with me for liking another girl. I didn't think so. She had a generous spirit—she'd want me to be happy.

Horas elbowed me and I looked up.

"Pup, I asked you a question," Father said, cold breath streaming from his mouth. Daylight had revealed a covering of snow on the mountain peaks, and flurries danced in the air around the clearing.

"I'm sorry…what did you say?" I stammered.

The lines on Father's face were deeper than I remembered. He frowned back at me and said, "This Watcher friend of yours—you trust her?"

"With my life, Father." I glanced at Horas, who nodded at me to continue. "She's loyal and kind, and her powers are extraordinary."

"Lord Quintus said she released the dragons from the mountain. What did she do with them?" Father asked.

"We rode on them into Purgatory. It was the only way we could enter," I said.

Several people gasped and Mother made a growling noise.

"Why go there?" Lord Quintus leaned forward.

I wasn't comfortable telling the wolves about Ember taking dark particles to change her horse into a human. The evil Watcher who had created Growlers was hated by our kind. He had combined dark particles with his own magic to build an army of animal people. Other Watchers had destroyed him for his deeds, but we lived with the curse of being split, instead of one. I knew the information would not be well received.

I thought quickly and told only part of the truth. "We went to save a dolphin Growler. He had been imprisoned there by an Angel a long time ago. Ember was helping a friend. That is her way." I thought back to the day in the Oldport High School when she'd stopped the other boys from picking on me. I had been smaller back then, and it seemed like a lifetime ago. It was that moment, though, when I knew I would follow her anywhere.

"Where are the dragons now?" Father asked. His dark blue eyes sparked the same as when he was hunting deer. The look made me more alert, and I sat taller.

"One died in Purgatory." Seeing the surprise in all the eyes around the fire, I quickly added, "There was another dragon there— she'd escaped from Hell. The two dragons we freed battled her and won, but Ormer was killed."

Father rubbed his chin and exchanged a glance with Lord Quintus.

"Why such interest in the dragons?" Sir Austin asked, pursing his lips. Youmi stood beside him, his eyes darting around the clearing as if he expected Hell hounds to arrive at any moment.

Lord Quintus looked at me when he answered. "Just think of it. A dragon is the most powerful creature ever to have lived. If one were to join our cause, we might have a hope of winning."

My stomach leaped into my throat. "No!" Ember had told me that Chumana had gone to raise a clutch of eggs. She had already sacrificed her mate, and she was the last dragon. "It's not her war. She was imprisoned for thousands of years."

"How did your friend Ember control her? What magic did she use?" Father asked. There was a hungry look in his eyes.

"There was no magic. Chumana wasn't controlled by anyone. She decided to help us, knowing the risks. Dragons are sentient beings. They are not slaves." My voice rose while I was speaking and a hush fell over the crowd. I lifted my head to see hundreds of staring eyes.

"Well said," Horas patted my back, and then faced the others. "What is coming for you is more than a single dragon can defeat. The armies of Hell are vast, and they've already arrived."

Mother stood, pointing a finger at the Demon. "They are far away from our land. You bring troubles to us that aren't our business."

"I'm afraid, my lady, it's inevitable. Evil will quickly spread everywhere, even here." Sir Austin looked solemnly around the gathering. All eyes were on the Watcher, and they were listening intently. "The one hope mankind, Watchers, and Growlers have is to band together. It's the only way."

"I will never fight at your side," Mother spat, before whirling and striding into the woods. A burst of colors was visible through the pine branches, and then she was gone.

"Please excuse my wife," Father said. "She's having a hard time with the news of the Apocalypse."

Sir Austin offered a curt nod.

Except for a few chirping birds and the breeze rustling through the leaves, the clearing was silent. My stomach grumbled and I swallowed down my hunger. It had been a day since I'd eaten anything. I glanced at Tamira again, and she hastily looked away. I hid a smile behind my hand. She didn't want me to know it, but she was curious.

Lord Quintus stood and faced the crowd. "You have heard of the Watcher's deeds. Now it is time to discuss this among your packs. Do we disperse, living out our days in hiding, hoping for the best? Or do we join with these Watchers and the humans and fight. We will take a vote when the moon rises again."

There was a hum of murmurs as the wolves began moving about. Smoke from campfires trickled into the frigid air. It would be a long afternoon, waiting for the sun to set and the moon to rise.

"What are you doing—I thought we were returning home?" Youmi whispered harshly to Sir Austin when Lord Quintus and my father had moved off. Out of the corner of my eye, I saw Tamira waiting at the edge of the gathering. I wanted to go to her, but hearing what the Watchers said was more important.

Sir Austin was gray haired, but stood straight, and was still strong looking. He crossed his arms, puffing out his chest. "The chain of events here lately are bothering me."

"How so?" Horas moved in closer, prompting Youmi and I to follow suit. The wolves might be my kind, but I'd bonded with these men, even though two were Watchers and one was a Demon. They, along with the German Shepherd pressing against my leg, were my pack.

"I've studied the Bible for centuries. My fascination with the Angels drove me to travel the world, seeking wisdom on the subject. After all, I exist because of one of their dalliances with a woman." He paused and searched the tree line with a hard gaze. We stared at the Watcher, waiting for him to continue. "Much has been written about the end of days, and yet nothing is happening in the expected order or way."

"Why do you think that is?" Horas asked, his eyes regarding Sir Austin with intensity.

Sir Austin licked his lips. "Perhaps this isn't supposed to be the end of the world."

"I call you friend, but you are mad." Youmi shook his head. "Angels are flying around in the open, the barriers are breaking and Hell beasts are pouring into this realm. The Horsemen have even arrived. How much more proof do you need?"

"Yes, yes, all those things are occurring. It is true. But the rapture should have preceded the Horsemen and the Hell beasts. We have witnessed Angels fighting among themselves, and the horn was blown by an adolescent man, rather than Gabriel himself. Something is amiss!" Sir Austin's voice rose to a level that caused some of the nearby Growlers to turn their heads. The Watcher leaned in closer and whispered, "A pocket of Hell spilling into Ila's valley is not right, I tell you. Devastation should be happening in all corners of the world if it is truly the end of it all."

Horas' mouth thinned and he glanced around. His sharp features and quick movements reminded me that he had been a Roman soldier a thousand years ago. He was clever and witty with good instincts. I waited anxiously to hear what he thought.

"If you're correct, and God hasn't decided to destroy the world at this time, then what do you think is going on?" Horas asked the Watcher.

Sir Austin threw his hands up. "Blast if I knew. It's a mystery. But I believe we should battle these evil forces invading our lands. We should attempt to drive them back."

Horas searched our faces with keen eyes, then a grin spread across his face. "I'm always in for a good battle, especially when my hope has been renewed."

I exhaled. "We need Ember and Insepth."

Horas curled his fingers around his chin. "Yes, yes, we do. How do we reach them? I've tried the cell phone, but neither has answered. They're with the Angels, and I'm sure their location is heavily warded."

"There is a way…" Sir Austin trailed off, shifting his gaze to Youmi.

Youmi held up his hands, shaking his head. "My water power gives me the ability to do it, but I haven't visited that place since I was a young man. I would surely fail."

"Ember is a dream walker. Her own powers should augment yours if you can just step your foot into the dream world and call her." Sir Austin's eyes were bright.

"It might work," Youmi conceded, scrunching up his brow in thought. "It would burn a lot of energy, leaving me weak afterward. It would be best if I made the attempt at night, when there's a better chance that Ember is asleep."

Sir Austin nodded and Horas flashed a smile my way. When I glanced over my shoulder, looking for Tamira, she was gone. I grunted, pulling my ball cap down further onto my head in a brisk motion.

"She's over there." Horas backhanded my shoulder and pointed toward the tree line.

My mouth dropped open. "How did you know?"

The Roman shrugged. "I'm a thousand years old, and I'm Italian. I know all about romantic attraction, and can spot it a mile away." He grinned, grabbed my cap and mussed up my hair before returning it.

"Go on, talk to her. At least someone in our group should be having a little fun." When I hesitated, Horas gave me a little push. "Whether Sir Austin is right or wrong about his end-of-days theory, time is something we may not have a lot of. Go on!"

I ran a few strides when Horas chased me, only slowing when he returned to the Watchers and I was almost to Tamira. She was plucking through her backpack when she looked up. Her eyes widened and she quickly stood.

"Oh, hello, Ivan." She looked down at her foot, digging it into the leaf covered ground.

"I am glad to see you again," I said, wishing she would meet my eyes.

Tamira swayed and snorted. "It's strange for me in human form. I've spent most of my years as a wolf, but Father insisted I attend the meeting like this." She spread her arms wide and peeked at me with a knit brow.

"You're a beautiful woman." The words were out of my mouth before I could stop them. My heart hammered and I added, "I meant, you're attractive as a wolf or woman." Her cheeks reddened and she didn't say anything. "I'm sorry. I barely know you. It's rude to say such things."

Tamira's face lifted and her smile was dazzling. "Oh, no. I think it's sweet. You're the nicest boy I've ever met." She laced her fingers and then unlaced them, fidgeting with her hands. "I'm surprised you even talk to me. You're—" She searched for a word. "—worldlier than I am."

I grunted and felt the tension leave my body. "Me, worldly? I don't think so."

"You've traveled to America and you spend more time as a human than a wolf," she argued.

I sniffed the air and caught her scent—meadow flowers and apples. A few strands of her black hair fluttered across her face. I couldn't stop myself from reaching out, catching the locks and tucking them behind her ear. Her cheek was warm. She looked up at me with parted lips, and I leaned in.

Our lips almost met when the first scream sounded and my head snapped in the direction of the clearing. An area that had been covered with people a moment earlier had fallen away, leaving a sink hole that was burning.

Loud barking echoed through the hills, the voices of creatures I would never forget. Smoke rose from the chasm, and from the acid mist, sprang the Hell beasts.

I grabbed Tamira's hand, dragging her back to the Watchers and Horas.

Angus barked at our arrival, and Horas pushed me and Tamira behind him. "Change to wolves!" he ordered.

Blasts of color erupted across the hillside and the screams turned to howls and yips. A wolf was decapitated just after making the change, and another was impaled on a spear that was carried by a half-lizard, half-man looking creature.

"We fight?" I asked Horas.

Horas' brown eyes were steady. "We fight."

Tamira changed first, and just as my skin became covered in fur, I saw Sir Austin thrust his hands forward. The wind he created spiraled, forming a funnel cloud that sped toward the gaping fracture in the ground.

Wolves leaped at the Hell beasts, crunching on necks and wherever they could get a good hold. The great numbers of Growlers and their instinct to work together slowed the onslaught emerging from the hole. Youmi pulled water from the creek at the base of the hill and slammed it into one of the three-headed Hell hounds.

Several explosions, one right after the other, shook the forest and I lurched backward. Wings flashed in the thick fumes. Hell's Angels had arrived.

Angus' growl made me search in his direction. A creature from childhood nightmares crawled toward him. Its eyes glowed red and its limbs were malformed like a giant spider. I rushed forward and sunk my teeth into the back of the thing's neck. It shrieked and rolled, pinning me beneath its bloated body. Tamira and Angus jumped in together, each biting into its multiple arms.

Horas appeared and grabbed the creature's head, twisting with a jerk. The crunching sound was followed by a gush of black ooze.

"Fall back!" Horas shouted.

As I gathered my muscles and got to my feet, I followed Horas' gaze.

It was Sawyer. And he was striding toward us with murder in his red eyes.

CHAPTER 13

MADDIE

"What did you see?" the U.S. National Guardsman asked. I would guess he was only in his twenties, but clutching the semi-automatic weapon in his hands, it didn't matter.

I exchanged a glance with Preston, who shrugged. He held the leashes of two dogs—a Rottweiler and a hound. He'd been focused on petting the dogs most of the morning.

A gray cloud still drifted over Oldport, and I coughed, trying to rid my throat of the scratchy feeling. I was calmer than I'd been the night before. My parents had survived. Hell's soldiers had changed direction when they'd reached my neighborhood, rampaging into the hills. They left a trail of burned devastation and then disappeared.

My eyes followed the swath of smoke rising from the mountainside. *The way to the cabin where Ember lived.* She had left with the Horsemen, but what of the others who were there? What happened to them? Were they ripped limb from limb the way Randy had been? Or maybe they'd burned to death like Lindsey.

My chest trembled and I struggled to catch a breath. I closed my tired eyes and pictured my boyfriend and my best friend the way they used to be—silly, happy and…alive. It hurt too much to think about what had happened and I forced the images from my mind. At least their suffering was over. I feared ours was just beginning.

I finally managed to inhale deeply, clearing the fogginess that had settled over me after the Angels had carried me and Preston to safety. When I opened my eyes, hot spots still smoldered and the scent of burning flesh was heavy in the air.

My lips were dry and cracked and it was difficult to speak without breaking down in a fit of sobs. I said a silent prayer to Jesus for help and found the strength to answer the man. "I'm not sure. There were explosions and the fire spread quickly," I lied.

The man stared at me, frowning. "We've heard stories about monsters…"

The inferno had been so hot that there was not much left of the school, stadium—or the bodies. Now, in the light of day, it just seemed like a really bad nightmare. But I wasn't fooling myself. It had been all too real.

I raised my face to the rumbling noise in the sky. Another pair of fighter jets streaked over the town. The power was out and there was no cell phone reception. Mom had told me that strange things were happening all over the country: random acts of violence, weather anomalies, and many fires. The National Guard was patrolling the streets of American cities, and more and more jets from the air base had taken flight.

"I'm sorry. I didn't see anything like that." I was determined not to make matters worse by creating a panic. Soon enough, the world would know that it was ending, and in the most horrible way possible. I wasn't going to be the one to freak people out before they absolutely needed to be.

The young man patted his gun and glanced up at the jet trails in the sky. "Well, if the rumors are true, we're ready for 'em."

As he walked away, I scowled at his bravado. I hoped he didn't have to meet one of the giant, three-headed dogs or the glowing-eyed creatures. I wondered how brave he would be if he did.

"It makes you wonder," Preston said, and I turned around. He was still petting his dogs. "If it came down to it, I bet an Angel wouldn't be a match against a missile."

"I don't know about that. Angels and those monsters that attacked the town are magical. I'm not so sure technology would be able to beat them," I shivered at the thought of the military fighting Satan's army.

Preston grunted. "It'd be a hell of fight, though."

"Maddie," Grandpa called out.

When I looked up, he was pushing through the throng of people who were waiting for bottles of water from a soldier standing on an armored truck. Some people were crying and others shuffled along the sidewalk in a daze. The loss of the half of the inhabitants of the town was a shock to everyone.

I rushed up to Grandpa, grasping his hands and tugging him away from the crowd.

"You're alive!" I hugged him fiercely, inhaling the smell of his aftershave lotion in a long breath. Being in his strong arms made the world a little brighter. "I saw that the church burned, and when momma couldn't find you, we feared the worst."

He pulled back and touched my face, wiping the tears away with his thumbs. "Oh, dear, Maddie! You are a sight for sore eyes."

"Randy and Lindsey didn't make it. It was horrible—"

He gave me a gentle shake. "Hush, child. Let those memories go. They are with our Lord and Savior now. He hasn't forsaken us."

"But He has!" I said loudly. Grandpa put his arm around me and guided me away from the curious glances. I rushed out in a lower voice, "Everything you've been preaching for years is true—the end of world is here! I've been talking to Angels. They say I'm supposed to be a Scribe of God, and Preston, too. But even the Angels don't know what's going on. God isn't talking to them anymore."

I knew I sounded insane, but Randy and Lindsey were dead, and so were a lot of other people. The world had gone crazy, and Grandpa, being a preacher, should understand better than anyone.

"Oh, child, He is with us always." His dark eyes twinkled. "Maybe the Angels have become arrogant and lost their way. It is *faith* that keeps Him close."

"You believe me?" I whispered.

Grandpa's smile was sad. "Yes, I do. Because the Lord warned me this was coming."

I swallowed, staring at Grandpa's face. His gray, tight curls were longer than usual, and there was coarse salt and pepper stubble all around his mouth and chin. His sweater was buttoned unevenly. I'd never seen him in such a disheveled state.

Just as Grandpa didn't question my words, I believed his. "What did He say?" I murmured.

"That He loves us, and that we should have hope."

"Hope?" Images of the night before, when monsters poured out of the ground and began ripping my friends apart flashed through my mind. "How can we be hopeful when the people we love are dying?"

"You trust me, don't you, Maddie?" Grandpa's voice was soft and coaxing.

I nodded, fighting back the tears.

"Go north to Cincinnati. You can stay with your Aunt Marcie." My mouth opened to protest, but he held up his hand. "He must go with you." He flicked his finger toward Preston, who had followed our movement. "There's no time to waste. You must be on your way."

"But what about Mom and Dad, and you?" Tears streamed down my cheeks and my stomach became tied in knots. "I can't leave you all, not now, with everything that's going on."

He pressed his finger to my lips. "You are a strong girl, and you have been chosen. It's a great honor." He smiled. "Swallow your grief and go. We'll meet again, whether in this life or the next. We'll be together again." He began to pull away and I pressed into his side, clutching him harder. "You must let me go so I can help people." He fanned his hand out. "They need me."

I sniffed into his sweater and nodded. He hadn't taken more than a few steps when the crowd folded around him. His voice rang out loud and clear, asking everyone to bow their heads in prayer.

I stood silently and listened to Grandpa's words of encouragement and love as I watched Preston hug his mom and pass the leashes to her. Her red hair was a mess and her face was as wet as mine. She had a shotgun strapped over her shoulder. I guessed that the bearded men with her must be Preston's uncles or cousins. They were also armed and clad in camo. They thought they were ready for anything. Preston's mom raised her hand at me and I waved back.

"Can you do this?" Preston asked, stopping in front of me. He had the keys to his truck in his hand.

I tried to ignore the burning smells, the military men, and the crowd of people praying on the roadway. Turning my face into the sunshine, I muttered, "I hope so."

CHAPTER 14

EAE

"**B**ut I have to pee!" Emily screeched.

The sound pierced my head, and I found myself rolling my eyes, mimicking the boy who was driving the car when he glanced my way. It was a miracle that we'd made it through five states without being pulled over. The boy's abilities had improved in the last couple of days, but it had been a frightening experience early on. The pillows had made a real difference. Now he could see over the dashboard much better. Joey was an amicable and intelligent child, but caring for the girls was proving to be more difficult than I had anticipated.

I searched the side of the highway for a place to safely pull over.

"I don't want to pee in the grass again. Can't we go to a restaurant and have burgers?" Emily hung over my seat, slipping her skinny arms around my neck.

Children were resilient. Once we were away from the chaos and the bodies of their parents, Joey, Emily, and Sarah came out of their shells, so to speak. The tears and trembling ended sometime in Utah, and now I couldn't keep the girls from touching me. They climbed on my lap whenever they could and the hugs never ended. At first, their affection had shaken me, but I was getting used to it. Angels weren't supposed to come directly in contact with humans, even an Angel without wings. It felt very wrong, but I couldn't correct the situation easily. I'd considered leaving the children in a safe place where they would be found by their own kind, but thought better of it. Hell was being released on earth, and I didn't want these little ones to suffer through that. When the time came, I would protect them the best I could. I was sure our Father would show mercy on them. But what I was going to do with them until then was a pressing concern.

They required regular feedings and breaks to relieve themselves. They didn't seem able to exist without attention, either. They talked constantly, making it impossible for me to think properly, let alone plan for the days ahead.

We passed a sign saying we'd entered the state of Missouri, and I could see the lights of a developed area off the next exit in the distance.

"We'll take that road." I pointed for Joey to see.

"Okay, Eae. I'll take it real slow," he said, leaning forward, his face tight with concentration.

"Not too slow, liked we talked about. If we are to make it to our destination, we mustn't be noticed." I gripped the door handle when Joey hit the gas pedal a little too hard.

"Ohio, Ohio, Ohio," Emily chanted, squeezing my neck tighter.

I tugged her arms away so I could speak properly. "Tennessee, child. We go there first."

She shook her head, whipping it back and forth. "Nooo. It's burning there."

I swiveled in the seat, staring at the blonde-haired, blue-eyed little girl. We'd taken a country road the previous night and pulled into a stand of trees for the children to sleep for a few hours. Emily had woken in the night, crying about the forest being on fire. There had been an odd feeling in the air when I'd questioned her about the ill dream, almost as if she'd had a foretelling event. I hadn't thought that possible—she was nearly a babe.

But now, I wasn't so sure. Her insistence was almost believable.

"Why don't you drive? You're the grownup," Sarah asked, squeezing in beside her sister.

"That way, Joey. Go to the right and pull into the back lot of that restaurant." I hung on as he made the turn a bit too fast, then I answered Sarah. "I've told you this already. My kind do not drive automobiles."

"You're so funny," Emily giggled, twirling some of my curly hair in her fingers.

She'd forgotten all about Tennessee and was looking brightly at the glowing sign with a picture of a piece of meat between two slices of bread. These *burgers* seemed to be the only thing the child would eat.

Joey found a space behind the one-story building and parked, turning off the engine. The machine was crooked, but I didn't say anything. I realized my expectations were too high for the boy. He dropped the keys into my palm and jumped out of the car. The girls followed all too quickly.

"Wait, stop!" I ordered, but the girls ignored me.

Grasping each other's hands, Emily shouted, "But we have to peeeee!"

"They are insufferable, disobedient creatures," I muttered.

Joey stared up at me with raised brows. "What does insufferable mean?"

His innocence was like a slap in the face. "It is not a fair description of your sisters. They are good children. And I am very proud of your resiliency. Your automobile operating skills are quite impressive as well."

Joey's mouth spread into a wide smile. "You really think so?"

"I sincerely do," I answered, giving him a gentle shove toward the restaurant.

"My dad wouldn't even let me mow the lawn, and now I'm driving on the highway. I think…"

The stream of his words disappeared from my hearing as I looked around. The street lights and signs were bright, but few cars were coming or going, and even fewer people were hanging about. A nearly full moon lit up the sky and the drone of traffic on the highway filled the crisp evening. A gust of wind caused dry leaves to dance across the parking lot and pelt us in a golden frenzy.

Joey laughed at the onslaught and I patted his back.

Bad things were on the wind and the child was oblivious.

We entered the empty establishment, and Joey took a left turn to the restrooms. I chose a table with four seats beside the window where I could keep an eye on the vehicle. The woman who approached the table was ancient looking. Her long gray hair was pulled up into a bun and the cane she walked with tapped on the hard, checkered flooring. She wore a server dress and held a notepad in her free hand. Her name tag read *Mary*.

All that wasn't as shocking as her eyes. A white film glazed over them. She was completely blind.

The children ran to the table together. Sarah and Joey took the seats across from me, but instead of sitting, Emily threw her arms around the old woman's legs. I briefly wondered about the child's show of familiarity with a complete stranger, but Mary didn't seem bothered by the display of affection.

"You're a sweet child," Mary said. She shuffled Emily into her seat and took everyone's orders.

I only wanted coffee and a slice of apple pie, two things I'd become quite fond of during my time in man's realm.

"You shouldn't have desert before dinner!" Sarah chastised.

I lifted a brow at the girl. "I am an adult and can eat the way I like. It is something you have to look forward to when you are grown."

After I said it, I regretted my words. Little Sarah would never get the chance to become a woman.

"Yes, it is a sad thing," Mary said, tilting her head at me.

My heart thrummed and my breathing slowed. "Who are you?"

She offered me a toothless smile that made my skin tingle with foreboding.

"Oh, surely, even without those glorious wings, you know me?" she said. Her tone was mocking and I stood, reaching out quickly to snatch the children from their seats and shove them behind me one by one.

"If I knew your identity, I wouldn't have asked," I said quietly.

Emily gripped my one leg, while Sarah and Joey pressed up against my other leg.

"I am one of the Virtues, Eae."

I dipped my head. "Forgive me! I have been cut off from Heaven and have lost my way," I said forcefully, wishing for understanding.

The Virtues were beings of light and beauty. They were in charge of delivering Heavenly miracles upon those humans whom God favored. They rarely came into this world, and only in times of great joy—or great disaster. They were there when Jesus ascended to Heaven after his death, and also during the human wars. They made heroes, giving them courage in the darkest of times.

Mary reached out and touched my head. "The Lord is with you. There is nothing to forgive. In this guise, I'm not so sure even Michael would recognize me in quick fashion."

I lowered my voice, despite the fact that the restaurant was empty, except for the children and us. "Why are you here?"

She pursed her lips and sighed heavily. "Bad days are upon us, and evil is spreading across this world. The balance is broken and

Angels run amuck. Some of us are here to restore that balance, others only to observe."

"Can you stop Samael and his army?" I whispered, searching the woman's white eyes, hoping to see some of my glorious Heaven there. But I couldn't see anything but an old, blind woman before me.

Mary snorted out a short laugh. "It is not my place to stop Samael or Gabriel or even the humans, who are amassing their weapons of destruction as we speak." She glanced down at the children as if she could see them, and when Emily peeked around my leg, Mary graced her with another smile like she knew the small child was looking at her. "I am merely here to give strength to those who deserve it, and to those who need it. And you, Eae, are one of those individuals."

She raised her hand in blessing. "May the light of our Lord Father shine upon you and give you strength." Blinding light rained down, and the children held onto me harder, squealing.

The warm touch of our Father filled my heart with hope until it was almost bursting. For the first time since I'd had my wings taken from me, I felt His presence. Tears rolled down my cheeks and I gladly let them fall.

"Listen to the girl, Eae. Go where she directs," Mary said.

The room dimmed and I opened my eyes. Mary was gone.

"Where did the woman go?" Joey asked, rubbing his eyes.

"She wasn't a woman, silly. She was a kind of Angel," Emily said, holding her arms out to me.

I bent down and picked her up. She wrapped her arms around my neck.

"How do you know that?" Sarah asked.

"She told me. Didn't you hear?" Emily yawned and laid her head against my shoulder.

"She didn't say anything at all!" Sarah argued.

"It's all right, child," I smiled down at Sarah. "Sometime we hear things, and sometimes we don't."

Joey looked around the empty restaurant, frowning. "I guess that means we don't get anything to eat."

"On the contrary. I don't think the owner of this establishment will mind if we take some pie and milk to go," I said.

"But that's stealing," Sarah said sternly.

"I am pleased that you are conscientious of that. But sometimes it's all right to take things for survival, and this is one of those times. Now hurry, Joey and Sarah. Gather up the food and we'll be on our way."

"Where are we going?" Emily murmured into my tunic.

"To Ohio, child, just as you said."

CHAPTER 15

EMBER

The loophole disappeared behind me and I ducked behind a bush. I felt for my Gaia and it came awake. Fire also erupted in me and battled with Earth, seeking escape. When Water joined Earth, they pushed my dominant element back. I took a shuddering breath. The Fire inside me was on high alert because there were Angels nearby. As I peered around the thorny branches, I was just happy I hadn't stepped into a warded place.

Ancient stones jutted out from the green and tan landscape. I felt the memories of millions of souls stirring my heart. People had built city on top of city on top of city over the course of thousands of years. There had been a lot of blood shed on this sacred ground.

The clouds were thick and the sun was setting to the west. A chill touched my skin as the air turned ashy. I had no time to lose. I reached out carefully with my Gaia, touching the birds perched in the stunted-looking trees, and then further, into the rats in the tunnels below me. The maze of underground paths left me disorientated and I drew back into my body. I hadn't seen any Angels, but I knew they were here, hiding somewhere. They wanted to ambush me. If I had any hope of saving Insepth, I couldn't let that happen.

I closed my eyes, searching for the element of Air inside of me. There had been times when I'd felt its presence, like when I'd scorched the Demons' compound and the Fire had gotten out of hand. Air had risen to create a rainstorm, putting out the flames. At the time, I wasn't sure what it even was, but now I recognized it. Unfortunately, it still eluded me. I tried to call upon it the way I did my other elements, but nothing happened.

Why was it staying away? I huffed in frustration. If I could control all of them and have them work together, I might be able to defend myself against Gabriel. Without Air, I didn't have a chance.

The sky dimmed even more and I stood completely still. In this place without any large amount of water, I'd have to rely on Fire and Earth. I only hoped they would be enough to rescue Insepth and get us out of there.

I didn't like being in the open, but in order to enter the maze of tunnels, I had no choice. I didn't dare draw any significant power. The Angels would sense it immediately. I'd have to rely on some good old-fashioned stealth to reach the entrance.

I left the cover of the first bush and sprinted to the next one, making sure to look around as I went. The distance to the fallen pillar beside the steps was farther than I would have liked, but I didn't hesitate. Running as fast as I could, I darted over the mounds of dirt and scrubby grass until I made it to the broken stones. I stopped long enough to catch my breath, assess my surroundings, and then stretched my legs to reach the crumbled steps. I jogged down them and into the dark opening, only stopping when I turned the corner.

I tried to slow my hard breathing and thumping heart. My organs were making too much noise in the shadows. I slid my back down the wall and paused, concentrating. This time when I let a little Gaia in, I entered a bat that was taking flight with dozens of others of its kind. It wanted to shoot though a hole into the evening sky to catch bugs, but I took it further into the tunnels instead. It used its sonar to navigate the black passageways. The little creature understood what I was looking for and it flew rapidly, turning left, then right, then straight again.

It entered a pathway that was brightened by moonlight and when I glanced up, I could see sparkling stars overhead. And then I saw him.

Insepth was hanging upside down, like a butchered animal. Anger heated my skin, and my Fire leaped forward. I embraced the flames but tried to hold them back, begging them to be patient.

Pain pierced my mind and I hit something. My sight went dark.

I blinked into the tunnel, forcing myself to be calm. *Angel warding.* Damn it.

How could I possibly get Insepth out of there if the room he was in was warded? I rubbed my temples, grasping for any idea that would help me.

The flash from the corner of my eyes made me bolt upright. I stared into the murkiness. It appeared again, hovered, and then shot away. I pushed my muscles, sprinting after the glowing ball.

I prayed it was what I thought it was.

The air was dank the further away from the entrance I went. My heart pounded in my chest as I blindly followed the ball as it zigzagged and turned. My lungs felt like they were about to burst when it finally stopped. It grew and brightened, lighting up the small room I'd stumbled into.

I drew in ragged breaths and waited, never taking my eyes off the light.

The ball suddenly exploded into a dazzling shower of sparks, and I covered my eyes until the radiance diminished. When I dropped my arm, I swallowed a lump in my throat and gasped.

"My dear, it makes my heart sing to see you."

Ila was a wispy apparition, but she was grinning.

⁂

"How are you here?" I resisted the urge to throw my arms around her. From experience, I knew I'd go straight through her with an icy chill.

Riley's ghost flopped down at Ila's feet. It was good to see them reunited.

"Barriers that have held for an eternity are crumbling. I escaped my confines in Purgatory with everyone else." Her lips tugged up in slight smile as if she was amused.

"But you're a ghost. Are you happy like that?" I whispered, eyeing my mentor from transparent head to foot.

This time, she was in the same form as when I'd first met her. An older, straight-backed woman with long gray hair held up in a heavy bun. Her features were sharp and foxlike, and her body was slender. She spoke with a slightly English accent that had always made me imagine her as the lady of a fine estate. But in truth, Ila had been one of the simplest people I'd ever met. She lived off the land, growing her own food and making soaps and candles by hand. She had loved her little valley in the Tennessee Mountains and the pets she took care of there. She had enjoyed her solitude, but had been ready to fight evil and protect the common folk when the need arose. Looking at her now, I felt a strong sense of relief. Ila would somehow make everything okay.

Ila shrugged her shoulders, becoming misty with the action. "It is a burden, but one I'm happy to bear at the moment."

"I need your help, Ila. Things are really bad," I prodded.

"I know, dear. That's why I'm here. We are connected through our blood and the elements. Even though I might not walk beside you in solid form, I'm never far from you."

"The Devil took Sawyer away." I quickly wiped the tears away that welled in the corners of my eyes.

Ila's lips quivered. Her form became more solid, glowing brighter. "I chose your guardian well. When the time came, he saved you, and that's precisely what he was meant to do."

"You knew all along it that would happen—and that's why you warned me about taking him to Purgatory," I said.

"You give me too much credit. I had an ill feeling about Sawyer going to that place, but I wasn't sure how it would play out in the end. As usual, you didn't listen to me—and I'm glad for it. His actions saved your life. The Angels would have most certainly killed you if the Dark One hadn't arrived."

I had to swallow down the hot surge of Fire that sprang to life in my gut. "But I lost him forever, Ila," I gulped. "And he might be suffering terribly."

Ila inclined her head and looked at me with the same stern look that used to give me shivers. "Be strong and keep your wits, girl! Sawyer made the ultimate sacrifice so that you could live. Would you throw away that gift on self-pity?"

"But I—"

Ila cut me off with a wave of her misty hand. "You miss him, you loved him—I know. But you're also filled with guilt that you can't save him." When my eyes widened, her voice softened. "I understand you better than you do yourself. You can't always succeed. There are forces at work in the world that are much more powerful than you. When you truly accept that, you will find peace, even when you suffer great loss." Her glassy eyes took on a faraway look. "I wasn't able to save my beloved, Montery, either. A part of him remained with me, giving me great joy."

I wondered what she was talking about and had opened my mouth to ask when she shook her head. "Not now, my dear. The remnants of the elements in my spirit make it possible for me to come to you in this way, but it's not easy. Soon my gathered strength will be gone and so will I. There are more important issues at hand."

"The Angels are acting insane. They're battling each other, and Gabriel has taken Insepth hostage," I blurted out, redirecting my thoughts.

"Yes, yes, I'm aware of all that." Her gaze narrowed. "Nasty business, if you ask me. The Angels aren't worthy to serve Him. But that's for another time. Now, we focus on Insepth."

"He's chained and hanging upside down in a warded room. I sense there are Angels nearby. I can't just waltz in there and save him. It's impossible."

"If you've learned anything, my girl, it's that most things aren't impossible."

I grasped my forehead. "I wouldn't even know how to find my way back to him. There are dozens of tunnels and they're all so dark."

Ila looked up and pointed. "I brought you to this particular room for a reason." Her smile was devious.

"We're below him?" My heart sped up as I raised my eyes.

"Directly," Ila confirmed.

"But how does that help?" I returned my gaze to her.

"It's not warded down here." Her smile grew. "Don't you remember what I taught you? Insepth and Adria as well?" I lifted my hands in frustration, and Ila added, "Sometimes moving objects in one location affects objects in another place."

The tingle of anticipation rolled through me. "He's bound from the ceiling where the warding is. Even if I can take the floor out, won't the warding hold him from above?"

Ila raised a brow. "That's where your Air element will help you. It's about time you learned how to use that magnificent power."

"I've wanted to touch the wind for so long, but it's elusive. How can you teach me how to control it in the short time we have now?"

"Your lessons and experiences of the past have prepared you for this moment. Fire is who you are, and Gaia is your closest friend. Water runs through your veins, and will help you when you're in need, but it's aloof. Air is the one element that you can touch, but it isn't inside of you."

"I don't understand," I said.

"It's something you can only call upon when you're in immense need, when you're in your darkest hour. It will only come to your aid for the greater good. Air doesn't help those who are selfish or arrogant or have evil intentions." She nodded to herself. "Sir Austin, for instance, is a noble man. He strives to do what's right in all cases."

"Sir Austin was there when Eae was forced out of Piper. He helped kill her."

Ila's body trembled and turned to mist for an instant and then took her form again. "He didn't know that the Angel's rendering would kill the girl. Neither did Insepth. At that time, the Angels were hidden to us, merely myths. How were they to know that their actions would result in the death of your friend?"

I pushed the memory of Piper out of my mind. "Perhaps the Air will never aid me. Maybe I'm not worthy."

She snorted and Riley whimpered. "Some things aren't black or white. You are neither good nor evil, but you're definitely worthy. Air has come to you before. It will again."

"But how?" I hated the whine in my voice. There wasn't time for me to learn what to do.

"You simply ask for it, my dear. It won't obey you the way the other elements do. It will decide the best path and take it. With this element, you must be prepared for anything."

Ila began to fade and the room grew icy.

"Don't go, not yet!" I implored.

"My strength is spent. I'm sorry, but I must leave you." Riley disappeared, and then her feet and legs became mist. "I wish you sweet success, Ember. It's up to you to free us all."

Her face dwindled away, becoming a thin haze, and then was gone.

"I love you, Ila," I whispered into the now pitch black room.

There was no response, but a chill swept over me and I closed my eyes. *Ila was always near.*

I opened my eyes and looked up. Fire rushed through me and I held my hand out to hold the flame. Gaia was ready, and even Water was at attention. I still didn't feel the Air, but from what Ila said, I didn't really need to.

I couldn't save Sawyer, but Insepth was another story.

CHAPTER 16

INSEPTH

Blood trickled down my eye, dripping onto the floor. I looked at the puddle developing, realizing it was the first time I'd gone such a long stretch without being able to heal myself. My circumstances had turned me into an ordinary man. I would much rather die, embracing my Earth power and giving Gabriel a fight, than to bleed to death like a slaughtered animal.

Gabriel paused, his fist in the air as he flapped his wings out behind him. "Do you sense that?"

Phanuel answered from the shadows, where he was leaning against a pillar. "I feel nothing out of the ordinary. More of our supporters are arriving, crossing through the barrier. Is that it?"

Gabriel straightened, resting his hand on the hilt of his sword. "I'm not sure. It was an odd feeling." He walked to the gap in the ceiling and peered up.

"The girl might have arrived," Phanuel said, pushing away from the column. He was suddenly alert and I smiled, though it hurt my face to do so. A mighty arch Angel worried about a Watcher girl—it was a moment to be savored, even given the rotten conditions.

"No, I don't think so. Nearly a hundred Angels are here, watching and waiting. She would only slip through by the grace of our Father. It's something different." I struggled to lift my head up to watch the Angels. "I will take a pass of the skies. Do not leave him," Gabriel ordered, pointing at me.

Phanuel nodded, and Gabriel flew upward toward the gap. The Angel barely made it through the opening. Dust sprinkled down from above when his wings brushed the old stone.

I cleared my throat, spitting out a wad of blood. "You're both arch Angels. So why does he order you around?" I asked Phanuel. "Is there a hierarchy among you I don't know of?"

Phanuel rolled his eyes. "I would think someone in your condition would save his strength, instead of wasting it on ignorant words."

"Ignorant? I simply asked a question." I grunted. "It must be a sensitive subject for you."

The Angel took a few steps closer and stopped. "I am wise to your intentions, Watcher. I will not be manipulated by you, and you won't turn me against my brother."

I was about to reply when more debris shook loose from the ceiling. Phanuel looked up and muttered, "What can that be?"

A wind stirred my hair and the sound of cracking filled my ears. The floor crumbled away in a blast of fire and rubble. Phanuel took flight, drawing his sword and spreading his wings in front of me.

"Run, Ember! Phanuel guards me!" I shouted.

Even if she had somehow gotten into the tunnels without Gabriel's notice, her powers weren't enough to break the warding that held me, or to defeat an arch Angel. She would be killed.

A flood of water entered the hall, flowing around the lip of flooring that hadn't fallen away. The walls broke apart, and I flailed sideways to avoid the impact. Phanuel was searching into the chasm and barely got out of the way of a falling boulder. Flames shot upward, scorching my hair and skin. My heart hammered and I coughed into the smoke. A jolt of excitement ran up my spine, but fear dampened it. The three elements weren't enough. Ember couldn't free me or save herself from Phanuel.

"Show yourself, Watcher!" Phanuel called out. "If you surrender, I will show mercy on you."

A gust of wind whistled into the room, gaining speed and volume until I was lifted completely sideways. Phanuel pumped his wings to stay in place. The expression on his face changed from annoyance to anger, and he raised a golden sword.

"So be it, then you die, girl!" Phanuel screamed.

Wind rushed from the chasm, carrying Ember with it. She lifted her hands and I saw the sparks on her fingertips.

"No! You die!" Ember hurled a blast of flame at Phanuel, pinning him against a fallen pillar.

The scent of burnt feathers filled my nostrils and I cringed. But I didn't waste the opportunity. Using the draft for propulsion, I bent and grabbed the chain holding my ankles. Once the metal was in my hands, I struggled to climb up the chain. If I could reach the warding symbols, I might be able to damage them enough to break the power.

There was a flash of light and the flames were extinguished. Phanuel was glowing, his features almost indistinguishable.

"Look away, Ember! Don't gaze upon him!" I began to squeeze my eyes shut, but hesitated, risking a glance at Ember.

She was looking directly at the Angel.

"You thought your childish Watcher games could destroy me?" Phanuel shouted, beating his wings, moving closer to where Ember now stood.

"No, I didn't, but this will," Ember said with smooth confidence that made me swallow hard.

Fire, Earth, and Water joined with Wind. They spiraled together and into the warded ceiling still suspended above my head. The blue flash was silent, lighting up the room.

"No!" Phanuel shouted, streaking toward me.

The explosion was deafening and rained chunks of the ruins down on top of me. The chains fell away from my ankles and I was falling. When I hit the ground, I groaned, but the surge of earth through me was pure pleasure. Chords of power rushed to the places that needed healing. I rolled out of the way just as Phanuel's sword dropped, striking the jagged rock beside my head.

The elements gathered again, slamming into the Angel and dimming his Heavenly light. He slashed with his sword, puncturing the stream of energy, and his scream caused a wave of air that knocked Ember onto the rocks beside me.

The use of so much energy had weakened her. I grabbed her hand and pulled her with me as I worked my still healing legs faster. The roar of Phanuel's power pressed into our backs.

"Now!" I yelled into Ember's ear.

She clung to my side and I drove my strength into the broken terrain at our feet. We lunged into the tunnel just as the earth rose up behind us.

"We can't stop!" I picked Ember up and ran with her. A small flame rose from her hand, lighting our way.

The passageway collapsed after us as we escaped just a few feet ahead of it. Ember's torch illuminated a solid wall rising up in front of us. I slid to a stop and braced my hands on the cold stone. With my lungs feeling as if they were about to burst, I let go of the energy and the rocks stopped falling away. A puff of dust filled the air and we coughed, falling against the wall.

I touched Ember's face. "Are you all right?" I whispered, not able to keep the sense of awe from my voice. She had combined all of the elements for the first time, and on her own with no instruction. Not to mention that she'd gazed at an Angel in all his glory and was still around to tell about it.

She cleared her throat and leaned into me. "I'm alive—we're both alive."

"How did you learn to call on the wind?" I asked, trailing my hand over her cheek and down her neck. She wasn't pushing me away, and more than anything, I just wanted to caress her.

"Ila helped me find you. She told me the way."

"But you should be stone. You looked at Phanuel when he lifted the veil and uncovered his true being."

The flame danced on her palm, casting shadows across her face. "It must have been all four elements blending together that protected me. I don't know. I just couldn't turn away."

Her voice quivered and I pulled her into my arms. The light went out and blackness pressed in against us. The only sound was that of our breathing.

"You came for me. Why?"

She exhaled and dust stirred in the cramped space. "We've had our differences in the past, but you're my friend now. We need each other to face what's to come."

"Friend? Is that all we are, Ember?" My fingers wrapped into her long hair and I brought her face closer to mine. She didn't pull back.

My Earth element filled me, probing at her Gaia, which came to life.

Waves of pleasure rolled through me as my lips brushed hers.

"Ember, I—"

The huge slabs of stone above our heads were lifted away, spilling moonlight on us.

Gabriel peered down into the opening, laughing. "I found the little mice."

Hundreds of Angels filled the sky beyond his form, their weapons drawn.

I was afraid our luck had finally run out.

CHAPTER 17

CRICKET

I clung to War's back as he streaked over thick, billowing clouds. His power, along with the other Horsemen, created the storm we were riding on. When I lifted my face to peek over the red horse's neck, wind pelted me painfully, and I quickly dropped back down. War's muscles worked between my legs and his loud snorts filled my ears. I was cold, but I tried to ignore the discomfort. I was astride a horse, instead of the one being ridden. It was something that never should have happened, but the world had gone mad.

I felt weak and small on War's back, a feeling I didn't like at all. I wasn't one of the Horses of the Apocalypse. Thundering over the clouds wasn't something I had the ability to do. But I could ride on War, and to get to our destination, I'd have to suffer the humiliation.

There! I heard Conquest shout to the others in my mind. He turned and the other three horses went with him. I grabbed War's mane tighter to keep from falling with the sudden change of direction.

Conquest slowed and War came abreast with the white horse. Death and Famine were right behind us.

There are a hundred of them, Conquest said. He tossed his head.

The clouds obstructed my view, and I risked leaning out from War's wide back to see better in the darkness. The storm calmed as we slowed, thinning and finally breaking apart as War's hooves struck solid ground.

I'd caught a glimpse of what Conquest was talking about. Angels hovered in the sky above the ruins of an ancient city. There were too many of them to count.

"What are they doing?" I asked out loud.

They are on a hunt. His nostrils flared and he stomped a front hoof in the sandy dirt.

Stars peppered the now clear night sky, and a nearly full moon shined down on the scene. The broken city was on a tall hill, and all around it were croplands and smaller hills. Lights twinkled in the distance, indicating that there were human settlements nearby. I wondered if those people had any idea an army of Angels was so close.

"What are they hunting?" My muscles tensed.

Watchers. Death lifted his head, flashing a brown eye my way.

I squeezed War's sides. "We must help Ember!"

None of the Horsemen moved. They stood quietly, like statues, surveying the situation.

Finally, War mind spoke. *They are part of the Celestial Host. We will be attacking Heaven's Angels.* He snorted, his breath jetting into the cold air. *It will be war with the Angels. Is this what we want, brothers?*

Their actions are inexcusable. They no longer follow the path of righteousness. We are in our right to drive them from this land. Conquest's voice was high pitched in my head.

Don't forget what they are, or the power they possess. The four of us versus a hundred of them are not good odds. Death said softly.

Yes, it won't be easy. There are no guarantees, but if we stand back and do nothing, we betray our nature and our purpose. War stepped in front of the other horses. *None of this is sanctioned by our Creator, and therefore, it is against the original laws. Angels were ordered to protect man, not destroy them.*

These are not 'men' they seek out. They are abominations, Famine finally spoke.

"They are still part human, and Ember fights to save the world of men. She is my friend. I will not let her die at the hands of the winged ones." I leaped from War's back and opened myself up to my true form. When I turned back to the horses, I was one of them. *I will fight them, even if you don't.*

What a mare, War said in admiration. He stepped forward and nuzzled my face. *You have much courage to go against an army of Angels, but it is a death wish. I am the Horseman of War. This is what I was created for, in one form or another.* He reared up, striking out at the air. When his feet touched the ground again, he swung his head toward his companions. *Are you with me, brothers?*

Conquest strode forward, touching War's nose with his. He looked back and nickered. Death and Famine stretched their necks and snorted together.

When the clouds began forming at their feet, I tossed my head and pranced in place. The Horsemen were with me, and my skin prickled. The rumbling of the building storm rattled my insides, and I couldn't stand still any longer.

I jumped forward, galloping onto the plain that stretched to the hilltop ruins. Faster, I pumped my legs, lengthening my neck and whinnying in defiance. Lightning flashed and thunder boomed in the sky. The sound of hooves pounding rang in my ears.

We had the element of surprise. The Angels would never imagine the Horsemen would attack. I only hoped it would be enough to offset the great numbers we were up against.

Because we were going to need a miracle as it was.

CHAPTER 18

EMBER

Raindrops hit my face as I huddled against Insepth's chest. Gabriel's head snapped sideways. He called out in the Angel language and darted away. Several of his black feathers that fluttered down were caught by the breeze.

"Now's our chance," Insepth whispered into my ear, pulling me beside him.

Dark-rimmed clouds appeared in the sky that was clear a moment ago, and the wind gusted, blowing dust into my eyes.

My legs were wobbly from the energy I'd used to draw all four elements. I swayed and Insepth caught me. My stomach rolled. I fought to keep the bile down. He bent and grabbed my legs, helping me up. With Insepth pushing, I cleared the opening and rolled to the side, reaching out to him. He took my hand and scrambled up next to me. Phanuel swooped down and caught one of our shoulders in each of his hands.

The Angel only managed to get about ten feet off the ground when fire streamed out of my hands, striking his wings. Insepth focused his Earth on the pile of debris below us. The ground erupted, sending boulders flying at the Angel. He let go and we dropped, hitting the ground hard. Two more Angels dove at us and Insepth grasped my hand, jerking me into a run.

"Can you weave the four elements again?" he called out, trying to be heard above the gathering storm.

I struggled to stay even with his long strides. "I don't think so. I can barely manage my Fire."

We dodged bolts of lightning from the Angels who pursued us, taking shelter behind a sprawling, bent tree. Insepth used his power to rip it from its roots and hurl it at the nearest Angel. The gray-winged Angel was struck and did a somersault in the air, but quickly recovered and came after us again.

"The air, Ember!" He whispered into my ear. Rain poured from the sky, thunder boomed, and a dazzling claw of lightning streaked across the inky sky. The plain lit up, illuminating Angels in flight and the rolling, billowing clouds that nature couldn't have made. I'd seen those clouds before, and the breath caught in my throat at the brilliance of it. Insepth held my face between his hands and forced me to look at him. His blue eyes were wild. "It's all around you—can't you feel the raw power that's waiting to be harnessed. You can save us!"

Not harnessed, but asked. My heart leaped with joy when I connected with the element immediately. The exhaustion left my body, and I felt the power leave me, pushing into the thick clouds. The wind gathered momentum, reminding me of the tornado Ila had summoned to destroy the Demons. I realized that Air might just be the deadliest of all the elements.

The spiraling cyclone crashed into the two Angels, sending them careening through the sky. Phanuel came into view, brandishing his golden sword. His platinum hair was blowing wildly around his head, and his war cry echoed across the valley. I reached out, touching the Air, pressing it faster, and it responded. Water cried out from inside of me and I directed the downpour toward the Angel.

But the storm elements weren't enough to stall his momentum. He broke thought the tempest, diving at me and Insepth.

Insepth pelted the Angel with branches, but the objects merely bounced off the glow that was building around the Angel. He was an arch. We'd been lucky to escape him before, catching him off guard, and his own arrogance at complete superiority, but not now. Phanuel wasn't underestimating us anymore. He was coming for us with everything he had.

Insepth shoved me behind him, gripping me with one hand, while his other hand continued to work the earth.

The sound of Phanuel's approach drowned out all other sounds, and the halo around him widened until there was only light.

Insepth faced me. "We gave it our best shot."

Galloping hooves drew my attention behind Insepth. A black horse skidded to a stop, bumping into us.

"Cricket!" I couldn't believe my eyes. I didn't hesitate and jumped on her back. Insepth scurried up behind me in a dream-like moment.

Her shrill whinny broke through Phanuel's war cry. Her muscles gathered and she was away, propelling me back into Insepth. He held onto her mane, wrapping his arms tighter around me. From the corner of my eye, I saw flashes in the sky and heard more battle screams. Shadows of beating wings stretched across the landscape, and the earth trembled.

Another whinny rent the air, but it wasn't from Cricket. I glanced up and saw them. The Horses of the Apocalypse slammed into Angels in the clouds.

Cricket was fast, but she couldn't outrun an arch Angel. Phanuel was gaining speed and I felt the heat of his Heavenly brilliance on my arms.

I turned in Insepth's arms, loosening his hold enough to extend my hand and send a stream of fire backward. The flames hit the light and fizzled, turning to smoke on the wind.

Phanuel was radiant, and his sword gleamed gold. It was so close to Cricket's hindquarters, I could see Angelic writing on the blade. He raised it above us and I dropped my head into Cricket's mane, squeezing my eyes shut. I'd done everything I could possibly do to save us, and I'd failed. The bitter taste of defeat dried my mouth as I waited for death to come.

The blade fell, but somehow Cricket managed a last minute burst of speed, skirting away from it. The force of the storm slammed into us, knocking me and Insepth from Cricket's back. I heard the sickening crunch when my arm made contact with the ground. I clutched it to my chest, opening to the little bit of Gaia I could wield.

A fiery chestnut jumped from the clouds, striking Phanuel with front hooves, sending him spiraling sideways. His light disappeared and he flapped his wings furiously to regain control. War didn't slow, though. He stomped at the Angel in the air, knocking Phanuel back down to earth.

Insepth jerked me to my feet. "We've got to find cover! We're powerless in this battle."

I pulled away, pointing at Cricket. She had charged into the fight, joining War. "I can't leave her!"

Insepth sighed and rubbed his forehead. Rain pelted our faces and the wind from the Horsemen pummeled us. I had to spread my legs to brace against the torrent. "Then we must link. It's the only way." His eyes narrowed, darkening. "But I must warn you. If we use what little power we have left, we won't be able to create a loophole to escape this place."

I nodded wildly. Insepth grasped my hands and I let my elements meld with his Earth. The Angel slashed at War and Cricket with his long sword. Blood spurted from a slash across War's chest, and Cricket jumped away just in time to avoid having her front legs hacked off.

Anger flooded my insides and the Fire awakened. I gave Insepth the surge of raw power and he took it, directing it into the ground below Phanuel. War joined our assault, rearing up to his full height. As he came down, he stretched out his mighty neck and went for the Angel with his teeth barred. He grabbed Phanuel by the neck and shook him back and forth. Blue blood spurted from the gaping wound and his wail came out as a wet gurgle. War tossed the Angel into the air and Insepth shook the earth, opening up a sinkhole that swallowed Phanuel up. A hollow scream followed, and Insepth frantically drew more power. He folded the soil back together, burying the Angel. War's victory squeal pierced the valley, sending shivers through me.

The rain came down harder, blurring my vision. But the beating of wings was still unmistakable. The sky lit up with the dozens of Angels that descended onto the place where Phanuel was buried.

Conquest and Death galloped out of the clouds and struck the ground with flying sparks next to War. Famine came more slowly, and when I blinked the water from my eyes, I saw a swath of blood on his heaving side.

Cricket trotted to me and her nose pushed into my chest. I clutched her face and pressed my cheek to hers. *Keep faith, Ember.*

I pulled back enough to gaze into Cricket's brown eyes. *There are too many Angels. We must leave here, or we'll all die,* I told her with my mind.

The explosion made Cricket leap away from me and I turned to see Gabriel drive his sword into the dirt where Phanuel was. "You've killed him—an arch Angel!" he screamed.

Insepth tried to tug me away, but I planted my feet in the saturated clay. "I won't leave Cricket or the Horsemen. They came to help us."

"Then we're all going to die," Insepth warned.

I barely heard him. The beating wind made it difficult to stand upright. I couldn't tear my eyes away from the horses as they pranced and pawed, courageously facing the Angels' wrath.

"It is your own doing Phanuel is dead! Do not blame us for your arrogant disobedience to our Creator." War's neck bowed and steam blew from his nostrils.

Gabriel took flight, stopping in front of the Horsemen. His pounding wings pushed back the force of their storm. His black hair curled around his head and his face was pale stone. When he spoke, it was with Angel power, carrying his words over the plain and through the driving rain with volume. "I am an Angel of the Lord. You will not defy me or my kind. We will ruin the four of you, strike you from this earth forever."

The horses reared up, mounting higher on the clouds of the tempest they'd created. The gust knocked me down, pinning me to the ground. Insepth rolled onto me, trying to cover my eyes with his hands. "You mustn't look!" he shouted.

But I shoved his hands away and opened my eyes more. Fire, Earth, Water and Air rose up to protect me, but I doubted they would be enough.

Gabriel charged upward, becoming light, and the rest of the Angels joined him.

The sky shuddered when the thundering storm crashed into the brilliance of Heaven.

The rain stopped and the wind died down. Cricket neighed and tears streamed down my face. The light magnified until the world was glistening white.

Pain exploded in my head, and then there was only cold blackness.

CHAPTER 19

HORAS

There was nothing left of Sawyer's humanity. I could smell the evil taint even from this distance. The creatures that loped beside him were from the very depths of Hell. They struck down the wolves, tearing chunks of meat from their victims in a feeding frenzy as they continued forward, heading directly for us.

Sir Austin's wind was gobbled up by the fires that erupted wherever the evil soldiers stepped. Smoke covered the hillside and I gulped when I reached pockets of fresh air. Even Youmi's Water had no impact on the Hellish flames. The blasts of liquid only seemed to provide fuel, fanning the inferno higher.

"Ivan, take Lord Quintus' daughter and Angus to safety!" I ordered, but the three continued to fight, biting at the monsters that came out of the haze.

A Demon rose before me, her head bent to the side and her eyes glowing. Like Sawyer, any connection she might have had to this world had vanished, having been replaced by the instinct to destroy everything in her path. I swept around her and buried my dagger into her neck. I'd already learned that killing wounds to their bodies didn't stop the Hell beasts. The removal of limbs slowed them, and taking off their heads brought them down for good.

I sawed away until the Demon's head fell into the mud, and then I moved to another and another. I was fast, agile, and strong. I'd fought in many battles over the thousand years I'd walked the earth, but nothing had prepared me for this kind of an onslaught. The attackers were mindless in their bloodlust. There was no reasoning with them and they didn't fear their own deaths. In a way, they were already dead. Their souls belonged to Samael.

When Sawyer crested the hill, I let out a ragged gasp. Fire moved with him, and it suddenly occurred to me that his one-time connection to Ember had made him impervious to it. His red eyes shifted from me to Ivan, and he changed course.

"Nooo!" I shouted, running to intercept the Demon who had once been my friend, slashing creatures down to clear a path.

Sir Austin and Youmi got there first. I saw them combine their powers, but they were exhausted, and Youmi had to hold Sir Austin steady while they directed a torrent of air and water at Sawyer.

Time slowed as I watched the devastating force moving with purpose. Sawyer motioned and three Cerberus leaped in front of him. They were each as large as a pickup truck and their bodies took the force of the Watchers' blast. The center hound was hit directly, severing one of its heads and ripping a hole in its side. The other two heads howled out in pain. Another hound bolted forward, and I watched in horror as one of its mouths crunched down on Sir Austin, ripping the Air Watcher from Youmi's grip. Blood splattered, and the Watcher hung limply in the jaws of the beast as he was shaken violently like a rag doll.

I increased speed and twisted out of the way of a snapping jaw. In a blur, I wrapped my arms around Youmi and rolled down the hill. We bounced, striking things that I wasn't even sure what they were until a tree trunk stopped our momentum with a sudden thud.

"My friend, my friend is gone," Youmi wheezed.

I grabbed him by his shirt and shook him. "Control, man. Stay in control."

"We are lost—"

I slapped him, forcing his gaze up. "We are not yet lost. You must reach Ember and Insepth—tell them what is happening here."

Youmi's eyes cleared. "I have to be in the dream state to find her. How will I manage that in the middle of this chaos?"

I drew my fist back and punched Youmi squarely in the face. His head lolled to the side and I dragged him into the bushes, placing him beneath the densest foliage I could find.

"There you go, Watcher. I've provided you with the sleep you need to find our dear Ember. Do not fail us."

CHAPTER 20

EMBER

Silence, glorious silence.

I opened my eyes and blinked. Massive white-barked tree trunks reached into the gray sky. There were no birds chirping or breezes rustling leaves. There were no clouds, stars, moon, or sun either. Just a thick, overcast ceiling that looked like a sheet had been pulled across the sky. In the distance, I could see the blue flames that ringed this world. Purgatory. I'd woken in the dream world.

I sat up, the injuries and pains from moments ago were gone. My gaze flickered around. The place was even more desolate than I remembered. A few of the giant trees were down, uprooted and broken apart. Samael had ripped the gateway into Hell here, near the acid lake filled with sea monsters. Ormer the dragon had died at the gate fighting Sin, the Angel who had been distorted into a dragon's body by her time in the Underworld. I caught a whiff of smoke and turned my head. Beyond the treetops I could see black tentacles rising. That must be the direction of the broken gate.

And not the way I wanted to go.

What was I doing here in the first place? Only a few minutes before, I'd been on the plain of Armageddon. I pressed my hand to my forehead trying to remember. Slowly, the cloud lifted and memories came trickling in. The Horsemen had been battling the Angels, and War, along with help from me and Inseph, had killed Phanuel. Gabriel and the rest of the Angels, in their Heavenly light, came for all of us. Then there was darkness—and now I was here.

A cold chill swept through me as I sucked in a deeper breath. "Am I dead?" I murmured.

"Unless all laws of physics have disappeared, I think you're still very much alive, but to find you in this God forsaken place makes me wonder for how long."

I whirled around and Youmi stepped out from behind one of the giant tree trunks.

The shock that nearly stopped my heart was quickly replaced with happiness. I ran up to the Water Watcher and threw my arms around his neck. He awkwardly patted my back and then disengaged himself, taking a step backward.

"How's Ivan and Horas, and Angus? Are they doing all right? And what about Lutz and Sir Austin—are they behaving themselves?"

I rattled off the questions, feeling giddy that I wasn't dead, and that I could finally get an update on what was going on back at Ila's valley.

Youmi frowned back at me without speaking. It suddenly occurred to me if the Watcher had travelled to the dreamland to find me, something terrible must have happened. I shivered and managed to say in a rough voice, "What's going on?"

"The forces of Hell, led by Sawyer, ravaged Oldtown and then set their sights on the valley. We didn't have much warning. Lutz barely got away, fleeing into the forest with Ila's pets. Cricket left with the Horsemen, and the rest of us escaped through a loophole Sir Austin and I managed to create."

I held my breath, horrible visions of what he was saying dancing through my head.

"We chose to go to Romania where the wolves were gathering. The Watchers of Light had been wiped out, and it wasn't very far from either Sir Austin's homeland or the Mediterranean Sea, which would replenish my powers. It seemed like as good a place as any to go."

A single tear sliced down Youmi's cheek and I touched his hand. "What happened?" I whispered.

He met my gaze. "Sawyer found us. Sir Austin is dead. I don't know about Ivan and your dog. They were fighting the Hell beasts the last I saw. Horas is the one who sent me here to find you" —he pointed to his bruised eye— "and bring you back to help us."

"Sawyer? Are you sure it was him?"

Youmi's voice held an edge that wasn't there before. "Yes. It was your guardian and lover who led the army that struck down my closest friend." He leaned in with narrowed eyes. "He followed us, Ember—from the valley and across the world, he came after us. The evil hordes have overtaken us—we're all going to die."

I pictured Sawyer smiling devilishly at me, black hair falling over his one eye as he bent to kiss me.

I shook my head. That man was gone. Samael had succeeded in turning Sawyer into a monster. And I was the only one who might be able to stop him.

I rubbed my face and my head hurt. The trees were losing their solidness, becoming hazy. A sharp, cooler burst of air hit me.

I faced Youmi. "I'm coming to help you!"

Youmi nodded, but he was disappearing, becoming mist, like the trees.

I jumped forward into the place he'd been standing and shouted, "Stay alive, Youmi. I'll save you all!"

CHAPTER 21

INSEPTH

There was a sound like a sonic boom, and the Angels' glow dimmed enough that I could blink up at the sky. Stars twinkled behind the scene that made my heart pound madly. Thousands more Angels spilled onto the plain from an opening in the clouds. Weapons of gold and silver flashed, and pounding wings filled the air.

Ember was motionless beside me and her body was limp beneath my hands.

"Wake up, Ember. We have to leave, now," I whispered fiercely into her ear.

She didn't respond. Her eyes moved beneath her lids and I pressed my ear to her chest to listen to her heartbeat. It was so weak I could barely hear it.

Cricket nudged Ember's shoulder, snorting warm breath over both of us.

Without Ember, there was no chance of building a loophole out of here. Even combining our powers it would be tricky. We'd both expelled most of our energy and the blinding light of the Angels had weakened us even more. The clashing sound of steel and the bursts of lightning made me rise to my knees. I gripped Ember's shoulders and gently shook her. "Wake up—you must wake up!" I whispered desperately.

A flurry of wind and feathers pushed my hair back. Cricket whinnied and I raised my eyes. Uriel and Raphael peered down at us. Michael, Raguel, and Azriel stood behind them. They all looked grim, except Raphael, who appeared to be working hard to not smile.

I rolled my eyes. I really hated Angels.

"Move aside," Uriel ordered me, but I stayed with Ember.

I was about to tell the Angel to go to Hell when Gabriel swooped in, landing in the middle of the cluster of Angels.

"Those two are the root of all our problems!" he bellowed.

Michael moved between Uriel and Gabriel. "There may be some truth to that, but your actions here"—he spread his arms wide—"haven't helped our cause, either."

Raguel twisted his thick neck, searching the crowd. Many more Angels hovered in the sky above.

"It has been decided, Gabriel. You and your followers will return to Heaven and await judgment on your actions. We have the entire Celestial Host at our backs. If you refuse, we will cut you down."

"And who will be the judge—*you?*" Gabriel snarled.

Raguel's eyes sharpened. "You know who will judge your actions."

"Really? Our Father has been absent of late. Perhaps He's condoning my actions by ignoring them." He tilted his head. "Have you considered that?"

Azriel dropped back his hood and his tattoos glowed when the moonlight struck them. "He has spoken to us, brother. We shall all retreat Heavenward. It has been ordered."

Gabriel's mouth dropped open and the Angels stirred with fluttering wings.

"Is this true?" His voice came out in a harsh whisper.

"Yes," Michael answered him. "We shall return home and leave mankind to their fate."

Gabriel strode forward and Uriel stepped in front of him just before he reached me and Ember. "They killed Phanuel, an arch Angel of the Lord." His eyes shifted to the Horsemen and he pointed his sword at them. "With their help. They cannot go unpunished!"

"The Horsemen will return to their stable. They are not needed to destroy the land of men. Samael and his army will perform their tasks, finishing off the humans in short order, as it is written," Raguel said.

"I think not!" War had changed into a man and pushed past the Angels. His flaming hair and beard stuck out in the dark night. He was close to the same size as the Angels, and when his brothers joined him, the power that emanated from the four could not be denied. "I believe you're fibbing, Azriel."

Azriel's face was stone, but he said nothing.

"There are only four of you and thousands of us. You can't win, Horseman. Are a couple of Watchers and humankind worth your deaths?" Michael said.

"It is written that we bring the plagues to this land, not the king of the damned. I don't believe that is how our Creator wants it all to end." Death eyed the Angels, a sprinkling of colors peppered the air around him as if he was close to changing back into a horse.

"Why does it matter who destroys this world, as long as it is destroyed?" Raguel said.

"Because there will be even more suffering if the creatures of Hell are allowed to take over this realm. The land will die, and then there will be only Heaven and Hell." Death licked his lips, letting his words settle over the Angels. "Samael won't end the human race—he'll keep some alive for pleasure and torment. When he grows bored, his eyes will shift toward the Heavens. And then he'll come for you."

"That is blasphemy! Samael and his army can never cross the threshold into Heaven. It is impossible!" Michael's voice rose, echoing over the plain.

"He never should have been able to break the barriers into this world without us unleashing the plagues first, but he did." War crossed his arms over his chest in a gesture of defiance.

Ember began shaking beneath my hands and her eyes rolled back in her head. "She's having a seizure!" I shouted as I tried to push my remaining Earth power into her.

"Allow me to assist my offspring." Uriel looked around, his gaze landing on Azriel. "Unless it is her time."

"I do not feel the strings of death with that one. She is invisible to me."

Raguel and Michael exchanged glances. It was Raguel who answered Uriel. "Do what you may with the girl. She means nothing to us." He looked back at Gabriel who was opening his mouth to speak. "Phanuel lost his life because he followed you, instead of us. His death is yours to claim. Gabriel, you will have a chance to make your argument before the council, but until then, we retreat to our homeland."

Uriel knelt beside Ember and grasped her head in his hands. Cricket stomped her hoof nearby and I balled my fists.

Raphael finally found his voice. "Just to be clear, brothers. It is your decision to allow our fallen brothers to rampage this land, and we will do nothing?"

"That is so," Michael answered.

Raphael nodded, lowering his head.

"Do you come willingly, Gabriel, or must more blood be shed on this day?" Raguel asked.

Gabriel smiled at me. "Perhaps giving them over to Samael is the most just thing to do."

He spread his black wings and flapped them hard, sweeping stones and dirt up from the ground into our faces as he flew upward. Taking his lead, the ones who attacked us moments before surged after him. Then the Celestial Host began to leave in legion formations.

Ember coughed and I pulled her into my embrace. I ignored Uriel's eyes boring into me.

Raguel faced the Horsemen. "What is your decision? Will you be as wise as Gabriel?"

War and Conquest laughed and Famine shook his head. It was Death who stepped up close to the Angel and said, "The numbers mean nothing to us. We have the pure power of destruction at our disposal—to use on men, monsters, or Angels. We stand down not because we are afraid of you, but because, unlike Azriel and his clever tongue, we have not spoken to our Creator. We will remain in this realm until He tells us to leave. And not before then."

"Your presence will disrupt the balance," Michael said.

Death smiled crookedly. "What—do you fear that we may impede Samael's march on this land?"

Raguel exhaled. "It matters not what you do, as long as your wrath is not directed at the Angels. I think that you'll realize, sooner than later, that humankind is a worthless cause."

Raguel nodded to Michael and Azriel, and with another rush of wind, they were gone.

Only the Horsemen, Cricket, Uriel, and Raphael remained on the plain of Armageddon with us. The sky was free of Angels and lightning, and the bushes rustled in the breeze. A night bird whistled in the distance.

Ember coughed again and finally opened her eyes. She looked around the group before her gaze settled on me. "Where is everyone?"

I chuckled. "Ember, my dear, you missed the battle."

She grabbed my shirt. "We have to leave now. The war has begun."

CHAPTER 22

EMBER

All was quiet, so different than what it had been when the Angels' light had knocked me out. Stars twinkled above and the breeze was pleasant. But looks were deceiving. In another part of the world, my friends were fighting for their lives.

I pushed myself up on wobbly legs, clutching Insepth's arm. "There's no time. Sawyer is leading an army from Hell and they're attacking the wolves in Romania. Ivan and Horas are there—so is Youmi. He's the one who found me in Purgatory and told me what was going on."

"Your spirit was in that place?" Uriel asked, stepping closer with a piercing stare.

I had lost all patience. A surge of energy made my heart pound and my skin tingle. I took both my hands and smacked the Angel on his stomach as hard as I could manage. His eyes widened, but he didn't move.

"You could have helped us!" I accused.

Uriel's mouth twitched before he spoke. "My loyalties are to my brothers and the oaths we made to our Father. I had to wait for the council to agree to bring Gabe and his followers home. It was not my decision to make."

I turned to Raphael. Fire roared to life inside of me as my Gaia was repairing the damage the Angels had done to my body. I blurted, "Why are you here? What is your interest in any of this?"

The brown-haired Angel snorted, throwing his head back. He was just as tall and well-built as Uriel, but he moved with a wiry stealth, and had never seemed as warlike as the other Angels.

"What else do I have to do? The glorious order of our kind has been reduced to chaos. No one knows what our path is, or what is even right or wrong." His mouth lifted into a smile. "So until order is restored, I will follow my gut."

"And your gut tells you to stay with us?" I narrowed my eyes and thrust my finger at him, a flame lighting the tip. "Or maybe you're a spy for the Angels?"

"That is a valid accusation," War said. He'd been hanging back with the other Horsemen, and the careful look he gave Uriel and Raphael made my stomach tighten.

"Oh, yes. I could be a spy." His smile deepened when he looked at me. "This is a time when you must trust your own gut. What is it telling you about my intentions?"

I stared at Raphael, searching my heart and mind. My thoughts were muddled, and I couldn't say for sure what my feelings about Raphael were, but I knew one thing for certain; I didn't completely trust any Angel, even Uriel. Time was running out. My friends needed me.

"I won't waste time on trying to figure out your motives. Unlike the Angels, I'm going to help my friends, and try to stop the Devil from destroying the world."

"You will die trying," Uriel said. "I cannot come to your aid any longer. Samael is marching into the lands of men, as was foretold in the Scriptures. The way it all came about is not what any of us expected, but so be it." His voice deepened. "Our Father's silence speaks volumes. I will not defy Him or my brothers any longer. I admire your spirit and bravery. Even though I wish I had never taken pleasure with your ancestor so long ago, I don't regret your existence. Everything about you is more than I hoped for." He stepped back, raising a brow. "Many blessings to you, child. I pray that your end is a painless one."

With a rush of wind, Uriel surged into the sky. He didn't even slow down to look back. He became smaller and smaller until he disappeared. A single red feather floated down and I caught it. Shoving it into the inside pocket of my jacket, I looked around. "Who's coming with me?"

Insepth nodded, a small smile reassuring me that he was ready for whatever came next. In a burst of colors, Cricket became a woman again. She stepped forward and said, "I will go. They are my friends as well."

My gaze rested on the Horsemen. War was the only one in man form, but he seemed to be communicating with them in mind speech. Conquest tossed his head and Death snorted. Famine was his usual quiet self, although he looked alert.

When War joined us, his face was somber. The three horses whinnied and whirled away, galloping across the plain with increasing speed. Clouds formed beneath their feet and lightning cracked across the night sky. The gusting draft made it difficult to stand, but I couldn't tear my eyes away from the Horsemen as the clouds carried them away.

The storm moved off and the wind died down to a cool breeze. I swallowed and looked at War. He watched his brothers as they sped away. Only when they were gone did he turn around and face us.

"My brothers are returning to Heaven's stable. They will not unleash their devastation on this world, but they won't fight, either.

Until our Creator speaks to them, they take the Angels' lead and stand down."

"You stayed," I said, noticing how close War stood beside Cricket, the back of his hand brushing hers.

"I have claimed this mare as my own. She has a stubborn nature, and wouldn't have come with me. So here I stay, until the end comes."

Cricket's cheeks reddened and she looked up at the Horseman. She nodded once at him. I saw a tear glint in the moonlight as it trickled down the side of her face.

A lump formed in my throat. "You should go with War—you'll be safe with him in Heaven."

The fierce look returned to Crickets face as she met my eyes. "The length of my life means nothing to me. It's what I do in that life that matters. I will not run away when my herd is in need. You are my herd, Ember, and so are Ivan, Horas, and Angus. I will fight for them alongside you."

My sight blurred with tears of my own, and I quickly rubbed them away. Raphael's gaze passed over each of us. "I will create the loophole, saving you the energy of the task. For you will need every last drop of power you can muster to fight the evil forces that await you. Mark my words, Ember. Samael is more cunning than any of us. If my instinct is correct, he has laid a trap for you."

Insepth's hand closed around mine and he smiled sadly.

He didn't have to say anything. I knew what he was thinking—that we were all going to finally die.

The Fire bubbled up inside of me, wanting to break free. I stroked the flames, promising them that they would soon be unleashed.

I would stop Sawyer. I had to. Even though it broke my heart.

CHAPTER 23

IVAN

Tamira rolled to the side as the mace swung down at her. She yelped and tried to scurry out of the ditch, but the monster's claw caught her haunches, dragging her down.

I sunk my teeth into the arm of the beast attacking me, tasting its acidic blood in my mouth. The fluid was like poison and I struggled to not swallow it down. Once free, I jumped into the pit where the she-wolf was trapped. Blood dripped into my eyes, burning them, and making it difficult to see. I smelled her fear, and let that instinct guide me.

I knocked into the red-eyed creature, unbalancing it, but it grabbed the scruff of my neck as it went down. Talons tightened around my throat and I whined. Tamira bit at the hairy, muscled legs, but it swung the mace again, striking her side. She whimpered and fell limply to the ground.

My heart raced as I tried to see Tamira, kicking with my legs in an attempt to escape. Blood splattered when another wolf was ripped in half by the heads of a Hell hound from above. Howls and human screams mingled as the sun rose slowly on the horizon, brightening the sky from early morning gloom.

I was so exhausted and my soul was broken. Tamira had fought bravely by my side and now she was down. I'd witnessed friends torn apart and great wolf warriors fall into pools of their own blood. My father had been speared, fighting beside Lord Quintus. They had both fallen.

My mind clouded from a lack of oxygen.

When the creature suddenly let go, I blinked, inhaling a gulp of air.

My mother had leaped onto the Hell beast. She bit into its face, her rumbling growls equaling the wailing noise the monster made. I struggled to rise, only to fall into a heap at the monster's feet. But my mother's squeal made my limbs come alive. I clamped onto the beast's ankle, crunching hard. The seven-foot creature waivered, and then collapsed on top of me. Mother's jaws closed around its neck and warmth oozed onto me from the kill.

I sluggishly clawed my way out from under the beast and went to Tamira first. She blinked up at me and whined as she jerked and rose on shaky legs. I nudged her nose with my face and she licked me. Her warm, scratchy tongue felt good, even as we faced death.

The yelp got my attention, and I loped to my mother. She lay atop the monster she'd killed, and at first, I didn't understand her pain. But then I saw its claws stuck into her spine. She was paralyzed and bleeding from her wounds.

I licked her face. *Mother, what should I do?* I mind spoke to her.

Her golden eyes shifted, staring at me. *Leave this place—get away! Take Tamira and hide deep in the forest. This isn't your battle. The only reason the Devil's beasts came here was because of the alliance the wolves made with the Watchers. You are more wolf than man. You might survive if you let go of your human side.*

Her pupils dilated and her mouth trembled. Her chest rose and fell, and then didn't rise again.

My heart pounded in my ears and Tamira howled. Another explosion ripped the air, yanking me to my senses. I nudged Tamira to climb on top of the dead creature, and over my mother's body. She skirted across them quickly, half-jumping, half-limping out of the ditch.

All around us were corpses and burning grass. The air was heavy with smoke and blood.

A Hell hound stuck one of its heads through the gray cloud, snapping blood-stained teeth with chunks of flesh hanging from them. *Go, Tamira! Flee into the trees!*

I won't leave you! she said, shrinking behind me, but still holding her ground.

When the second and third heads appeared in front of us, another hound stepped up from behind. Lutz was almost the same size as the Hell hounds, and had he been there, he might have been able to fight one off, but not two. Tamira and I were like pups to these two monsters. As the hounds closed in, I looked into Tamira's eyes.

We die together. That is a good thing, she said.

My heart filled with incredible sadness at her words.

Something bumped into me and then one of the hounds' heads reared back. It whimpered and the head lolled to the side. Blood spurted from the cut to its throat.

"This way!" Horas called out, slowing just enough so that I could see him. He was covered in blood and his clothes were torn.

Tamira and I sprinted after him, dodging swinging dogs' heads and leaping over the bodies of wolves.

The ground was slick with blood and the rancid scent of death made my head dizzy. I tried not to inhale too deeply as I raced after the Demon.

Horas stopped suddenly and we nearly ran into him. Dark Angels swooped into the melee, swiping their swords to cut down the fleeing survivors. There were possibly hundreds of the Devil's soldiers in the air and thousands more on the ground. There was nowhere to go.

"Damn them!" Horas shouted.

I panted heavily, pressing into Tamira's side. The shaking of her body joined my own.

Horas held out his arms to protect us, but there was nothing he could do as the forces of Hell descended. This wasn't a battlefield; it was a massacre.

A Dark Angel paused above us, screaming out a war cry as he raised his black sword and dove for us.

I couldn't look away. His face and body was tattooed and his black hair was long and tangled. There was no glow to his body, not like Heaven's Angels. Where Uriel's eyes blazed life, this Angel's eyes were black and empty.

The fire bolt that struck the Angel spun him in the air and another blast melted his feathers.

I turned back to see Ember striding into the meadow with Insepth by her side. Cricket was in human form and sitting atop the mighty red stallion, War. My heart jumped to life when Insepth pointed to where several hounds were tearing apart the corpses of more wolves. The ground heaved and shook, opening up and swallowing the monsters.

"Thank God! They made it!" Horas brushed the top of my head with his hand before he lurched toward our friends.

I stretched my legs, taking off, and Tamira stayed close.

Bright orange flames flew from Embers hands, striking the Hell beasts. Even though they seemed impervious to the fire, Ember's flames still pummeled them into the mud. Out of nowhere, a storm gathered overhead, suddenly filling the clearing with lightning and pelting rain. Tamira yipped from the assault, but I ignored the stinging of my open wounds.

The red horse leaped into the air with Cricket atop him. Wherever he went, wind and lighting struck, destroying hounds and beasts alike.

We had almost reached Ember and Insepth when I heard the clash of steel and looked up. The brown-winged Angel that Ember had left with days before was darting through the skies, striking down the Dark Angels with a golden spear that shimmered even in the smoke-filled gray sky. His body gave off a glow that made Samael's Angels look away, shielding their eyes from his onslaught.

The ground shook again and more of Hell's beasts fell into the crevices, only to be crushed when Insepth brought the earth together, closing the gaps. Youmi jogged from the other side of the clearing, reaching Ember and Insepth just as we did. He raised his hands and turned the downpour into a twisting funnel of water. When he released the spout, it ravaged the nearest fires, spraying soot and steam into the air.

Tamira ducked behind Ember and I rushed to the Watcher's side. Ember paused and pressed her hands into the fur between my ears.

"I'm so glad you're alive!" Ember exclaimed. Her eyes darted around. "Where's Angus?"

I looked up at Horas, who began searching the smoldering field around us.

I left wolf form to answer her. "I don't know—he was with us not long ago," I said, my heart dropping into my stomach.

"Is this what you're looking for?"

My head jerked in the direction of the brittle voice.

It was Sawyer. He held Angus in his arms.

CHAPTER 24

EMBER

Sawyer stood in the midst of the gore, holding my precious dog in his arms. I'd dreamt this moment a long time ago, and I choked back a sob that it had become reality.

Any love I might have had for Sawyer dissolved with his evil smirk. I didn't care that he'd been corrupted by the Devil. Or that my Sawyer, the one who'd guarded me with his life and loved me with everything he'd had, might still be in that red-eyed body somewhere. I didn't care about anything at that moment—except vengeance.

War's storm destroyed Hell beasts on the ground and Dark Angels in the sky. Insepth directed the earth to swallow up the enemy, and Youmi worked the rain to drive the evil creatures back. But Sawyer remained in place, untouched by the turn of events our arrival had brought. A strange black fire burned at his feet—dark particles. The evil substance that had created Growlers and Cricket, and even the bloated dragon, Sin. Those particles were from the deepest part of Hell, and in pure form they corrupted everything they touched. Thousands of years ago, Watchers had cleaned the taint from the Growlers and I'd done the same thing when I'd changed Cricket, but no one did that for Sawyer. The particles had altered him, making him one of Samael's soldiers.

My head throbbed and the world calmed around me. I stared at my former lover and friend. I had no choice but to kill him now. I could never forgive him for what he did to Angus. He had to be punished.

His smirk deepened as he raised Angus above his head. A three-headed hound slunk toward him, eyeing the prize he held. My eyes widened and the sounds of the raging storm and battle disappeared.

"A fine treat for my pets," Sawyer said.

Fire erupted out of me in a burst like none before, barreling toward Sawyer in a burning ball. His laughter on the wind brought tears streaming down my face. But just before the fire reached him, Raphael dropped out of the sky and grabbed Angus from Sawyer's hands. The flaming ball struck Sawyer with a blinding explosion that shook the ground and set the nearest trees that weren't already burning aflame.

My clothes were in tatters from the eruption of fire out of me and my strength waivered, sending me to my knees. Insepth's arm was around me and he was saying things, but his words were like a bee buzzing in my head.

Tears burned my cheeks. Sawyer had killed Angus, and I had killed him. The world, whatever was left of it, was a darker place than ever before. When would it stop—when would the suffering finally be over?

The dust cleared and I squinted to see the place where Sawyer had stood. There was a roar of something undefined, but deafening. Insepth gripped my shoulder and Tamira whined behind me. Ivan knelt beside me in human form.

"We should go…" he muttered near my ear.

"It can't be!" Horas exclaimed.

I stood, pulling away from Insepth.

Samael's black wings unfurled, exposing an undamaged Sawyer.

"Really, love, if you're going to use any element against my soldiers, don't choose fire. It's a personal favorite of mine." He grinned and arched his brows. His lithe form walked on land as well as he soared through the skies. And he was coming with hundreds of fresh Dark Angels taking flight from a newly gaping fissure in the earth. Smoke curled out of the hole, and other things were stirring.

My heart pounded frantically as I remembered the nightmares I'd had when I'd first gone to live with Ila. Blazing red eyes stared out from the shadows. The growls and hisses of the monsters hammered in my mind. I'd seen distorted faces with bodies that were a horrible blend of human and animal features, and with tails that were covered with flashing scales.

And then there had been the people. Their wails reached straight to my soul. They were the ones the Devil had imprisoned in Hell. I heard them again, and I was frozen in place. My limbs refused to move.

Samael drifted like a wraith toward us, with his black soulless, hungry eyes. The push of his power proceeded him, blowing my hair back with hot, putrid wind. I was frozen in place. My eyes watered, but I couldn't look away. He controlled my Fire, and it receded deep inside of me, afraid of its master.

Insepth, Youmi, and Ivan were tethered in place, the same as me, but Tamira paced at our backs, and Horas leaped in front of me. "Snap out of it. We can still escape."

He was a Demon and it occurred to me that the Devil already had his soul, so there wasn't much else to do to him, besides kill him. But not us. We had something Samael wanted more than anything—fresh souls.

A few of the wolves not lucky enough to have already died, yipped and whined as they thrashed on the ground. The Hell beasts from my dreams devoured them as they swept over the field, like rampaging insects.

Samael's voice carried across the meadow as he rapidly closed the distance. "It puzzles me your reaction to the death of a dog. I can only imagine the torture you'll experience when I kill your friends and your family. Especially your brother and his unborn daughter."

Tears burned my eyes. The blood and smoke covered hillside was gone, replaced by a burning city. It was a vision I'd seen before. I easily found Timothy and Chloe huddled on the boat. Chloe was crying and clutching her swollen belly.

No, please no. The picture disappeared and the Devil's army rose again from the ashes. The drumming noise of their movement exploded in my ears and the stench of Hell choked me. My Fire was still hiding, but my Gaia joined with Water and Air in a flurry of snapping branches in my mind.

I broke eye contact with Samael, and gazed into Sawyer's red eyes. He focused on me with pure hatred and I swallowed the lump in my throat. The change in the clouds caught my attention, and I let the swirl of elements fly free.

Insepth, Youmi, and Ivan woke from their trance just as War streaked down from the sky, his shrill whinny snapping Samael's glare his way. The horse's red hair glinted in the grayness and his arched neck and pounding hooves showed his power. Cricket clung to his neck, burying her face in his long mane as the stallion gained speed.

The elements I'd unleashed raced toward War's storm in a blurry glow that stretched high into the sky. Their pull made me stumble forward and Insepth caught my arm. Earth, Water, and Air collided with the squall with a sickening roar. The wind snapped to greater force and changed directions, driving into the Devil's army. Rain poured onto the battlefield in a torrent that made it impossible to see anything except streaking, falling water. Lightning crashed and thunder bellowed. I could hear the wailing screams of the Hell beasts as the hurricane attacked them from all sides. I squinted, trying to see through the deluge. Ivan struggled to stand upright, and I grabbed his arm, pulling him against me and Insepth.

"This way, Ember!" Horas shouted.

I followed where he was fixated. There was a circular glow not too far away. In the middle of the brightness, I saw a golden hued mountaintop. A faint, dry wisp of air reached my face, causing uncontrolled tears of relief to stream down my face.

"Come on!" I urged Ivan and Insepth into a run toward the light. Youmi was a few strides ahead and Tamira, in wolf form, loped along with us.

Raphael's wings were draped around the loophole he'd created. His expression was intense and focused.

"Stop them!" Samael's voice rang out above the gale.

I didn't look back even though the baying of his hounds rose above the storm, and the slapping of many feet pounded the puddles behind us. The hiss of Hell's fire rose in my ears and its heat seared my back. The Devil's army broke through the tempest with the explosion of sparks and smoke.

Insepth clutched my hand tighter and I pumped my legs harder, holding my gaze on the autumn landscape beyond Raphael's opening.

Youmi jumped into the glowing ring first, and Ivan and Tamira were right on his heels. As the scent of clay earth and pine needles assailed my senses, I slowed, daring to look over my shoulder.

Samael's pitch black wings were fringed in fire and folded into his sides as he rushed at us like a torpedo. Three-headed hounds and Hell beasts chased after him, and running ahead of the grotesque mob was Sawyer. Dark Angels swooped down from the clouds, brandishing gleaming black swords and axes.

Samael smiled and his ebony eyes brightened.

We weren't going to make it.

I whirled and threw my hands out, calling on my Fire. It responded, surging out of me in a deafening burst of release. I prayed that my flames wouldn't go to the master of the inferno.

They didn't. Fire and Air joined, creating a smoking tornado that ripped into the Dark Angels, sending them somersaulting through the sky.

Samael ignored the screams of his fellow Angels as they fled the funnel cloud. His own deathly wind preceded him, knocking me and Insepth to the ground. Horas appeared, holding his hands out to us, and I reached for him, shutting my eyes tightly, and bracing for Samael's impact.

A neigh pierced the air. War skidded to a stop and Cricket leaped from his back. She grabbed me and shoved me into the glowing ring. Horas helped Insepth, following right behind us.

Sunshine warmed my face and a meadowlark whistled as I hit the ground, rolling with Cricket.

I looked back. War turned and struck out with both his hind feet at the instant Samael slammed into him. A flash of lightning shot out of the Horseman's hooves, knocking the king of the Dark Angels backward.

War gathered his muscles and surged through the window just as it blinked out. Standing where the opening had been was Raphael. His eyes were wide and sweat dripped down his forehead. But a small smile touched his lips when our eyes met.

Cricket squealed and ran to War, throwing her arms around his neck. He bent his head and nickered to her.

Thanks, Ila. You were right about Cricket, and changing her, I said in my mind, hoping she'd somehow heard me.

Insepth crawled to my side, his chest heaving. "He'll follow us here," he huffed.

"This place is protected now," Raphael replied. He shook his wings and feathers floated to the ground around us.

Parts of the valley smoldered, wispy tentacles of smoke rising into the air, and the barn was leveled, but I saw the metal roof of Ila's cabin glinting in the sun. Many trees still stood tall and strong. A new barn could be built, and the grass would grow back in the spring—if there was a springtime.

"How?" I managed to say, sitting up. My heart still hammered, but it was slowing.

"Uriel and I set warding over the valley after the evil horde came through here the last time." His eyes fell on me. "It was Uriel's intention to bring you here—to a safe place in the coming storm."

My skin tingled. "Why?" I asked.

Raphael laughed. "You don't know? He has helped you at every turn. You are from his own blood. He cares for you."

I grunted as I jumped to my feet. "He went with the rest of the coward Angels! If he had been with you back there, he could have helped defeat Samael, and maybe even have saved my dog."

My voice was angry, but it was only despair I felt. With shoulders slumped, I began to cry. Cricket left War, sprinting over and wrapping her arms around me. I pressed my face against her shoulder, rocking both of us with my sobs.

"This dog?"

Uriel's words thundered in my head as I whirled around.

He stepped out from the trees and gestured with his fingers. My gaze followed the direction that he pointed.

I heard a whimper and I was running before I even saw him.

Angus pushed through the bushes and yipped, sprinting toward me. I dropped into the dry leaves and buried my face in his fur, reaching out with my Gaia for his injuries.

There was nothing—not even any residue of damage.

His prickly tongue licked the tears from my face. "I love you, boy. I love you so much," I cried into his fur.

When Angus flopped onto my lap, panting happily, I finally looked up. I dried my cheeks with my sleeve and blushed. Everyone was watching me, even the red stallion.

"Thank you for healing my dog." I swallowed back fresh tears.

Uriel came forward to stand beside Raphael. "I didn't heal this beast. I brought it back to life."

"You can do that?" Insepth asked, kneeling in the grass beside me and stroking Angus' head.

"Of course, it is one of my gifts as an arch. Such a blessing is usually bestowed on only the most noble of humans." His lips thinned and his eyes rolled. "I think I'm the first Angel to waste the rebirth prayer on a pet. When Raphael deposited the animal at my feet, I felt compelled to bring him back."

I scrambled to my feet and rushed to Uriel, throwing my arms around his middle. "It wasn't wasted, and you know it. Angus is the most noble of all of us."

He let me hug him for only a few seconds before he grasped my shoulders and picked me up, depositing me a couple feet away.

His face was flushed. "You and your friends can enjoy safety and peace in this valley for a while," he said with a curt nod.

Ivan was on the ground with Angus, butting heads and letting the dog lick his face. Tamira sat close by cross legged. She had changed into a girl when I hadn't noticed. The lines on her face pronounced her grief. She'd lost her parents and her entire pack, but there was brightness in her eyes when she examined the valley. Ivan looked up and his expression reflected the same hope.

War had also transformed into a man and his arm was thrown around Cricket's waist. Horas and Youmi shifted on their feet uneasily, and Insepth stared at me with a raised brow.

I turned to the Angels. "Why didn't you fight Samael and his fallen Angels—aren't they your enemies?"

Raphael looked to Uriel, who sighed, and said, "It is not in your nature to follow rules and orders, is it? The rebellious human inside of you is forever trying to alter the future—change destiny. And it's the arrogance of your kind that spurs you into action, even when the outcome is dismal at best."

He paused and looked around the clearing. His voice rose, becoming stern when he continued, "We are Angels, and the main thing that separates us from the fallen ones, is that we follow the strict orders set forth by our Father. Chaos would ensue through the universe if we began doing whatever we wanted." His narrowed gaze settled on me. "We choose order over chaos, even during this time of instability. It is not our task to stop Samael from rising or the destruction of mankind on earth. Raphael and I have already interfered too much in the lives of humans and Watchers. We will not separate ourselves from our brothers or our Father any longer. We have provided you with a haven for respite. How you use this gift is your decision. But our time here is finished. We are returning to Heaven."

Uriel looked at everyone in turn. "If you choose to do something that puts your lives in peril, we will not come to your rescue. This is goodbye."

I opened my mouth to argue, but quickly shut it when Uriel shook his head. What Uriel said made sense, but I disagreed that God wanted the Angels to do nothing. Who was I to tell that to an arch Angel? Uriel had been around since the dawn of time, and he knew things I didn't. I was just lucky that he'd broke from tradition as much as he had. And he'd brought Angus back to life. That more than made up for his departure.

I swallowed the lump in my throat. "Thank you for everything you've done—and you too, Raphael." I smiled at the soft-spoken Angel and he smiled back. "Perhaps we'll meet again."

Uriel's face scrunched in uncertainty and his brows raised. "I doubt it, child. But hope springs eternal." He glanced at War. "Choose carefully your course, Horseman. You do not want to be trapped in this world when the end comes. Samael would like nothing better than to tether you to a heavy cart and whip you daily. He will not allow you a warrior's death."

War nodded. With a gust of wind and a spray of leaves, Uriel was gone. Raphael paused long enough to wink at me before he bolted into the darkening sky. I watched the dual streaks that were Heaven bound. When they met the blinking stars, they disappeared. Icy wind blew in from the woods, bringing the scent of damp smoke and decaying leaves.

The smell was comforting and I inhaled deeply. If the forest had time, it would recover. I reached into my pocket and squeezed Uriel's feather between my fingertips. Even if I never saw him again, I'd have it to remind me that he really did exist, and that he'd helped me when I needed him most.

Horas' voice broke the silence. "Is anyone hungry?"

"I could eat," Ivan grinned. He reached out for Tamira and she grasped his hand, letting him pull her up. When she was standing, he didn't let go of her hand and she didn't try to pull away. During the few days we were apart, Ivan had bonded with the wolf girl. It was a good thing.

When Tamira glanced shyly at me, I smiled back. "I'm sorry about your family, but I'm glad you're here with us."

"Thank you," Tamira said quietly before wiping away a stray tear.

"I'll help you with dinner," Youmi offered, slapping Horas on the back as he walked past him.

Cricket came forward with War. He bowed his head ceremoniously to me. I raised my hand, stopping him. "I can never thank you enough for what you did back there—attacking the Devil's army, and kicking him in the face." I chuckled, fighting not to grin.

War leaned in. "Unlike the Angels, I found it quite exhilarating to battle such an adversary. I only wish my brothers had been there. Between the four of us, we could have buried the army of the dead."

"So you'll continue to fight with us?" I asked slowly.

War looked at Cricket and back at me again. "I didn't think you'd heed Uriel's advice." He spread his arms wide. "Spending the last of your days in this pleasant place isn't nearly as appealing to you as dying a miserable and painful death, is it?" I saw humor in his eyes.

"You said so yourself that if the other Horsemen joined our cause we could win," I said.

"That is true. We might be successful against Samael's army, but we could never stand against our Creator. And we never will."

My heart plummeted into my stomach.

"We will not be the ones to destroy the lands of men as is written, but we won't disrupt the Creator's will by stopping it, either. When I raised my powers for the destruction of Samael, I weakened. The Creator left me and I felt His absence."

Cricket squeezed War's hand as she stared at him. I knew that look. She was in love.

My chest constricted and I took a shallow breath. I remembered love. Samael had stolen it away from me when he'd taken Sawyer. I closed my eyes, picturing Sawyer in his faded blue jeans and black leather jacket, smiling at me.

I wouldn't take that from Cricket. I loved her too much.

"Where will you two go?" I forced the words out.

They exchanged glances and Cricket nodded. I frowned, looking at them.

"I'm going to join my brothers in Heaven's stable. Cricket has chosen to remain with you for the time being," War said.

"No, you have to go with War. You'll be safe with him," I urged.

Cricket shook her head. Her eyes were glistening with sadness. "I don't care about safety. I will miss him, but if I left you, I'd feel the same way." I began to protest, but she silenced me with a stern look. "I will not hide, waiting for the world to end. War has promised to come back for me when my death is near, but I will not live my life in a place without grass and trees. I am of this world, and will die along with it."

War was red faced, his chin raised.

"I'm sorry," I mouthed to him.

"The short time I have spent in the company of this Horsewoman has been the best moments of my long life. I have no regrets, and I will honor Cricket's courageous spirit. I pray that our Creator changes His mind about this beautiful land of men. When this mare travels to the other side, whether it be in days or in years, I will come to collect her spirit. "

He bent and cradled the sides of Cricket's face in his palms. Unspoken words passed between them, and I saw a tear trickle down the side of War's face. When he pulled back, there was an explosion of colors and mist rose from the meadow floor. The red stallion tossed his head, whinnied loudly, and galloped into the clouds.

I reached out and took Cricket's hand, tugging her to face me. She dropped her gaze from the sky. Her eyes were wet.

"You'll see him again."

"I know," she murmured with a sniff and a bob of her head.

"They definitely leave in style," Insepth muttered.

He was staring into the sunny sky with an expression of awe I couldn't remember seeing on his face before.

"You've been awfully quiet through all this," I commented.

Insepth's face lit up. "We're still alive and back in Ila's valley, which is now protected by arch Angel wardings." His eyes burned into mine. "It's time to celebrate, dear Ember—celebrate the time we have left."

My face heated. "You're giving up, then?"

He snorted. "We've faced monsters of all kinds—dragons, Angels, and the Devil himself. It's a bloody miracle we're still alive. Maybe the fellow upstairs has been watching out for us all along, and now it's time for us to finally have faith in Him."

I licked my lips, staring at Insepth. He was tall and muscular with an angelic face. His eyes matched the color of his long pony-tailed, golden hair. The glory of his Earth power draped around him, reminding me of how star struck I'd been by him the first time we'd met.

If the proudest man I knew was ready to lay down his weapons and walk away from the war we'd waged together since the beginning, I could hardly blame him. I was so very tired, and Sawyer had killed Angus. He would have killed me if War and Raphael hadn't gotten us out of there. I didn't want to ever face his void black eyes again.

Insepth offered his hand. "Shall we see what Horas and Youmi are throwing together for a feast?"

My heartrate sped up. It would be so easy to take his hand and hide away in Ila's valley. A shiver passed over my skin and I knew Ila was glowering at me. *Some things are more important than ourselves, dear,* I heard her say in my head. Whether it was just my imagination or for real, I didn't know. But my stomach growled and Insepth's grin deepened. Regardless of what I did, I needed to eat, rest, and recover.

I reached out to him and Angus barked. Our heads followed the dog's gaze into the shadows at the edge of the forest.

Leaves crunched and bushes shook. I grasped my Fire and Insepth took hold of the Earth. Cricket trembled as if she was about to change into a horse.

The branches broke apart and a giant black bear barreled at us. He stopped close enough that his breath tickled my skin. A flurry of movement at his feet caught my attention and I saw rabbits darting out into the grass and several cats slinking around his feet. Hens flew from the cover of the underbrush, squawking over our heads. I watched them cross the meadow and enter their coop that had somehow managed to escape damage. A chorus of bleating noises brought the goats bounding into the meadow. They kicked out their legs and rose up to bump heads before sprinting off into the deeper grass.

I faced Lutz and rested my hand on his broad forehead.

You came back. I wasn't sure if you would, the bear snorted heavily in my mind.

It's so good to see you, Lutz. And you kept all of Ila's pets alive. Thank you.

Lutz shook his giant body and groaned. *It wasn't easy. I took them to a cave I knew of and we stayed there until the fire and the monsters passed by. The goats have difficult natures. They only think of food and play.*

I pressed my forehead to his. *I'm glad you're home.*

It is a good place to be right now." He eyed me. *"Are you staying?*

It would have been impossible to look at my friend's face and say anything except yes.

So I lied for his sake.

CHAPTER 25

EMBER

Chickens pecked the ground by my feet as the sun peeked out above the mountains that surrounded Ila's valley. The air was crisp, but the sun promised a warmer afternoon. Cricket was back in horse form and grazing in the dewy morning grass with the goats. If it weren't for the darkened pockets of burnt forest on the mountainside, I might be able to pretend that the Devil's army hadn't passed through here, like everyone else was doing.

Horas had put together a tomato sauce from canned goods stored in Ila's cabin and served it over pasta the night before. Youmi's contribution had been the strawberry wine he'd discovered stashed in the attic when he and Sir Austin had taken care of the place the last time. Our group had spread out in the little cabin, sitting at the table, on the couch, and in Ivan and Tamira's case, on the floor. We ate and laughed, all too relieved that we were alive and monsters weren't banging on the door. It had been a short time of respite from the devastation of our losses. Sir Austin had died, and so had Ivan's and Tamira's families. Sawyer might as well have been dead. There was nothing left of the Sawyer I'd fallen in love with. Eae was gone, too.

I understood why no one talked about our losses. It was too much to contemplate at this point, let alone discuss. But while we enjoyed some much needed peace and quiet, people were dying out there. The world was crumbling and soon there would be nothing left of it.

I groaned. Cricket lifted her head and looked at me, her mouth still full of grass.

I held my hands up. "I'm okay."

"No, you're not."

Insepth had snuck up behind me. A long stem of straw hung from his mouth. He looked relaxed in a cream button up shirt and brown corduroy pants. A few stray curls covered his one eye and he tucked the strands behind his ear as he leaned against the tree I was sitting under.

"You're up early," I said, picking a lone daisy that had survived the fire and frost. I began mercilessly plucking the petals without looking up.

It was harder to ignore the Watcher when he dropped into the grass, bumping into me.

"I'm grotesquely bored," he said.

Fire spurted to life in my veins. "I bet Sir Austin would like being bored right now."

Insepth chuckled, and the sound made me face him.

"Quite right. But he was a soldier at the heart of it all. He died a warrior's death in a time when others won't be so lucky."

"How can you be so casual about your friend dying? I only knew the man a few months, and you'd spent centuries with him."

Insepth cast me a sideways glance. "We all don't mourn the same way, Ember. His loss means a lot to me, but life goes on for the living. Sir Austin understood that."

"So you're going to just go on living while the rest of the world burns around us?" I snapped.

He exhaled and dropped his head back against the tree. "It's always black and white—live or die—with you, isn't it."

He sounded tired, but my heart was racing when I rested my chin on my knees. "How long do you think this blissfulness is going to last—a week, maybe two? Then we'll face the same fate as everyone else."

"Not necessarily," he said.

I didn't miss the wicked tone to his words, as if he knew something I didn't.

"Spit it out," I demanded.

His eyes were bright and his lips trembled. "The warding that protects us was created by two arch Angels. It might very well protect us long after the collapse of the world as we know it."

My brow knitted as I processed what he'd said. "You believe that after the Devil overruns the earth, we'll be safe and snug in our own little utopian world?"

He shrugged, smiling timidly.

I barked out a laugh and jumped up, placing my hands on my hips. "When the Devil is done destroying the beautiful earth that we love so much, he'll be more powerful than ever, and he'll break through the warding to kill us, or maybe to torment us forever." I narrowed my eyes. "I didn't take you as a fool, Insepth."

He rose and ran his hand through his hair. "There's nothing else we can do! If the Horseman hadn't come to our aid, Samael would have ripped us in two. I'm all for fighting when the odds aren't completely absurd," he thrust his arm out, "but going back out there is suicide. If I only have weeks to live, I'd rather I wasn't spending them on a fool's errand."

I grimaced when he'd thrown my words back at me, but the anger I'd felt a moment ago lifted. Who was I to dictate how anyone should live their final days?

"You're a walking contradiction, you know that?" His brows lifted and I plowed on, "You say you're bored, but you choose to stay and do nothing here."

Insepth stepped closer. His eyes darkened and my heart thumped harder.

"There are things we can do to occupy ourselves, Ember." He touched my cheek.

My Gaia was begging me to walk into Insepth's embrace and kiss him. Warm honey spread through me and I swayed toward him, my mouth parting. A hawk screeched and the sound was a jolt to my senses. There were still birds and animals and people who needed help. I ducked away from Insepth and out of his reach.

He snorted, a smirk rising on his lips. "I never took you for a tease."

I rounded on him. "Oldport was destroyed! I had friends there, I don't know if they're alive or dead. No ones' cell phones are working and I haven't been able to get a hold of my brother."

Insepth strode to me. "I know it's going to be hard—"

I swatted his hands away. "I will not stand by and do nothing while they all die!"

"You can't save them. It's beyond all of us!" Insepth shouted.

"So the worst thing that happens is I die along with my family and friends. What's wrong with that?" Hot tears welled in my eyes.

"Everything! You don't have to die at all, Ember—and neither do I. We've got the blood of Angels in our veins. We might be able to eke out an existence in the new world."

"New world? You really are delusional. The Angels aren't going to save us." I shook my head. "You were the one who wanted so desperately to stop the Angels and the Apocalypse, and now you're okay with it?"

He looked away and then back again. The tension had left his face. "I was arrogant to think I could make a difference. After witnessing the tower fall in Los Angeles and coming close to death several times in a matter of hours, I'm humbled." He paused. "I was wrong."

Insepth's admission touched me and I released my Gaia. It intertwined with his Earth and my insides sighed when I stepped into his arms.

I stared into his passion-filled eyes, and felt the pounding of his heart against my palms. His lips touched mine with butterfly softness and I leaned into his kiss. He groaned with me and our mouths became more urgent. I wrapped my arms around him, savoring the life that pulsated through me. Soon it would be yanked away. This moment with Insepth was all we had.

He suddenly broke from the kiss and pulled back. "Don't do it, Ember. Please don't go off and get yourself killed," he said with the fierce intensity of a caged lion.

I forced a smile and sniffed, feeling a tear make a trail down my cheek. "I have to go."

Insepth pressed his face against mine and whispered, "Then I'm coming too."

CHAPTER 26

EMBER

"How do you know where to go?" Ivan implored.

The sun had set a few minutes earlier and the sky was the dull gray of dusk. A few birds still whistled their calls and the breeze had picked up, bringing cooler air.

Everyone was gathered in front of Ila's cabin. The group had worked hard to clear debris out of the yard and a pile of branches was pushed to the side. The mounds for Ila's and Riley's graves were undisturbed and I stared at them, wondering where they were. I'd done everything I had known to contact my mentor the night before, even traveling into the dream world. But my prayers and calls for help went unanswered.

I lifted my gaze to Ivan. "I've known for a long time where it would happen—where I need to go."

"You saw those monsters. There's no defeating them!" Ivan's eyes bulged and his face was red.

A strange calmness had filled me when Insepth had told me he was going with me. It seemed fitting that he be there at the end. He had his own demons to face, and not in the literal sense. He also had the uncanny ability to escape peril with his life. I was betting that even if I died, he would find a way to plug on, and that made me feel better.

But seeing the distraught looks on everyone's faces, my chest tightened. This would be the last time I'd see any of them.

"The pup is right. You cannot hope to stop them. It would be madness to try," Lutz said in his bellowing, loud voice. He had worked alongside the others in human form all afternoon. His sleeves were rolled up his arms and soot smudged his face and shirt.

I held up a hand, growing impatient. "You're all right. It's a suicide mission, I know. But one I have to do. My family is out there. I have to help them."

Horas pushed away from the porch railing. "Why are you taking Insepth and Cricket, but forbidding the rest of us to accompany you?"

I faced the Demon. "I'm not taking them, I'm letting them come along because there's nothing I can do to stop them. But it's different with the rest of you." I looked around. "You're safe here in the valley, and you've all risked your lives enough for my causes."

"But it's okay for Insepth or Cricket to give their lives in your service?" Horas defiantly lifted a brow.

Cricket snorted, stomping her hoof, but I ignored her. "Cricket has her own business where we're going, and I'm sure War won't let anything happen to her." I glanced at Insepth, who stood with his hand resting on Cricket's shiny black shoulder. His smile made my insides tremble. "If things get bad, Insepth is going to make sure Samael doesn't take either of us alive." My eyes hardened, landing on Ivan. "That's something I know you wouldn't be able to do."

Everyone fell silent. The only sound was the wind rustling the dry leaves.

Lutz cleared his throat. "I will remain here and care for the other animals. It is a small thing to do, but I'm proud to help you in that way, Ember."

I gave him a quick hug. Even in human form, he had a musky scent that reminded me of what he really was—an enormous bear.

I chewed on my lower lip and looked at Ivan, who stared at the ground with his ball cap pulled down low on his forehead. "You're the best friend I could ever have. You've done everything I've asked and nearly died for it. I have one more favor to ask of you, something only you can do for me."

Ivan slowly raised his head and met my gaze. "You know I would do anything for you."

"Please stay here with Angus. Take care of him—and let him be a part of your pack."

Emotions passed swiftly across Ivan's face. He looked honored and resentful at the same time. I waited, holding my breath.

"I will do this for you, but I do not like staying behind."

I breathed easier, hugging the wolf girl tightly before throwing my arms around Ivan. He buried his head in my hair. "You must come home, Ember. A pack needs a leader," he muttered.

I grasped his shoulders and nodded firmly, but I didn't answer him. I wasn't going to make promises I couldn't keep. And I knew if I opened my mouth, I wouldn't be able to hold back the flood of tears that threatened to break free.

Youmi formally saluted me, but I stepped up and squeezed him in a quick embrace anyway.

"I will not be here if you return. I'm going back to my people. That's where I will wait in these final days," Youmi said.

"Thank you for everything you've done and for being loyal. I'll never forget you," I said through clenched teeth, hating goodbyes.

Youmi nodded and passed by, striding over to Insepth who already had the loophole open for him. The Japanese warrior paused only long enough to raise his hand to us before stepping into a green land that met the sea.

I heard a seagull's shriek and caught a whiff of salt water when the opening blinked out.

I turned to Horas with a lump in my throat. "You'll stay, won't you? I need you take care of everyone," I forced the words out.

"If this is truly what you want, I will honor your wishes." He looked around the yard. "I never thought that my final days would be in such good company." He kept his voice level. "I don't believe your greatness has been fully revealed, young Watcher. Until we meet again."

I couldn't keep the tears from falling any longer when Horas wrapped his arms around me and patted my back.

Angus pushed against my leg and whined. I saved the last goodbye for my furry boy. He licked the tears from my face and barked at me when I rose and gently shoved him toward Ivan.

I swallowed a shaky gulp of air and didn't turn back. If I did, I was sure I would change my mind.

As darkness settled over the valley, I pulled myself onto Cricket's back. Insepth already had the loophole waiting and I squeezed Cricket's sides.

Tears blurred my sight as we trotted through the opening and away from my friends for what I knew was the last time.

⅄

"I think it would look odd to the locals if the horse was walking about on its own without saddle and reins," Insepth commented as he stopped beneath the trees next to the high school stadium—at least, what was left of it.

The turf was torn up as if a burning plow had been turned loose. The goal posts were down and the remnants of the carnage still smoldered. A handful of military personnel wandered over the terrain, and several police cruisers' lights flashed at the end of the field. The rest of Oldport was dark. The electricity was still out.

"No one's here to ask about my friends. We might as well move on." I muttered. Cricket dropped her head and I rubbed her neck.

"I wonder what he's up to."

I followed Insepth's gaze. An elderly man was talking in the parking lot. He stood on top of something I couldn't see and a small crowd was gathered around him. Some of the people held lit candles and others used battery powered lanterns. I couldn't hear the man's words exactly, but his voice was comforting, almost mesmerizing.

"Maybe we should find out." I left the cover of the branches. "Stay here, Cricket. We'll only be a minute."

Cricket nickered and I stretched my legs. The stench of Hell was strong, and seeing the school grounds destroyed made it difficult to think clearly. A soccer game was going on when the attack had happened. Colby was on the team. That meant Lindsey would have been here, and maybe even Maddie and Randy. I quickened my pace when I thought about Preston. He rarely left Randy's side. They all could have been killed.

I stopped when we reached the back of the crowd and glanced at Insepth. His lips were pursed, but he didn't say anything.

"Our Lord tells us in Revelation 3:10, 'Since you have kept my command to endure patiently, I will also keep you from the hour of trial that is going to come on the whole world to test the inhabitants of the earth.'" He raised his face to the sky. "The time has finally come, friends. Our Lord will call us home, and how glorious it will be."

"When, Pastor Holt—when will it happen?" a woman called out.

Pastor Holt—Maddie's grandfather?

He smiled at her. "It is written in Mark 13:32, 'But about that day or hour no one knows, not even the Angels in heaven, nor the Son, but only the Father.'" Murmurs rippled through the crowd and hands shot up, and the Pastor raised his palms. "Please, we must be patient as our Lord has directed us."

"There were monsters! I saw them killing people—friends and neighbors!" A middle-aged man cried.

"The authorities are denying everything, even though we saw it with our own eyes!" an older man shouted.

Pastor Holt nodded and everyone quieted. "Of course they would deny it. It takes faith to recognize the evil that's coming forth. For some of those who have faith, but are still in denial, they are simply trying to stop the chaos that will surely arrive in time."

A small, gray-haired woman called out in a thick southern accent, "What if He's forsaken us? The people of Oldport didn't deserve to be mutilated and murdered. There were believers that died, Pastor. How do you explain that?"

The pastor rubbed his eyes, suddenly looking tired. When he lifted his gaze, his voice came out strong and steady. "Some things are not able to be explained. Without faith in our Lord, all is lost. I'm talking about your eternal salvation, not the short time you spend on earth."

People nodded and there were many "Praise God" and "Amens" called out. Pastor Holt's focus landed on me and his eyes widened in recognition, but that was impossible. I'd never met the man before.

"Go back to your families—be with them while you can. And pray, friends. Pray for guidance and mercy!"

In a more fluid movement than I expected of the aged man, he stepped down from what I could now see was a wooden box. He touched hands and kissed cheeks as he made his way through the crowd that was breaking up. Men, women, and children dispersed onto the dark street, their quiet conversations a sad drone in the evening the air.

"He's got a way with words," Insepth said, but I ignored him, watching the pastor come straight toward us.

Pastor Holt stopped a few feet away. His eyes shifted to Insepth and then rested on me.

"In the presence of Angels," he said softly.

Insepth chuckled and I shook my head.

"Why would you say that," I asked.

He laughed, showing white teeth. His dark eyes sparkled and the crinkles at the corners of his eyes deepened. "I can see the glow around both of you."

I glanced at Insepth and he shrugged, suddenly looking uncomfortable.

"You're my dear Maddie's friend. She's waiting for you, you know," he said in a persuading way.

His words replayed in my mind. "You are Maddie's grandfather!"

He opened his arms. I went into his embrace without hesitation. The scent of his cologne was familiar and reminded me of my own grandpa who'd passed away when I was ten. The smell blocked out the odor of death in Oldtown and made the world seem normal for an instant. But what he said rested heavy on my heart.

I stiffened against his shoulder and inclined my head. "Where is she?"

His smile broadened even more. "Don't be afraid, child. The Lord is with you—always with you."

"Ah, are you sure of that? He seems to be missing," Insepth said a little too condescendingly.

The twinkle disappeared from the pastor's eyes and impatience crept into his voice as he looked at Insepth. "It's your arrogance that keeps Him away," his eyes shifted to me, "and your confusion."

Fire flared in me, flushing my face. "I'm sorry, but if you'd been through everything we have, you wouldn't be so confident that He's coming to help, either."

The pastor licked his lips. "You were born for a reason, child. One that only He understands at this time. But if you don't trust Him and give yourself to Him fully, we will all be lost."

I stepped away from the pastor. "The end of the world isn't my fault," I growled.

Pastor Holt's hardy chuckle brightened the dark and empty street. Everyone had left without me noticing. The silence made my heart drum faster.

"Of course not. We've all contributed to this—men and Angels. You have a part to play, as does my Maddie and the boy who went with her."

"Preston?" He nodded and I plowed on, "Where did they go— tell me!" I demanded.

"You already know—" he poked my chest with his bony finger "—in here."

"Why must everything be a riddle? Just out with it, old man," Insepth ordered.

The vision of the burning city rose again in my mind. The pastor was right. I knew where they went.

Goosebumps began to rise up on my arms. A mist rose and I turned my face into its chill.

It's beginning. There isn't much time. Go, my dear. Go to your destiny. Ila's voice was a soft keening noise on the wind, but I'd heard her loud and clear.

Clip-clops struck pavement behind us and I clutched Insepth's arm, pulling him away from the pastor.

"I'll do my best," I called out, forcing a smile.

"Have faith, child!"

His words echoed in my mind as Insepth lifted me onto Cricket's back and then jumped up behind me. We trotted around a partially collapsed building and then we were out of sight.

"Has your plan changed?" Insepth raised a brow, his hand wavering in the air.

"No. Open the loophole. We're running out of time," I said.

CHAPTER 27

EMBER

We rode into a wall of smoke that choked me. Cricket reared up and Insepth almost came off her backside.

Steady, girl. Let's not panic yet, I told Cricket.

Her reply was muddled and loud in my mind. I pressed my hands into the sides of her neck, using my Water power to calm her. It worked. She dropped her head and walked forward slowly as I squinted into the heavy air.

"What happened here?" Insepth whispered near my ear.

I didn't answer him. I was afraid to utter a sound when I realized where we were. I knew this exact spot on the highway. It was same mile marker that the semi-truck had lost control and jackknifed into the path of our vehicle. Dad had been driving and Mom was in the passenger seat. I was in the back. Our car had crumpled into the side of the giant, shiny cylinder full of gasoline. Our car exploded, and I'd seen them burning. I had seen Mom and Dad burning in the flames.

I shivered and Insepth squeezed me. "Ember, are you all right?"

For a moment, the smoke and abandoned cars with their doors flung open, disappeared.

There was bright sunlight overhead and the wails of sirens in my ears. I was sitting naked in the ashes. A kind fireman draped a blanket over my shoulders and picked me up.

At the time, I had thought that was the worst thing that would ever happen to me. I'd been so wrong. That day was just the beginning of the end. Now, years later, I was back again, in the very same spot where it all had happened. Coincidence? After everything I'd been through, I highly doubted it.

I peeked into the shadowy interiors of the cars we passed. There weren't any bodies or blood, or anything.

"It's as if everyone just disappeared," I murmured.

Guiding Cricket with my legs, we walked between an overturned truck and a school bus. I strained to hear noises of any kind, but the highway was quiet, except for Cricket's hooves striking the pavement and her gentle snorting.

"I don't like this one bit." Insepth continued to whisper, and for the first time I heard fear in his voice. "It might be a trap."

I would think the Devil would be too busy to come after two Watchers, but Sawyer was another story. Whatever Samael had done to him had erased any humanity the Demon had left. He'd thrown his life away to save me, and now he only wanted me dead. It was hard to even imagine, but it was true.

We came around the bus and the city skyline rose in front of us. The buildings were dark and none of the streetlights were lit. The full moon provided the only light to see by, but gray-fringed clouds passed over it, casting long shadows from the buildings and the overpass.

Cricket pulled up and I heard pebbles dropping and striking rocks.

"My God," I gasped.

The clouds separated and moonlight sprayed down, revealing a gaping crevice across the highway. A car was teetering on the other side. Wind gusted and there was a rhythmic scrapping sound. I grasped Cricket's mane.

She backed away from the edge, but not quick enough. The car came loose and fell with loud, metal scraping noises. The sounds went on an unbearably long time, echoing over the roadway and into the city. When the falling car finally hit bottom, dust billowed up from the deep hole.

"We should get out of here," Insepth urged.

"We can't leave without my family and friends—" I stopped talking and stared into the shadows beneath the overpass. I could see shapes gathering. Blood red eyes blinked—thousands of them.

Cricket whirled, shooting into a gallop. She darted through the abandoned vehicles, not needing my urging. Tapping sounds, like giant insects, followed us and I bent down to peer under Insepth's arm to see.

The vision that Youmi had showed us in the water had come true. These weren't Hell-beasts or hounds chasing after us. They were grotesquely shaped humans, pale and filthy, with sunken faces and hollow eyes. These creatures came out of the darkness slowly at first, gaining speed with spiderlike movements as they alternated between running and crawling. They made *smacking* sounds that made my stomach churn.

More creatures spilled out from unhinged doorways and alleyways. The pale shapes moved in clusters, crashing into each other as they pursued us with unnatural speed. Saliva flew from their gaping mouths, and what was left of the clothes they'd worn in their human lives was tattered and bloodied. Even with Cricket galloping as fast as she could, two of the creatures grabbed for her hind legs and she kicked out, striking one in the face and the other in the chest. Black liquid splattered my arms from their wounds.

It was nearly impossible to tell that they had once been humans. The evil smoke I'd seen in Youmi's water vision had risen from the crevice that split the highway. Wispy tentacles had reanimated the dead. But what about the rapture? Had it also happened?

The creatures caught up and came abreast of Cricket. She swerved, knocking several down. But they kept coming—hundreds of them. A bony hand shot out from the thrashing bodies, catching my ankle. Insepth stabbed at the hand with his dagger, but it wouldn't let go. It tightened, yanking me into the gnashing teeth. Insepth held on and Cricket kicked sideways. There was a cracking noise, but the creature still clutched me and was crawling up Cricket's side.

I hadn't used my powers, afraid they would be a beacon to Samael that we were here. But I didn't have a choice anymore.

Delicious Fire surged through me and out my fingertips. I aimed for the creature that was hanging on, pummeling it with flames.

Insepth wrapped his arms tightly around me, holding on while I worked my Fire to free myself.

There was a nauseating sizzling sound, and the smell of burning flesh. My heart leaped into my throat when the creature's back bubbled and cracked. The scorched skin stretched and snapped apart, revealing puffy new reddened skin.

Insepth bent over me and sawed at the hand with his dagger. Black blood squirted and when he met bone, he yanked the wrist backward until it crunched loose. The creature squealed as it fell, disappearing into the flailing limbs.

Cricket turned down a narrow street, dodging abandoned cars and jumping over fallen street lamps. More and more creatures poured out of the buildings until the street was covered with writhing bodies that looked like a swarm of ants. And they were all focused on one thing—us.

Cricket slid to a stop and reared. A tractor trailer was overturned, blocking the entire street. There was nowhere to go.

I clutched Cricket's mane as she kicked off creatures with her hind feet and struck out with her front.

"We have no choice!" Insepth cried. Earth flooded my senses, and I called on my own Gaia. Fire didn't work on these evil things, but dropping a building on them might do the trick. There would be no hiding once we unleashed our combined powers.

The swarm of creatures was too much. Clawed fingers snatched at us, cutting into Cricket's hindquarters and slashing my legs. The fresh blood turned the mob scene into a frenzy of pawing hands and lapping tongues.

Insepth linked with me.

"Here! Over here!" A familiar voice shouted from one of the buildings.

An incredibly tall figure was silhouetted in an open doorway across the street. He was waving at us.

Insepth growled, the power fluttering around him.

"Samael will come for us," I choked out.

Cricket saw the giant in the doorway and made the decision for us. She whacked her head sideways, clearing a path and leaped forward. It took every muscle I had to hold on.

The black horse bit, reared, and kicked her way through the horde. We were almost to the doorway when all the creatures turned as one and charged us.

The crowd caught us, slamming into Cricket. Insepth and I went airborne and skidded along the street, and Cricket was knocked to the ground. She rolled, thrashing to rise on her hooves. Monsters clawed and bit at me, dragging me away from Insepth.

A cry echoed between the buildings and the creatures paused their attack, flicking their heads in the direction of the sound. The pause was only the length of a drawn breath, and I pushed up on my hands to see what they were looking at.

A sword sliced the air, decapitating several of our assailants. Black ooze rained down and I scurried up and shimmied past falling bodies to reach Cricket.

Her shrill neigh pierced my heart, and I caught a glimpse of her buried beneath the mob. Insepth was beside her head, stabbing at the backs of her assailants. He was covered in gore, and his blond hair was slicked back with the stuff.

All my elements reared to life inside of me. To Hell with Samael and his Hell beasts finding us. That death wouldn't be any worse than this one.

I inhaled deeply and closed my eyes. I could hear every snapping jaw and snarling hiss. The smell of my own blood filled my nose as I was knocked to my knees. I didn't feel the teeth biting into me. The power rippled and grew.

My eyes flew open and the world was blood red. I was about to let the power go when I was jerked off the ground and slung over a shoulder.

The sword swiped at the creatures that had Cricket down and their severed limbs covered her. She rolled to her feet, ducked, and galloped through the door, clearing a path for us.

I was dropped into Insepth's arms and he shouted, "That way!"

With an explosion of colors, Cricket changed into a woman and followed Insepth's outstretched arm that pointed to the path. My mind registered that this building was a bank and we were aiming for the vault.

Little hands waved from the darkness and I blinked, unsure of what I was seeing.

"Hurry! Come on!" children's voices shouted.

Yes. They were kids—a boy and two smaller girls—urging us to run faster.

My heart pounded and I grasped Insepth's shoulder, pulling up so I could see the man brandishing the sword.

He was spinning, holding his sword out. Creatures dropped to the floor in piles. A faint glow surround him and I gasped.

Insepth turned and shouted, "Come on!"

The warrior gathered his muscles and leaped, covering the distance in a single stride.

Insepth slammed the vault door shut and there was complete blackness. The scratching noises on the vault door faded away after a moment.

A light burst to life and a boy was holding up a lantern.

The warrior who had saved us was bloodied and bruised, and two little girls clung to his legs, but there was no mistaking who he was.

I saw Eae through a blur of tears. And then I was right alongside the girls, hugging him for dear life.

CHAPTER 28

EMBER

"That one is Joey," Eae nodded at the boy stretched out on the floor, and then at the girls in his lap, "and these are Sarah and Emily."

Emily stirred. She yawned and nestled against Eae's large chest.

My gaze lifted. "Where did they come from?"

"After we were separated in Los Angeles, I discovered them. They were alone and afraid. Their parents had been killed." He grunted. "I couldn't bring myself to leave them."

"How did you cross the country—did Angels help you?" Insepth asked.

Eae slowly shook his head, careful not to disturb the sleeping girls on his lap. "I would have gotten no aid from them. Azriel offered to take me up to Heaven, but I refused."

"Why?" My hand paused on Cricket's hair. She'd fallen asleep with her head resting on my leg. Even though I'd healed her injuries, she had been too distraught to say much. I wasn't sure if it was because she'd come so close to dying or that War hadn't come to her rescue.

"I am an Angel no longer. I would only be a burden in Heaven, with no purpose to our Father or anyone else." His green eyes clouded. "In the land of men, I thought I could help you, Ember. I am sorry that I failed."

"You didn't fail!" I whispered fiercely. "You saved all of us from being eaten."

He sighed deeply. "And now we are trapped in a vault, surrounded by monsters. I only prolonged your death."

I licked my lips and glanced at Insepth, waiting for one of his witty comments to ease the tension.

He just stared at the wall, saying nothing.

"There has to be a way for us to escape," I said.

"If we use our powers to break free and destroy the horde of creatures beyond that doorway, Samael and his army will know we're here. And they'll come for us," Insepth said.

"If we do nothing, we'll die of starvation," I replied.

"We will more likely succumb to suffocation before we starve," Eae commented nonchalantly.

"Thanks for the reality check," Insepth muttered.

I sat up straighter and ignoring Insepth's comment, I glanced between the wingless Angel and the Watcher. "Then we must try!"

Eae's face softened and he bent his head. "Since you were a babe, you were my responsibility to watch over. But now, I also have these young ones." His eyes glistened in the dim light. "What will become of them if we open those doors? I fear if the destruction you wreak doesn't kill them, the creatures will. A quiet death within these walls would be a mercy, don't you think?"

I swallowed down the knot in my throat and pressed my lips together. Eae was right.

I stared at the lantern, wondering when the batteries would go dead. The darkness would frighten the children, too.

I inhaled, clearing my mind. Something wasn't right.

"Do you remember when Youmi showed us the vision in the water?" I asked Eae.

"Of course. That was the day my wings were taken."

I nodded, trying to block the image of Eae's butchered back from my mind. Insepth looked away, but not before I saw the shadow of shame pass over his face.

"We had seen people drop to the ground and long golden threads leave their bodies. Michael had appeared. He'd raised his sword and there was a boom that had parted the sky, revealing a place beyond that was too bright to see. The threads had streamed toward the opening, passed through, and joined the blinding light. And then the rest of the Angels had arrived. They had lined up in the sky, their golden and silver battle armor shining, and their weapons drawn." My eyes narrowed. "Do you remember?"

"Yes, that is what I saw as well," Eae agreed.

"Did any of that happen before people changed into those things out there?" I worked to keep my voice level, but my heart was racing.

Eae's brows rose. "The rapture didn't take place. If it had, these innocents would have been the first claimed by our Father."

I leaned in. "The Angels aren't going to collect the good souls." Eae's eyes widened and I continued, "They're letting the Devil and his army march over the earth, killing and torturing everyone along the way." I looked at the girls. "There's no salvation coming for them."

"I don't believe that. You must be mistaken," Eae said firmly.

"She's right. I was there when Michael and Raguel said it. The Angels have achieved what they always wanted—the annihilation of mankind. They don't care about the souls of the righteous," Insepth said.

Eae shook his head. "No. Our Father would not allow the souls to be taken by Samael. He wouldn't."

I sat back. "I don't think so, either."

Insepth cast me a sideways glance. "How is this a good thing? What is going through that busy head of yours, Ember?"

The scratching noises had stopped some time ago and when we weren't talking, the silence was achingly thick. The air was stale and if my imagination wasn't playing tricks on me, the lantern had just dimmed.

"What time do you think it is?" I turned to Insepth.

He snorted and lifted his eyes, thinking. After a pause, he said, "I'd estimate it's early morning by now. The sun is probably rising."

Eae looked at me with sharp eyes and I swallowed, trying to slow my heartrate.

"None of this is supposed to be happening." I squeezed Cricket's shoulder and she twisted away, rubbing her eyes. I bolted to my feet and looked down at Eae. "This isn't God destroying the world—the Devil is doing it."

"What are you saying, child. Speak clearly," Eae ordered.

I knelt in front of him. "The Bible says that the horn will be blown calling the Horsemen to spread destruction across the earth, right?"

"Yes, but the exact details are not recorded in the Book. There has always been room for interpretation of the words."

"The Horsemen work for God, right?" I asked.

Eae nodded.

"They said they couldn't find Him, so they left. They didn't want to destroy His creation if it wasn't what He really wanted." I lowered my voice. "Somehow, Ila knew they were the key to our salvation. That's why she told me to change Cricket into a Horsewoman—so she could convince them not to go through with it."

Eae was losing patience. His voice was rough when he asked, "What of it? It doesn't matter whether the Horsemen or Samael bring the final Apocalypse. The world still ends, either way."

His words tempered my excitement. "Maybe. But unless God has left for good—or is dead—then this story doesn't have a definite ending."

"We can't fight those creatures out there, Ember. Even with all of the power combined between you and Insepth, there are thousands of them. And the same thing might be happening in every city across the world. It's hopeless," Cricket said, tears welling in her eyes.

I took her hand and pulled her into an embrace. I couldn't bear to see her afraid. Even though she was a woman now, she was still my horse—the beautiful, strong, and brave mare I loved so much.

I opened my mouth to try to comfort her. *Caboom.* The vault shook and crashing noises could be heard coming from the other side of the door.

Emily screamed and Eae rose with the girls in his arms. Joey jumped to his feet and pressed against Eae's leg.

"What's going on?" the boy asked.

"I do not know," Eae said.

"Perhaps Samael has found us?" Insepth braced his hand on the wall when another explosion rocked the vault.

The door shuddered and we huddled together. I opened to my elements, and the shock of Earth energy next to me confirmed that Insepth had done the same.

The sound of the girls crying was awful, but Eae's cooing voice trying to sooth them was even worse. If terrible things came through that door, Eae would have to end their lives. It would be the most merciful thing for the poor kids.

Light poured into the vault when the door swung open. I blinked, trying to see.

Two figures were outlined in the dusty light, and they were alone.

When I heard the laughter, I sagged against Insepth and Cricket ran into the light.

"You came for us!" she cried.

"We came for you," War said, wrapping his arms around her.

Insepth held up his hand, helping me out of the vault and over the broken floor.

"It's a good thing we found you when we did," Conquest said, with a grave look tightening his handsome features. "Samael's army has arrived."

I looked around. "Where's Death and Famine?"

"They stayed back with the Angels. They will do nothing more until instructed by the Creator," Conquest replied.

"Will you fight with us?" I looked at the tall men, one with chestnut colored hair and beard, and the other with long platinum hair. They moved like horses and even smelled like them.

It was War who answered. "Yes, we will fight beside you against the evil that is coming."

"What changed your mind?"

War glanced at Conquest and then said, "It is the right thing to do."

CHAPTER 29

EMBER

Morning sunshine blinded me when I stepped out of the building. The street was littered with body parts, overturned cars, and downed lamp posts. Wires sparked while a layer of rank smoke hung in the air. I wrinkled my nose, trying to avoid looking at the carnage. I took shallow breaths and followed the Horsemen past an Italian restaurant I'd eaten at a few years ago to celebrate Timmy and Chloe's engagement. The front door hung on one hinge and the stained glass was broken. I caught a glimpse of green tablecloths and a chandelier in the gloomy interior. I had to look away. That had been a happy occasion with my family. Now Mom and Dad were gone, and I feared for the lives of my brother and sister-in-law.

If I still had my cell phone with me, and even if it had worked, I didn't think there was any chance that I'd get a hold of them or anyone else. The end of the world had arrived. Cincinnati was a large city and it was all but deserted, except for the creatures that used to be its human inhabitants. Was this what all the cities across the world were like now?

My head throbbed with the craziness of it all. And I was so very tired. The only thing that kept my feet moving was the desperation that somehow I'd find my brother alive.

A droning noise filled the air overhead. The sound intensified and I stopped in the middle of the street and looked up between the tall buildings. Only a small space of blue sky was visible. There were a few puffy white clouds and a lone bird.

The noise grew and grew until two dark shapes crossed my line of vision and then were gone.

"It can't be," I gawked at Insepth.

His brow lifted. "The humans are making a last stand."

An explosion shook the nearest building and Insepth grabbed my arm.

Another blast rocked the city and a cloud of dust billowed onto the road.

"I believe we're going in the right direction," War said, winking at Cricket.

Our eyes met. Her wide-eyed look told me she was terrified, but she didn't say it out loud.

Emily was still crying in Eae's arms and the other two children shuffled along with him. I wasn't sure how he was even able to move with them attached to him like little crabs.

Eae tilted his head, listening. "Others are coming."

Three more jets streaked by and my pulse quickened. I pulled away from Insepth and broke into a run, passing the Horsemen. I turned onto another street, dodging vehicles and broken glass. I followed the booming sounds of explosions, knowing where I was heading.

The buildings blocked out the sun and everything appeared to be abandoned. I heard the others huffing behind me as they ran, but I ignored them. One more turn and I should be almost there.

A city bus was sideways across the street and I had to skirt around it, climbing over the debris of a collapsed store front. Insepth cussed and I heard Conquest suggest to War that they change into their horse forms, but I didn't slow to hear War's response.

The street dipped and I finally saw my destination. The Ohio River. I stopped to catch my breath, sucking in a gulp of air.

Cricket was beside me and dripping with sweat, but when her gaze settled on the place I was staring at, she grasped my hand and shuddered.

At the center of the river, between the pedestrian and vehicle bridges, the water was bubbling and rolling violently.

"Heaven help us." I heard Eae say.

"I believe that ship has sailed," Conquest replied.

"Over there!" Insepth pointed at the burning football stadium.

The jets came by for another pass, firing more missiles. One hit the stadium, blasting a gaping hole into its side, and the second one struck a roadway beside the stadium. Thousands of creatures were crowded together there, looking like spiders crawling all over each other.

My heart froze when the missile met its mark, cratering the pavement with a cloud of smoke. The screeching wails of dying creatures could be heard on the wind.

The giddiness that spread through me lasted only a few seconds. A rumbling groan was accompanied by the ground shaking. I nearly lost my balance as my focus returned to the bubbling river. Water shot into the air like geysers in a long line.

"This is bad," Insepth said into my ear. "There isn't much we can contribute to this madness."

I shot him a look that made him glance away quickly. The Horsemen watched the river, and Eae tried to calm the children.

Giant waves sloshed in the river and steam rose from the bubbles. The water level rose, spilling over the banks and flooding the sidewalks and businesses that were alongside the river's edge. A barge was dragged into the current, and began to spin. It tipped sideways into the churning water.

The ground heaved again and the river fell away, leaving behind only damp rocks and a giant chasm. Two of the fighter jets had circled back and were directly over the hole when dark objects streaked into the sky. I squinted and took a few staggering steps forward when I realized what the objects were.

Two of the Fallen Angels intercepted the jets. They produced a wall of wind that hit the jets, causing the first one to spiral out of control and crash into buildings on the Kentucky side of the river. The second jet did a complete flip and landed in the river with a fiery splash.

Hundreds more Dark Angels took flight, and Hell beasts spilled out of the hole. That's when I spotted Samael. He was suspended in the air, his great black wings pounding furiously. The gale he created was so strong it drove the river back so that his army could pass onto land.

When I heard the other jets approaching, my head whipped toward the Horsemen. "The Angels are going to bring them down, too!"

War nodded and changed into a horse at the same time as Conquest did. The storm gathered around them and they surged into the sky.

The Hell beasts and hounds moved swiftly, charging onto shore and up the winding concrete serpentine wall that pedestrians usually strolled along. Fires flared to life everywhere they stepped. They were close enough that I could hear the chomping sound of the hounds' mouths.

I looked over my shoulder at Eae. He was hugging the children so they couldn't see what was coming. His eyes were bright and his voice cracked with fear when he shouted, "I must protect the children!"

I offered a small smile as tears slid down my cheeks. "I know," I mouthed. I turned away and grasped Cricket's shoulders. "Help Eae with the kids. Don't let them suffer," I told her.

"I want to come with you," she argued.

My own Fire gripped my insides and anger burned inside me. I didn't want to lose Cricket or Eae, but I had seen the little boat on the river—the same one that had been in the dream I'd had so long ago that night in Ila's cabin. I had to go to it.

I inhaled and cleared my mind, forcing my voice into the commanding one I used on Cricket before I'd changed her into a Horsewoman—when she was just my beautiful horse. "You will do as I say. If God wills it, I'll come back. But until then, you have to do whatever you can to stay alive—along with those kids."

The sound of the jets' engines roared above and the thunder and lightning of the Horsemen's storm cracked the air. Sweat dribbled down my forehead from my inner Fire.

The world went silent when Cricket spoke. "You better come back to me."

I touched her face and then whirled around. Insepth ran with me, and without words, we linked.

He harnessed my Earth powers and thrust it into the rocky shore that the Hell beasts were scrambling over. As Insepth caused an earthquake that collapsed the river bed at the edge of the water that Samael was holding back, I directed my Tempest into the river. The water hesitated for a brief moment, and then pushed back against the Devil's wind.

Between the collapsing earth and the fighting water, Samael lost his hold on the river. It swooshed back into the channel, swallowing the monsters of Hell and their fires. The hounds that hadn't made it to shore yipped in the foaming water.

A wave of creatures made it out of the channel before it flooded. They clamored up the steps of the walkway with determined speed. I threw fireballs at them while Insepth attacked them with chunks of earth that he sculpted into crude earth beings, hastily created.

The sky darkened and a jagged flash zigzagged across the angry clouds the Horsemen forged, catching my attention. The red and white horses galloped into the line of Dark Angels that waited for the jets. When their storm reached the Angels, there were sparks of lightning and crashes of thunder. The Angels couldn't get past the Horsemen and the jets released their missiles, speeding by.

Samael barely escaped the dual detonations that struck the breach leading into Hell.

Fire streamed from my fingertips, not killing the beasts on land, but strong enough to knock them to the ground, buying some time to get around them. Insepth was still with me, but there wasn't time to look his way. I heard his grunts as he hurled debris and brought the pedestrian bridge crashing into the river on top of dozens of enemies.

I couldn't slow to think about the devastation around me. It was like a distant dream or a movie playing in another room. I had eyes for only one thing and one thing only—a small tug boat being batted around in the waves.

"Ember, look!" Insepth shouted.

The panic in his voice turned my head. The smoke where the missiles had struck was settling. A swarm of Hell beasts crawled out of the holes, spilling into the street.

I pushed my legs faster and was almost to the river when something hit me from behind. I was airborne for an instant, my arms flailing as I tried to break my fall. I hit the broken concrete with cracking ferocity and rolled to the edge of the water. When I looked up I was staring into the soulless eyes of one of the hound's heads.

It was too close to do anything else. I opened myself to my Gaia, pulling it back from Insepth and diving into the beast's mind. There was a solid wall, but wanting to drive it crazy, I punched at its mind with everything I had. It lurched forward and I rolled to the side as it dropped heavily to the ground.

Its saliva smattered my face as I scrambled to my feet. The hound's other heads bashed into each other, biting and yowling.

I focused all my Earth energy into the hound's minds, and with the feeling of a bursting bubble, its walls broke apart. One head went limp and the others growled as it fell over.

I swayed, pushing off from its extended paw. Insepth was surround by beasts, but I didn't go to him. I turned back to the water and called on that element to help me.

The waves separated just enough for my feet to touch the pebbles beneath the surface. Water sloshed at my sides and I feared I'd soon be swimming. I felt Samael's gaze before I saw him across the expanse of the river. His black eyes found me and his beating wings forced the waves against me. Water sprayed my face and a wave went over my head. My connection with the precious water was gone and I was swimming for my life.

I closed my eyes and desperately searched for ways to use my powers to control the elements that were in chaos. Wave after wave struck me, somersaulting me through the cold, churning water. I caught a breath when I finally managed to bob to the surface.

Something struck the side of my head and lights flashed beneath my eyelids.

I reached for my Tempest, but the darkness spread in my mind and I knew I was drowning.

CHAPTER 30

EMBER

Arms closed around my wrists and I felt myself being dragged through water. I tried desperately to push away the dizziness that clouded my head. The river was cold and dark, but I saw a fuzzy light above the crashing waves and I focused on that place, kicking my legs to get there faster.

My face cleared the surface and I took a gulping breath as I bumped into the wooden side of a boat. Hands reached down and I grabbed them. Behind me, my rescuer shoved me upward and I was pulled over the railing. I slumped on the deck, coughing up water and shivering. A man-sized jacket was flung over my shoulders and I blinked, looking at the three faces that stared back at me.

Timmy squatted beside me and pulled me into a tight hug. He was soaking wet and taking rasping breaths. It was Preston's jacket on my shoulders, and Maddie's hands on my knees.

"You found us!" Maddie exclaimed. Her brown eyes glinted with the same light I'd seen in her grandfather's gaze.

I swallowed. "I was looking for my brother and his wife. I didn't think I'd find the two of you with him."

"Maddie had a dream last night. He showed her the way," Preston said.

My brows rose. "He?" I asked carefully.

Maddie nodded. The light in her eyes brightened even more. "I prayed for guidance and this is where we were led to."

An explosion ripped the sky above us.

Timmy leaned back, but held onto my hand. "We were trying to get down river to escape those *things*, but the water drove us back." His eyes were wild and my heart stuttered at the sight of his fear. I'd had months to prepare for this moment. I'd seen monsters and dragons and knew magic existed. My poor brother was in shock, and he didn't know what to do.

My insides trembled when the sky lit up again. Dark Angels dashed through the clouds and I caught a glimpse of the silhouette of a horse rearing. The city was burning and smoke choked the air. My nightmare had come true and the day I'd dreaded was here.

"Where's Chloe?" I asked, my eyes darting around the small deck that was covered with puddles and pieces of broken wood.

Timmy's face paled and his focus shifted to the cabin. The door was ajar. "It doesn't look good." He stood and pulled me up beside him.

Preston looked away and Maddie frowned. My heart hammered as I stepped into the tiny dark space. Chloe sat on a cushion in the corner. I dropped in front of her, picking up her cold hands. There was bright red blood on the blanket covering her legs. The last time I'd seen my sister-in-law, she hadn't even looked pregnant. Now, her stomach bulged.

Her eyes rounded when she recognized me, and tears ran down her face. "Oh, Ember, I didn't think we'd ever see you again."

The boat rocked harshly and I spread my knees to keep from tipping over. Chloe groaned.

"She's two months early, Ember." Timmy's voice cracked. "Her water broke and she began bleeding." He ran his hand through his wet hair. "If your friends hadn't showed up and helped us into the boat, we—" the boat dipped and he grabbed the doorframe "—wouldn't have made it."

"It's started, hasn't it?" Chloe breathed. "The end of the world—and we're all going die. Even my little girl."

Samael had said I was going to have a niece, but hearing Chloe actually say it, spurred my movement. I placed my palms on her belly and let my Gaia flow through me into Chloe.

Closing my eyes, I saw the baby floating in the womb. Her little finger was in her mouth and she was sucking it. He eyes were sealed shut and she kicked out with her feet. And there were pockets of blood drifting in the fluid. She was too small to be born—her lungs weren't fully developed. But my Gaia knew what to do and I let it go. The power drained from me, flowing into Chloe's womb, embracing my little niece.

"It's going to be all right," I told Chloe.

"Ember is special, Chloe. She can help you and the baby." Timmy sounded confident and I didn't want to dash his hopes. Even if I managed to save the baby, I couldn't stop what was happening beyond the boat.

A wave sprayed over the railing and I heard Maddie scream. We hit something and the boat creaked. A splintering noise rang out.

"Ember, I think you need to come out here!" Preston shouted.

But I ignored his plea. My Gaia had done the only thing that might save my niece's life, and now sweat poured down my face from the use of power. I met Chloe's terrified look. "She's coming. You have to push."

"It's too soon!" Chloe squealed as a contraction convulsed her body. Through the healing connection, I felt the same pain and I doubled over, gritting my teeth until the awful cramping passed.

"Trust me, Chloe. Do as I say," I found my voice and ordered.

Timmy squeezed in behind Chloe and pressed her head back against his chest. "You can do this," he told her.

Preston and Maddie stood in the entrance, their faces drained of color, but they didn't say anything. Screams and wails could be heard in the distance, and the sky had darkened to a nighttime hue beyond the windows. The rumble of the storm continued past the windows. Rancid smoke drifted into the cabin and I took small breaths trying to keep my head clear.

I felt another contraction coming and lifted the blanket. "Push, Chloe—you have to push."

"What's the point?" Chloe lifted her head. Her eyes were filled with pain. "The world is coming apart."

Tears flooded my eyes. She was right, but I couldn't sit back and let my family die without trying to save them.

"There's still hope," Maddie cried. She knelt at my side and began praying aloud. "Please, Lord, deliver this baby safely into the world, and protect us all from evil. Deliver us to a peaceful place. Amen."

I licked my lips and looked around. Timmy whispered a string of soothing words to Chloe and Maddie's eyes were tightly shut, although her mouth continued to move as she soundlessly prayed. Preston mouthed the word "hurry" to me. He ducked when something small and sharp flew through the air, nearly hitting him. It impaled the side of the boat with a thud. Water lapped over his feet, spilling into the cabin. The boat was sinking.

I focused on my Gaia working its magic inside of Chloe's womb. The baby's heartbeat was strong and the Gaia had shifted her position, dropping her head down into the birth canal. The contraction built and I flung my head backwards, clenching my teeth.

What a horrible time to be born—into a world that was destined to become a part of Hell. Maddie had prayed from her heart. She hadn't asked for everything to stop, only that we die in peace and salvation. I admired her strength in her faith, but I was selfish. I wanted my niece to grow up and ride a pony and date a handsome young man. I wanted her to get married someday and hold her own baby in her arms.

My face flushed with anger and my Fire stirred to life, taking the bite out of Chloe's pain. Two of the Horsemen were fighting against Hell rising, and there was still the drone of aircraft in the sky. I wasn't ready to concede just yet. I had to fight for my baby niece.

"What's her name going to be?" I looked between Chloe and Timmy. For a brief instant, I saw a spark light up their faces.

"Faith. We'd talked about calling her Faith." Chloe glanced sideways at Timmy and he nodded his head.

"It's a fine name for our little girl," he said quietly.

Icy, brown water lapped at my feet and the boat rocked, tilting sideways. Maddie fell against me and Preston put his arms around both of us.

"We're going to drown if we don't get out of here." The urgency in Preston's voice made my heart thrum harder. I couldn't risk losing my Gaia to work with the Water element.

I looked over my shoulder, through the swinging door, toward the shore. Creatures crawled over the bank and three-headed hounds howled.

Insepth, where are you? I need your help, I spoke in my mind to him.

There was silence and my chest froze.

Chloe cried out and arched her back. My Gaia wrapped around baby Faith, growing her body and developing her organs. The power it took to do it made me dizzy and nauseous, but I didn't let go. Even though my other elements were tugging at me to break away from Chloe, to save us all, I didn't let go.

I heard the rumbling, and then crashing noises behind me, but I kept my gaze locked on Chloe's face. "One more push," I begged.

Chloe closed her eyes and her face reddened with her strain. With a long groan she pushed. Faith's head crested, and then there was a gush of warmth as the baby slipped into my hands.

"Is she okay?" Chloe gasped, pushing away from Timmy to sit up straighter.

Faith was limp and pale in my hands. I called on my Gaia again just as Maddie pulled a tissue from her pocket. She vigorously wiped Faith's nose and guided my hands to hold the baby in an upright position. The power of the Earth rushed through the newborn's tiny body and with a jolt, she sucked in a wet breath and squawked loudly.

I sagged in relief as Maddie took my niece and handed her to Chloe. The umbilical cord was still attached and Chloe was bleeding. The boat rose out of the water and rolled backward. Water rushed out of the cabin and I looked up. Insepth was at the water's edge, his hands outstretched.

"I can't hold the land bridge for very long!" Insepth shouted. He was drenched, muddy, and splattered with blood.

I pushed to my feet. "What's going on?"

"Samael controls the river—the Horsemen have been giving him fits, but they can't hold off the Dark Angels much longer."

"Cricket and Eae?" I forced the names out.

"They're battling those creatures on the shore." I followed Insepth's pointed finger.

I could see Eae was using a long piece of metal as a sword and Cricket kicked and struck out with her hooves at the never-ending swell of creatures clamoring up the pile of rubble where they were making their stand. The three children were huddled on the ground between them.

"We've got to help them," I said, taking a step toward Insepth. Maddie's hand snaked out, grabbing me.

"I think she's bleeding too much," she said.

Timmy held Faith and Chloe's head lolled to the side.

"Please help her," Timmy pleaded through tears.

A gust of wind and a towering wave crashed into Insepth's land bridge, crumbling parts of it. "I can't hold it, Ember! We have to go now!" he yelled.

Preston faced me. "Tell me what to do," he said calmly.

He was ready to die. I saw it in his eyes.

"Help me get Chloe up. We have to get to shore."

"But the monsters are waiting for us!" Maddie said.

Chloe's voice was weak, but her words sharpened in my mind. "Save baby Faith. There's no time…"

"We're not leaving you," I said.

"You can't save anyone if you're dead!" Insepth complained, but he sunk down beside Preston and helped pick Chloe up.

My Gaia was mostly drained, but the small amount I had left I gave to Chloe, healing as much of her insides as I could.

A crash of lightning lit the black sky and I saw the shadow of a horse falling through the clouds. I followed the plunging image as it hit the surface of the river with a great splash.

The roof ripped off and wind pummeled my face. The boat's walls broke apart, and then we were lying on the rocks and dirt that Insepth had worked so desperately to hold together. Wings flapped in the sky and a loud laugh shook the air.

"Nice try, love. But I grow weary of this game. It must end," Samael said with a booming Angelic voice.

I didn't look up. Maddie grabbed my hand, pulling me with her. I bumped into Timmy who was holding his baby tightly. His eyes were hooded in fear when he turned and held Faith out to me.

"Take her, Ember. Take her to safety. I have to stay with Chloe."

"No, we're going together," I said, but I followed Timmy's gaze along the shore.

To my horror, Hell beasts scrambled from the shore onto the rocky bridge, coming for us. Insepth and Preston set Chloe down and she wobbled. It was Maddie who took Faith from Timmy so he could help his wife.

There was nowhere to go. We were surrounded. Debris-filled waves slammed the sides of Insepth's creation and monsters blocked the only way to shore. The sky above was filled with Fallen Angels and the Devil himself was there, waiting to strike.

Insepth wasn't giving up. He crashed the part of his bridge covered with the evil beings into the raging river, and he hurled boulders into the sky at the Dark Angels.

I saw Eae go down and Cricket rear up as the creatures pushed against her. The screams of the children were drowned out by the barking of a frenzied Hell hound.

Sorrow wrenched through me. I'd tried so hard to prevent this from happening, but I had failed. Everyone I loved was going to be murdered in the most horrific ways imaginable. I couldn't stop it.

Faith's cries reached my ears and I closed my eyes. Faith was all I had now.

Lord, forgive me for being so arrogant to think I could stop Your wishes. I see now what a fool I've been. But please, please save my family and friends. Don't let them suffer.

"It's a little late for prayers to Him, love."

I opened my eyes, and Samael was suspended in the air above me. His black hair blew back from his handsome face, and his white shirt was perfectly clean. It struck me once again at how Samael didn't look like what I'd always imagined the Devil to be. "But if you pray to me, I'll save them from the gruesome deaths awaiting them. I'll save them all, sweet Ember."

His voice was warm honey and the world quieted around me. The burning city and raging river disappeared. I could barely hear Faith crying.

I could save them from being torn apart. And how easy it would be.

Samael smiled with twitching lips, and I began to open my mouth when I spotted the glowing ball at his shoulder. It darted in front of me and a cool mist spread out below it.

Ila stared at me with a stern face and Riley yipped at her feet. The apparition lasted only a few seconds when Samael's wing smashed through it, scattering it on the wind.

You can win without surrendering your soul.

The words were just a murmur in my ear.

My elements surged to life and I opened up to them, letting them fill me.

"You're making a mistake, love. Even if you summoned all of your power and were fresh and strong, you couldn't beat me. I'll kill you, and then I'll let my pets eat the rest of your party. The baby will be my special snack, and you'll be the cause of it all."

For an instant Samael's face contorted and became sunken and skeletal. His teeth were like daggers and his fingers long and bent. This was what the Devil really was—he had been deformed by his evilness, just as Sin had been altered from her time in Hell, changing from an Angel into dragon form.

I had glimpsed his true face. But should I trust that Ila was right, that I really had a chance at beating the Devil and his army? If she was wrong, I was condemning my loved ones to gruesome deaths and perhaps no afterlife.

But I'd seen what had happened to Sawyer when he'd made a deal with the Devil. I wasn't going to make the same mistake.

I narrowed my eyes, standing straighter. "I think you're afraid of me."

His glorious face returned and his chuckle turned into a hearty laugh. The vibrating sound rolled across the river and echoed between the buildings.

"Help me do this, God," I asked before raising my hands and closing my eyes.

Even with my Gaia diminished, it still streaked out of me, joined by Fire, Water, and Air. The four elements weaved together in a tightly intricate pattern. The pattern grew into a steady stream that I aimed at Samael.

"Ember, no!" I heard Insepth shout.

As the elements left me, I felt my life being torn away.

The sky exploded into a million beautiful falling stars, and then there was nothing.

CHAPTER 31

EMBER

"Open your eyes, Ember. It's over."

I knew it was Insepth speaking, but the words were fuzzy, distant sounding. My head throbbed and something sharp jabbed into my back. My lids were heavy and my stomach rolled.

I couldn't ignore the prodding hands or stifled crying. I was afraid to open my eyes, but I blinked, seeing purple dots and darkness.

Through cracked lips, I said, "Is he dead?"

Insepth's face sharpened into focus. Tears made trails down his smudged face. His blond curls whipped around his head in the wind and his lips quivered.

"You tried—you gave it everything you had—but it wasn't enough."

His words shot through my mind like a bullet and I pushed up on shaky knees.

The strange bubble of quiet that I'd been in when Insepth had first spoken disappeared and the world came to life with sickening madness.

A few feet away, Preston and Maddie huddled together. Maddie's mouth moved and her eyes were closed. She was praying—and she was still holding Faith.

Chloe was crumpled on the rocks and Timmy stood in front of her, holding a broken oar in the air. Disjointed creatures with gray, slick skin, crawled out of the river and onto the rocks. Their eyes were dead and meat clung to their teeth. I couldn't see Eae or Cricket. They had disappeared in a sea of monsters.

It was difficult to move my mouth and tears stung my cheeks. "What happened?"

Insepth's arms went around me and he whispered, "You released everything you had, and many Dark Angels fell from the sky, but not Samael. He fled."

"We have to help them," I choked out.

"We're spent—we've done everything we can." The sky lit up, but Insepth's hands held my face, forcing me to look at him. "I regret many things in my life, now more than ever. But you gave me something I never thought I'd have, and I'm forever your servant for that gift. I love you, Ember."

His Earth trickled in, entwining with the little bit of Gaia I had left. They blended, filling me with peace.

"Kill her!" Samael called out from the clouds.

"Don't look," Insepth begged, trying to hold my face against his, but I found some strength and pulled back.

I turned toward the heat. Creatures and Hell beasts dropped away, allowing something to pass by. My heart suddenly came to life, pounding in my rib cage.

It was Sawyer.

His red eyes were fixed on me. Flames sprang to life wherever his feet touched the ground. His expression was hard and pale, and his lips were cruel.

He moved with demon speed and raised a large, blood-stained sword he carried into the air. Insepth turned and flung his arms wide, shielding me with his body.

The sword fell, piercing Insepth's chest.

No, no, no...

Insepth slumped and his blood spilled onto my hands. He blinked up at me with pained brows, mouthing something I couldn't understand. When the light left his eyes, I finally looked up.

Samael hovered above Sawyer. "Kill her—kill her now," he prodded gently in an almost hypnotic drawl.

Sawyer raised the sword again.

I was ready to die, along with everyone else I loved. But not this way—not by Sawyer's hand. And Samael knew it. He understood that being murdered by my former lover and friend was even worse than death.

"Please, Sawyer, you don't have to listen to him." My throat burned and my voice cracked. Insepth's blood was all over me and Faith was crying. The world seemed to pause, waiting, as the sword trembled in midair.

Sawyer's eyes glowed a blistering red and his pale skin was stretched tightly over his face. His hair fell in matted tangles around his head, and his clothes were splattered with blood. Where had my beautiful Sawyer gone? This monster glaring down at me certainly wasn't the man I knew and loved. Samael had corrupted Sawyer, tainted him with an evil so foul that I couldn't undo it.

He was lost to me.

I remembered the first time I'd seen Sawyer, and our first kiss. From the beginning, there had been an intense connection between us. I'd known he was a Demon, but I hadn't been afraid of him. I sensed goodness in him. He hadn't approved of what his Demon leader, Garrett, was doing to humans. There had been compassion in him that Ila and Ivan had recognized. And he'd only made a deal with the Devil to save me. It had always been about protecting me.

The swell of hatred I'd felt toward Sawyer for killing Insepth, my friends, and my dog, dissolved into tattered numbness. I blew out a deep breath, and I let it all go. The resentment and smoldering anger I'd carried with me since the day my parents had died disappeared, and my raging heart quieted. I was filled with a feeling of contentment I had never experienced before.

"I love you, Sawyer. I forgive you," I said.

I lifted my chin and closed my eyes, waiting for the end to come.

CHAPTER 32

SAWYER

I love you, Sawyer. I forgive you. The burning flame that had filled my vision for so very long lifted and I *saw* Ember.

She crouched on the rocks, and her dirty face was wet with tears. I heard the mad beating of her heart and felt the stir of her breath in the air. Insepth lay dead at her side and her brother swiped furiously at Hell's soldiers, defending his wife. The human football player and Ember's cheerleader friend huddled nearby, and I briefly wondered what they were doing here.

Then I heard the crying of a baby and my eyes shifted to search out the sound. The humans were holding a squirming, naked child, wrapped in a bloody blanket. I could smell the remnants of afterbirth still clinging to its newborn skin. I also sensed the familial connection to Ember.

All of these observations happened in an instant, and the place where my soul should have been swelled with horror. Years of soul eating pummeled my mind. *I am evil, I have always been evil.* But the day I'd seen fiery Ember walking out of the school with Ivan, everything changed. She had touched a part of me that had lain dormant for more than a hundred years. My humanity had been rekindled and I'd come alive. Ember had given me the one thing I'd craved most in the terrifying world that I belonged to—and she didn't even know it.

"You are a soulless Demon. If my Father gets His way, you will suffer an eternity of pain for your sins. But if we succeed, you will be a revered member of my court. I will give you everything your heart desires. But first, you must kill the Watcher girl. She is your enemy. She stands in the way of your true salvation," Samael whispered to me. "*Do it. Do it now.*"

I screamed and swung the sword.

CHAPTER 33

EMBER

Sawyer's wail made me dare to look. There was a *whoosh* of wind in my face, as the blade passed over my head and flew through the air with a hissing sound.

Samael's eyes widened but he wasn't quick enough. The sword pierced his chest and he fell backward onto his own writhing soldiers. His bellow reached over the river and onto the shore. Hell beasts scurried away from the flapping black wings, knocking against each other and sending others jumping into the water.

Sawyer's eyes were brown once again and his features softened, returning to their former handsomeness. Tears trailed over his cheeks as he held out his hand.

I didn't hesitate and grabbed for it.

I was once again in the protection of his glorious arms. His black hair tickled the sides of my face when he said, "You are my love and my life."

Sawyer's lips touched mine and my Fire awakened, giving me the strength to cling to him.

I drew in a shaky breath. "You killed Samael."

His hand pressed into my stomach. "I did it for our family," he groaned into my ear.

He stepped back and a red stain spread across his shirt. The gleaming end of a blade stuck out of his chest.

I screamed and covered the wound with my own hand, pushing my Gaia into him. His mouth lifted in a slight smile as he buckled forward. Preston rushed over to catch him, and helped me lower him to the ground.

The sword had entered his back and sliced through his heart. My Gaia couldn't help him because he was already dead.

Samael's maniacal laughter spun me around. There was a slash in his white shirt and blue blood stained it, but his wound had already healed.

"I'm immortal, love. A simple sword blade cannot kill the Prince of Darkness."

His words meant nothing. Sawyer had saved me again, and died for it. Insepth was gone, and Eae and Cricket, too. Timmy embraced Chloe and creatures crawled over them. Uriel and Raphael hadn't come to save us. And neither had God.

All was lost.

Maddie placed Faith in my arms. The baby stopped crying and gazed up at me with an open mouth. I brought her against my heart and held her tightly as Preston stepped in front of us.

"I might not have superhuman powers or wings, but dammit, you're not going to kill my friends or this baby!" he shouted at Samael.

Samael's black wings unfurled and he smiled. "Don't worry little man. I won't kill them for a long time. Death would be too easy."

A familiar screech vibrated in the sky and I lifted my face to the sound. Something like fire streaked through the clouds and my insides were awakened.

"It can't be…" Samael hissed.

He took flight, and just as his feet left the ground, he was snatched out of the sky.

Chumana's claws held him tightly and she dove into the abyss that led directly to Hell. An explosion of smoke followed her decent. The creatures dropped where they were, their distorted features changing back to human forms, and the Hell beasts and three-headed hounds exploded into puffs of black dust. The dark particles streamed back into the hole that was caving in before my very eyes.

The rock bridge that Insepth had created was breaking apart. The river rose, reclaiming its banks. Preston grabbed my hand and tugged me along with Maddie. I held onto Faith and searched the place where Timmy and Chloe had been. I saw a hand reach out from beneath the pile of now ordinary bodies, covered in tattered clothing.

"There!" I shouted, stopping Preston.

He saw the hand too, and went to it, pushing the dead away. Timmy scampered up, pulling Chloe with him.

I met Timmy's relieved gaze, and when he saw that I held Faith in my arms, his face brightened.

"No time!" Preston urged us forward, helping Timmy carry Chloe over the rocks.

Maddie clutched my arm and together we stumbled toward shore. I glanced over my shoulder just as a wave took Sawyer's and Insepth's bodies away.

The baby in my arms and the friend holding onto me were the only things keeping me from turning back. The river rose, carrying away corpses and wreckage, and putting out the many fires with a sizzle. Timmy hoisted Chloe onto the bank, and Preston offered his hand to Maddie, who grasped it.

The rising flood caught my legs and knocked me under. I tightened my hold on Faith, lifting her up to keep her above water. I called on my Tempest, but felt nothing at all. It was as if it wasn't there anymore.

The giant hole that Chumana had plunged into had been was completely covered by the fast moving river.

Panic clenched my stomach as I struggled to stay afloat in the current. I heard a splash and I bumped into something. Hot breath snorted at the back of my head. I reached out and grasped Cricket's mane. Her strong muscles worked hard to go against the flow of the water as we inched closer to shore.

Before we reached the bank, Timmy jumped into the river and met us. He held onto me and Faith as Cricket pulled us the rest of the way to safety.

When we made it to shore, I handed Faith to Timmy and leaned against Cricket, my arms slipping around her neck. She nickered and touched her nose to the side of my head.

Are you all right, girl? I thought I had lost you. Where are the Horsemen? I implored with my mind, but there was only silence as a reply. I pulled back and looked into the horse's large brown eye. *Can you hear me, Cricket? Talk to me!* Again, only silence.

I reached for my Gaia and there was nothing. I shuddered and grasped at the Fire.

My heart pounded in my ears. There was only emptiness in the place where my elements had been. It was different than when the Watchers had used their combined powers to sever my connection to the elements. That time I'd still felt the powers just beyond my grasp. This time there was nothing at all, as if they'd never even existed.

Sunbeams sliced through the clouds and onto the still smoldering city in long, brilliant streaks. Other than the buzzing sound of helicopters overhead, everything was quiet. There weren't any strange storms or Angels zipping around. It was just an ordinary sky. A cool, misty breeze lifted from the river and I inhaled. It carried with it the scent of life.

A hand closed around mine and I looked up.

"He hasn't abandoned us after all," Maddie said.

Her usually perfectly styled black, shiny hair was a complete mess, and the side of her face was bruised. Dried blood smeared her arm and her clothes were torn in many places, but she was smiling broadly.

I hesitated, not sure what to say. In the end, Sawyer had saved me, but he'd died in the process. And so had Insepth and many others.

I should have been relieved that it was over at last, but I wasn't. A dragon had saved us, not God.

Faith's cry snapped my head sideways. Chloe was sitting up with the baby in her lap and Timmy was beside her. My brother and his wife were teary-eyed and sniffing as they stared down at their baby, born during the Apocalypse. The heavy weight in my chest lifted at the sight.

Not far behind my family were the three children Eae had rescued. The littlest girl was in Preston's arms. Emily held his hand and Joey was talking, motioning at things with sweeping gestures. Eae was nowhere to be found.

People began to appear in the street, walking in small, dazed-looking groups. The wonderfully familiar sound of sirens filled the air. The river had washed away most of the carnage, but there were still bodies lying around. It seemed that the humans that had been transformed into spiderlike creatures, returned to normal when Chumana took Samael away. But they were still dead. The Hell beasts had turned to dust and followed their master back to Hell. I wondered how history would retell what had happened here. I wasn't sure myself. At that moment, it just felt like a really bad dream.

I caught a glimpse of a ball of light. It danced above the rubble, and then darted behind the debris of the collapsed bridge.

"I need a moment alone," I told Maddie.

Her brows raised and her hand stopped me. "Are you okay?"

I forced a smile. "I'm fine. It's just a lot to absorb—you know?" I lifted my chin in Preston's direction. "I think he can use your help with those kids."

Maddie followed my gaze and nodded. When she looked back at me, there was sadness in her eyes. "I'm sorry about your friends, Ember. They sacrificed their lives for you—they wanted you to live."

She squeezed my hand and then walked away. I marveled at her ability to understand so well. Not so long ago, I had thought she was just an ordinary teenager. Now I knew why she'd been chosen to be a Scribe. The world would know what happened here because of her and Preston. They'd tell the story like it was.

I climbed up and over the twisted metal and chunks of pavement, causing fresh cuts on my legs and arms. I barely noticed though, as I made my way down to the water's edge. If I craned my neck, I could just see the tops of the tallest buildings and I could still hear sirens and the muffled calls of people in the distance. But in the shadow of the collapsed bridge, I was alone.

Bumps rose on my arms and a shiver raced up my spine. The sun brightened and I had to shield my eyes with my hand. I heard the flap of wings and felt cool wind on my face before I saw anything.

My heart pounded and I held my breath, squinting to see.

"Who's there?" I whispered into the light.

"It is I, your guardian Angel."

"Eae?"

"Yes, child. My wings have been restored."

The light dimmed enough that I could finally see him. Eae stood before me with his cool gray wings unfurled and spread wide. He wore a white tunic with a golden belt. His body glowed with a radiance that was almost blinding. And he was grinning.

"How did this happen?" I murmured.

"I chose to help the children and you. Even when all hope was lost, I kept faith in the Lord."

"He gave you your wings back?"

Eae's smile deepened. "And my first task was to bring this one from the water. His light was not completely distinguished and I was able to breathe life back into his body."

I followed Eae's gaze. A hard lump formed in my throat and tears welled in my eyes. Inseph lay beneath the Angel. His eyes were closed and his lips were parted.

"What about Sawyer?" I struggled the words out and met the Angel's sympathetic expression.

"That one I could not save. It was not his destiny to walk alongside you." Eae tilted his head and his voice softened. "But he earned salvation, and I'm here to bring him Home."

Eae stepped aside and the fog thinned, revealing Ila. Her gray hair was piled up neatly in a bun and her hand rested on Riley's head. She smiled, but I dragged my gaze from her to search deeper into the mist.

The haze separated and Sawyer stepped up. He was a ghost, like Ila, and I knew that if I ran into his arms, I'd pass right through him. I kept my feet rooted in place and stared.

"Thank you for saving me, Ember," he said.

"But you died for me." My lips shook.

The side of his mouth lifted. "My soul was saved because of your love. That love broke through the spell that bound me to Samael. You gave me a reason to believe."

I covered my mouth with both hands, swallowing down the tears with a quivering gulp.

"You're a strong girl, Ember. You'll be fine, even without the magical elements. I'll take care of Sawyer—he won't be alone," Ila said.

"Are they really gone?"

"I'm afraid so, my dear. It's all part of the reconstruction. Change can be good, and you have many more adventures awaiting you."

"It's time for me to take them Home," Eae said.

Eae's wings stretched wide, blowing my hair back. "Wait don't go, Eae. I have more questions!" I shouted.

"My time of walking by your side in this world has come to an end. But remember, I am always here, watching over you."

The three forms faded and the breeze began to carry them away.

I ran into the cool mist, reaching for Sawyer. "Wait, please, Sawyer. You said we were a family—what did you mean?"

He chuckled on the wind. *"Soon enough, you'll understand. As far as your magic is concerned, if anyone can work a miracle, it's you,"* Sawyer's voice touched my mind, like the brush of a butterfly's wings.

Riley barked and there was the sound of flapping wings. The wind that touched my face was warm and sweet smelling, sending tingles across my skin.

When they left, I expected the air to turn normal again, but the world was still swallowed with shimmering eternal brightness.

I spotted a dark figure through the blurry light and I followed it, stretching my legs to catch up.

"Stop! Who are you?" I shouted, breaking into a run when I thought the form would get away.

My feet squished into wet grass and the light dimmed, changing into the fog of a rainy afternoon. I stopped and looked around. Tombstones and old trees surrounded me. *I know this place.*

There was a monument close by, and I recognized my parents' names engraved on it. Raindrops splashed down harder and I wiped my eyes, swallowing hard.

"Are you so very surprised by who I Am?"

I turned slowly and faced the being who had spoken.

He was an old man, dressed completely in black except for a small square patch of white on his collar. He was standing under the thick branches of an ancient maple tree. Drips of water fell from the priest's black hat, one by one, the same as they did the day of my parent's funeral when I'd met him for the first time. It was the day my story began.

"Father Palano—what are you doing here?"

CHAPTER 34

EMBER

The priest smiled, tilting his head. "Do you remember what I told you the last time I saw you?"

A ray of sunlight cut through the clouds, landing on Father Palano. I shivered and my mouth was dry. "You told me that I was good, that there was light in me, and that I had a choice."

His head bobbed and his eyes lit up. "Yes, that's right. All of My children have choices." His smile thinned. "Sometimes they follow the path of goodness, and other times, they wander down a dark road."

"Your children?"

His gentle smile returned. "Nature and all its creatures. Angels. Mankind. Watchers. Growlers, dragons and even Demons. They're all My children."

A dozen questions flashed through my mind, but the only thing I managed to say was, "Where have You been?"

The rain stopped and a breeze rustled the wet leaves. The grass was dappled where the sun came through the tree branches. I inhaled the fresh air slowly and stared at His wrinkled face.

He chuckled. "I've been here all along—watching and waiting."

My courage grew, along with my curiosity, and my heartbeat quickened. "Waiting for what?"

"To see what you would do."

"Me? Why would my actions matter at all?"

He tipped his hat back, revealing a bit more of His still handsome features. "My child, you were the result of Uriel's poor choice and defiance." His bushy white brows scrunched. "I thought that because of My first children's sins, your kind would not have survived. But they did, becoming separate beings—different from Angels and men. I waited to see if balance would be restored without My direct intervention. But with your kind's evolution, the world became more unstable. And then you were born. A being that could wield all four elements, something akin to the Angels."

I felt sick. "All the horror and death is because I was born?"

He shook His head. "No, child. Samael rose up and unleashed Hell on earth because of the choices made by Angels, Watchers, and men over the course of thousands of years. You were simply the catalyst to their whimsy. Your birth tilted the balance too far toward a world of magic—and that I couldn't have."

Anger pumped through my veins. I remembered Oldport and my human friends—Lindsay, Randy, and Colby—and their terrible deaths. "So You let the Devil go on a killing rampage?"

His brow lifted, but His face remained relaxed and friendly. "Samael has been returned to Hell and the walls have been sealed. His time on earth is over."

"Yeah, because of Chumana," I retorted.

The wind gusted and leaves took flight, spraying into the air. I felt hot breath on the back of my neck and looked over my shoulder.

Chumana dropped her head to my eye level. Her red scales rippled when she mind spoke. *Little one, you speak unfairly to our Creator. It was He who instructed me to capture the Dark Lord and return him to his prison.*

I reached up and placed my hand on her leathery forehead. She closed her eyes and leaned into me. The vibrations of her drumming trill soothed my mind and spirit.

I'm glad you did what you did, but you should have killed the devil, I told her with my mind. I glanced at Father Palano, not too worried that He would strike me down for my thoughts. *If he's imprisoned, he could break free again someday.*

It was the Father who answered. "That is true. But balance had to be restored. In order to have goodness, there must be evil."

I looked up at the dragon. *But He let your kind be destroyed by Angels and men. Why do you listen to Him at all?*

Her laughter rattled my head. *My kind were not perfect. There were those among us who caused mischief in the world. The war between us was not one sided, like some wars.*

Her admission made me stand straighter, and I looked back at God. "Why are You disguised as a priest?"

His smile spread. "You couldn't even comprehend My true form, so I visited you in a way that your simple mind could relate to."

With my hand still resting on Chumana's snout, I swallowed and asked, "Why did You decide to stop Samael?"

"I saw a forsaken Angel, who had been mutilated by the off-spring of other Angels, offer up his life for three children he barely knew. A mother and father sacrificed their lives for a newborn, and two young people with strong faith followed My guidance. But for all that, it really came down to the moment that a Demon, fully corrupted by Hell and Samael's fury, chose to save you. That selfless act changed the course of the universe."

My chest heaved and more tears fell from my eyes.

"The pain will ease with time—I promise." He tipped his hat. "I must be going."

"Wait! Is magic really gone?"

His lips pinched together and His eyes narrowed. "I have cleansed the world from the taint the Angels made when they mingled with women so very long ago. Things will be the same, and yet different when you return."

"What happened to the Horsemen, and will I see Raphael and Uriel again?"

"The Horsemen have returned to their place in the stars. As far as the Angels are concerned, they are busy with reconstruction. Until the time you pass into the next life, you will not meet them again."

His face relaxed. "Some partings are a sign of good things to come."

The sun brightened, obscuring Him in a hazy glow that spread across the tombstones and through the trees.

Chumana stepped heavily past me, entering into the light.

"Will I see you again?" I called after Chumana.

On special nights, when the moon is full and the wind whispers long forgotten stories, I'll meet you in your dreams. Her wings spread wide and she pushed off.

I shielded my eyes from the brilliance and tucked my chin when a blast of air hit me. The sounds of sirens and voices shouting broke the quiet and I opened my eyes to the lapping waters of the riverside.

I dropped beside Insepth and gave him a gentle shake.

He groaned and opened his eyes. "Are we in Heaven?"

I barked out a short laugh.

The river water was brown and fast moving and filled with bobbing debris. The bridge was still collapsed and pockets of smoke billowed above the city. So many people had died. Sawyer was gone and Cricket was just a horse again. But sunshine warmed my head and Timmy walked toward me with little Faith in his arms.

I had finally talked to God.

Things had turned out better than I thought they would.

CHAPTER 35

EMBER

The breeze through the open car window carried with it the scents of pine needles and dried leaves. We turned the corner and the tangle of nature thinned, revealing the rock wall. The shade lifted and Ila's long, green valley came into view. Yellow flowers dotted the meadow and the surrounding hills rose up in brilliant autumn splendor. The places that had been burnt were covered with fallen leaves and even the swath of downed trees blended in with the live ones. Like nothing bad had ever happened here.

I leaned farther out the window. The mountain air invigorated my senses. Broken boards were piled high where the barn had once stood and the flock of chickens pecked the ground around it. I spotted several long-eared rabbits in the yard and a cat lounging on the wall.

But it was the barking that made my stomach do a somersault. Before Timmy had the car stopped, I swung the door open and jumped out. I ran the rest of the way up the driveway, not stopping until Angus and I collided. He licked my face and whimpered, and I mumbled silly compliments into his fur.

I heard the vehicles roll to a stop behind me, but didn't bother to look back. Angus was in my arms, and at the moment, that's all that mattered.

"Have you been a good boy? I bet you have," I cooed to him.

Angus' tail thumped the gravel on the driveway when I stood up. I kept my hand on his head as I faced everyone.

Preston had parked his pickup truck alongside the wall, and was opening the horse trailer door to bring Cricket out. Maddie stood beside the gate, waiting for him. I focused on Timmy and Chloe, who were taking Faith out of the infant car seat. Chloe moved slowly, obviously sore and tired from the apocalyptic birth a few days earlier. Timmy, on the other hand, had a spring to his step as he took the baby from his wife and walked up to me.

Insepth stood back. He glanced at me and then away, seeming distracted and uncomfortable. A tightness formed in my chest as I looked at him. Ever since he'd woken, he'd been strangely quiet. I knew part of the reason was his disconnect with the earth, but I sensed there was something else going on with him.

"Are you sure about this, Ember? We'd love to have you live with us in Ohio," Timmy said, handing Faith to me when I held out my hands for her.

Faith's dark blue eyes stared and she shook a tiny, balled fist. I squeezed her hand and clucked to her. The baby was born a couple of months premature, but she was eight pounds and completely healthy. My Gaia had saved her, and now that power was gone forever. I tried to push the thought aside, not wanting to dwell on the loss.

"I'll visit—I promise. But after everything that has happened, I need some down time."

Timmy ran his hand through his hair and snorted. "Yeah, I know what you mean. I don't think I'll ever really understand what went on back there—it's kind of a blur now."

If it wasn't for Faith's weight in my arms, I might have pretended it had all been a nightmare myself. I still remembered everything vividly—from people becoming spider-like creatures and eating each other, to the Hell-beasts and hounds pouring into the city. It had been a scene from a horror movie and something no one should ever forget. But people were forgetting—droves of them. Cell phone and cable TV services were back up and running, and at first, news stories showed interviews with people who'd seen monsters rampaging through the city, men with swords flying through the sky, and horses galloping in the storm clouds. Many people had survived and seen the chaos, but as the days passed, fewer of them talked about the supernatural causes of what they'd witnessed, focusing on natural disasters, like the earthquake that shook Los Angeles, and the tornado and floods in Cincinnati. Sure, I knew that these weren't normal weather phenomena—that the boundaries breaking between earth and Hell had caused all of them. But to everyone else, all the memories of monsters and magical creatures were quickly being forgotten.

I looked up and Timmy had his arm around Chloe and her head rested on his shoulder. Maybe it was for the best for everyone to forget.

"Are you going to be all right living up here alone?" Chloe asked. "I'm not comfortable with you being so isolated and taking care of yourself. You're barely an adult."

Her blonde hair was short and spiked and the stud on her nose glistened in the sun. Even though she was in her twenties, she seemed younger than me. But then, she hadn't seen everything I had over the past few months, and she didn't know the things I did. She hadn't battled with otherworldly powers or killed people. In truth, she was innocent compared to me.

"I'll be fine. I have my dog and my horses to keep me company."

I shifted my gaze to Insepth. He had the lead rope of a chubby Quarter Horse between his hands. Piper's mom had gladly given the gelding to me when I'd visited her the day before. She was one of the lucky ones who had survived, but without her daughter, she was filled with a deep sadness that had nearly overwhelmed me when we'd met. It hadn't been that long ago that my dear friend had been accidently murdered by Insepth and the other Watchers. Even though I'd forgiven him, accepting that he really didn't know that severing her connection to Eae would bring back the cancer that should have killed her when she'd been a child. It was done and I couldn't go back, and having her beloved horse here with me lessened the pain slightly that still filled my insides at the loss of my closest friend. Plus Cricket had her best friend back, and that was even more important. For a moment, I wondered if she remembered the love she had shared with the Horseman, and then I shook my head. Many of my questions would never be answered now.

Maddie opened the gate, and Preston and Insepth led the horses into the meadow. They unsnapped the halters at the same time. Cricket tossed her head and whinnied before she dug her hooves into the dirt and took off. Rhondo bucked and snorted, chasing after her. The black mare slowed to a prancing strut so Rhondo was able to catch up to. She nipped at him, but he didn't shy away. When they reached the herd of goats, there was a flurry of rearing and bucking before the pair finally settled down and dropped their heads into the grass.

I exhaled at the sight of the horses and goats grazing. Things would never be the same, but they were good.

"Don't worry about Ember. She is going to be fine," Timmy said. He put his arms around me and brought his lips to my ear. "Thank you for saving us."

I kissed Faith on her forehead and gave her back to my brother, wiping a tear away from the corner of my eye. "Take care of the little munchkin. Next time I see her, she's getting in the saddle with me."

Chloe's eyes rounded, but Timmy chuckled. "I guess with you as her aunt she has no choice but to become an equestrian," he said.

"That's for sure," I replied.

A lump formed in my throat as I followed the little family back to their vehicle and watched them get in.

"We love you, Ember." Timmy held his hand out the driver's side window and I took it in both of mine.

"I love you all, too."

"Don't be a stranger, and stay out of trouble!" Chloe called out the window.

The silver SUV bounced down the gravel driveway, sending a cloud of dust spraying into the air. When they had turned the corner, out of sight, I finally faced Preston and Maddie.

"I'll unhitch the trailer and then I better get Maddie home," Preston said.

I noticed his hand on her back and how she stood close to him. I glanced between them and sensed the beginning of a romance. I couldn't keep my smile from spreading. Preston must have read my thoughts. His face reddened and he removed his hand and hurried back to the trailer.

"My mom wants Joey, Sarah, and Emily to stay with us until we can locate any living family they might have out west," Maddie said, shrugging. The corner of her mouth lifted high. "Mom's really in her element taking care of them." She snorted softly. "I got the feeling they're going to be with us for a while. But Preston and I will come back over the weekend to check on you, and perhaps even bring the kids up to see the animals."

I nodded absently. "That would be nice," I was unable to stop myself from asking the question I'd been holding in for hours. "Do you remember what actually happened?"

Maddie raised her face to the sun, closing her eyes. "I'm a Scribe of God. I remember everything. When things settle down and Oldport is rebuilt, I'm going to begin writing about it."

I exhaled in relief. "Everyone else is forgetting. I was a little worried it would happen to you and Preston."

Maddie looked back at me with clear brown eyes. "I think our Lord wants to help them heal. If they all knew that monsters really existed, there would be fear and chaos. It's easier if people believe that it was only a plague of natural disasters."

"But what about the real story you're writing? No one will believe you."

Maddie smiled, hugging her sweater tightly around her when the breeze picked up, sending a bunch of leaves dancing all around us. "It's kind of the same thing with the Bible, isn't it? Miracles and stories about Heaven and Hell, Angels and Demons, are believed by those who have faith—and that's who this story will be for."

I cocked my head. She was right. Perhaps memories were stolen from people so that they wouldn't remember, and they'd need faith. It was the type of question that would keep me from sleeping, I was sure.

I stepped closer and lowered my voice. "I met Him, Maddie. I talked to God."

"I know. He told me."

My brows rose and I shook my head. This beautiful cheerleader was constantly surprising me.

She gave me a tight hug and then wagged a finger at me. "No more trying to save the world. We've been given a second chance, and we should all rejoice. Life is sweet."

"Don't worry about that. My powers are gone. I'm just an ordinary girl now."

Maddie left me with a laugh, and said, "It wasn't those crazy abilities that made you special, Ember. It was just you."

Insepth joined me and we quietly watched Maddie and Preston head down the driveway. I waved back as hands came out the windows. The act of doing something so normal was comforting.

"It's time. We have to see what's happened to our friends," Insepth said, eyeing me with a serious face.

"I know." My skin tingled as I started up the dirt path leading to the little log cabin.

CHAPTER 36

EMBER

The frost had killed Ila's flowers and only wilted stems and dried petals remained. I went ahead of Insepth, passing my red pickup truck and taking the porch steps two at time. Angus inclined his head, looking up when I paused at the door. The stiff breeze made the rocking chairs go back and forth and I shivered. I was nervous and reached for my powers, but of course, they weren't there.

"You spent most of your life not knowing about the elements or working with their powers, and the loss affects you so. Think how difficult it is for me after nearly three hundred years of touching the Earth's power."

Insepth's blond curls blew around his chiseled face. He looked like he was twenty-five and I often forgot how old he really was. I wondered how he would handle the aging process, but it was his keen ability to read my thoughts that made me stiffen.

"How did you know that's what I was thinking about?"

The side of his mouth lifted for the first time in days. I didn't realize how much I'd missed his arrogant smirk until just that moment.

"Nothing magical, I assure you. Over the centuries, I've become very adept at reading people—I guess it's one of the few abilities I still have."

"It's hard for you, isn't it?"

He shrugged. "Of course. We were practically immortal, and now" —he spread his hands wide—"we're just like everyone else."

"It's going to be an adjustment. You'll be okay," I offered, not sure I was telling the truth.

"The thing I hate most is not feeling nature. As we drove up the mountain, I longed to reach out to the trees with my senses or to take flight with the majestic hawk in the sky. Those days are gone and I feel completely empty."

My chest tightened. It had only been a few months ago that I'd first touched Fire and Earth. My time with Water and Air was even shorter, but still, I felt as if I'd lost an organ. I could only imagine how bleak it felt for Insepth.

I grasped his arm and his blue eyes darkened as he leaned in. He stopped just short of my mouth.

"Perhaps I'm feeling a little something after all." He grinned and I pulled back, swatting his arm.

Butterflies erupted in my belly and my cheeks burned. I pushed the door open, wanting to escape his laughing eyes and pouting lips. Our relationship had never been decided. I wasn't even sure what I wanted it to be.

Cold wind stirred through the window, lifting the red curtains in the air. I shoved the window down and looked around. Colorful quilts were still draped on the couch and chairs the same as when I'd left. The charred scent of the remnants from a fire in the stone fireplace hung lightly in the room, and late afternoon sun spilled in through the paned glass. The door leading into the bedroom was ajar and the one to the storeroom was closed. The books were still overflowing the shelves. When my eyes paused on the pile of dishes in the sink and the plate on the table with a half-eaten pancake, my heart sped up and my gaze met Insepth's.

He crossed the room and peeked into the bedroom and storeroom in turn. After shaking his head, I went through the back door and down the steps.

"Where is everyone?" Insepth said, jogging to catch up to me.

I lifted my chin and pointed as we entered the forest. "Over there. I see smoke."

"I wonder what we're stumbling into…" Insepth muttered, trailing off when I shot him a stern look. His grin returned. "You can't shoot fire from your fingertips any longer. Don't forget that."

"Yeah, and no one else can, either," I huffed, lengthening my stride with Angus running beside me.

I ignored the branches that scraped my arms and skipped over exposed roots and rocks on the trail. I'd first taken this path a long time ago. It led to the place I had learned to wield Fire. Ila had been with me, teaching me about the plants and animals of the forest. I shook my head, erasing the images from my mind. It seemed like a hundred years ago that she had guided me through the trees, and so much had happened since then. Ila and Sawyer had died, and without the power of the elements, I'd never see them again in this life. The only conciliation I had was that they were together, wherever they were.

The smell of wood smoke became stronger and I sped up. Angus entered the clearing first, barking. I stopped and Insepth bumped into me.

The sight that greeted us took my breath away.

CHAPTER 37

EMBER

"**Finally, you've returned** from the greatest story," Horas said, rising from the log he sat on. He held a glass of dark liquid in his hand and he raised it to us.

Ivan jumped off the log he shared with Tamira and ran over. He nearly brought me down when he slammed into me.

There wasn't the familiar musky scent of wolf clinging to him, and when he leaned back, I saw that his eyes were no longer golden. They were light brown and moist with tears.

For a moment neither of us could speak. When he'd finally sucked in the emotions, he blurted out, "What has happened to us, Ember. I am only human. The wolf is gone."

When I began to speak, my voice cracked and I paused. The loss Insepth and I were feeling was nothing compared to what poor Ivan was experiencing. He'd spent most of his life in wolf form and now it was forever lost to him.

"I'm so sorry. I had no idea this would happen if we succeeded." I put my hand on his chest. "I'm no longer a Watcher, and neither is Insepth."

"The Demon has left me as well," Horas chimed in. He shook hands with Insepth, who slapped him on the back, and pulled me into a quick hug with his one free hand. When he stepped back his eyes twinkled. "I can't say as I miss my former self. I'll have to get used to surviving only on human food, instead of the souls of convicts and predators, and the other limitations, but it's a small price to pay for freedom after a thousand years of servitude to the Dark One."

"I wasn't sure about Demons. I was afraid you'd be pulled into Hell with the rest of the Hell beasts," I admitted, taking a seat beside Tamira. She smiled and looked away, fidgeting with her fingers in her lap.

"That was probably the fate of many of my kind, but I'm proof that those of us who tried to live as morally correct a life as possible, could find redemption in the end." He returned to his stump, and Insepth picked up a stick and squatted beside the fire, pushing the burning logs around.

I sat straighter and glanced around. "Where's Lutz?"

Horas and Ivan exchanged glances. It was Ivan who answered me. "When it happened, Lutz was in bear form and that's how he stayed." When my mouth dropped, he quickly added, "He lives in the woods like an ordinary bear now. He can't mind speak anymore, and ignores me when I follow him." He shrugged and smiled a little. "He's happy, though. I'm sure of that. He liked being a bear more than a man."

"The same happened to Cricket," I said in a weak voice.

Silence hung over the clearing. Even the breeze quieted. The birds stopped singing and the trees sighed.

Horas cleared his throat, interrupting the melancholy, and turned his sharp gaze on me. "How did this come to be? Forgive my impatience, but the day we all changed," he motioned to Ivan and Tamira, "was sudden and quite dramatic."

Insepth continued to push the firewood around and nodded for me to tell the story. A quiver raced through me as I thought back on my arrival in the city. Maybe in time I'd share all the details, but not at this moment. I didn't want to mar our reunion with too much talk of the sinister things Insepth and I had seen.

"It was like the vision Youmi showed us. People became evil, crawling creatures. Beasts and hounds flooded out of a chasm that opened in the river. The humans fought back, firing missiles into the city, but they weren't powerful enough against Samael and his Dark Angels." I closed my eyes, remembering the chaos in the skies above Cincinnati. "It was awful. Buildings exploded and fires burned in the streets. Eae found us in the wreckage and saved us." I looked up. Horas and Ivan were wide eyed and even Tamira had perked up and was staring.

"He had three little kids with him, and just as we were changed, so was he. He got his wings back."

"I'm glad to hear that," Horas said.

"So he's a real Angel again?" Ivan asked.

I rubbed Angus' head and he whined, flopping down on my feet. "I don't think he ever stopped being an Angel."

Ivan nodded. "Did you destroy Samael?"

I smiled. "I tried, I really did. But he was too powerful for me and Insepth. War and Conquest put up a good fight, too, but it wasn't them, either." Seeing Horas open his mouth, I intercepted his question. "They returned to the stars. At least that's what God said."

Horas' hands went up. "You talked to God?"

"Yeah, but I'll tell you about that later." The sun disappeared behind the mountain and the air turned crisp. I leaned closer to the fire, holding my hands above the glorious warmth. I knew what would happen if I lowered them into the flames, but I was still tempted to do it to see if the fire would really burn me. That too was something to save for later. I looked up and everyone was watching me, even Insepth.

"It was Chumana who arrived and took Samael back to his prison in Hell. She picked him up with her clawed foot like she was scooping a fish out of a pond."

"And that ended the war?" Horas asked.

I shook my head and tears welled in my eyes. I wiped the wetness away with my sleeve and swallowed down the pain that had been shredding my heart.

"It seemed God needed proof of our worthiness—the descendants of Angels. It wasn't until Sawyer, a Demon in Samael's army, sacrificed himself for me that He was finally convinced. The Apocalypse ended because Sawyer loved me."

With a heavy sigh, Horas leaned back, and Ivan dropped his head into his hands.

"I knew deep down Sawyer wasn't evil. He came through in the end, saving us all," Ivan said.

Angus whimpered and I stroked his broad head, tilting my face to the heavens. Snowflakes began falling from the sky, one by one at first, and feathery soft. The cold taps felt good on my skin.

"It's snowing," Tamira muttered.

Ivan put his arm around her and she snuggled in deeper against him. Silence blanketed the forest as the snow fell harder and the fire sizzled. Sawyer had talked about spending a cozy winter together in Ila's cabin. It was something I didn't dare look forward to. From the beginning, I feared our love story would end tragically—and it had. I'd lost my love, but Sawyer had died so that I could live and I wouldn't squander his sacrifice. As difficult as it was, I had to move on and survive in this new world without magic and prophecies—without my guardian by my side.

I drew in a breath of cold, clean air. "Is anyone hungry?"

Ivan grinned. "I'm starving," he said quickly, dodging Tamira's hand as she swatted at him.

"You're always hungry," she teased.

"Some things never change." Horas stood. "I'll see what kind of supper I can scrounge up from the storeroom."

I rose with him. "What will you do with your new life?" I asked Horas.

Snowflakes peppered his black, wavy hair and his eyes became dreamy. "I wish to travel the world—only this time I'll see it from the eyes of a humble, good man, instead of a monster." He snorted lightly. "Who knows, perhaps I'll meet a beautiful woman who will enjoy the adventure with me."

"I want this to be your second home, Horas. You're always welcome," I said with a heavy spirit.

"I am glad for that. I have become quite fond of these mountains, and those that live here." His eyes glistened and he looked away, clucking to Angus. "Come, Angus. I believe there's a bowl of dog food waiting for you."

My dog looked up at me for approval and I motioned with my hand for him to go with Horas. He bounded into the darkness of the trees with the former Demon behind him.

"There was something I wanted to talk to you about," Ivan said. He pressed his ball cap down further on his head and shifted on his feet.

I became worried, my brows furrowing.

He inhaled and rushed the words out. "I would like to stay here in the valley with Tamira. We can build our own cabin and we'll help you care for the animals and do any work you need. Please don't make us leave."

I reached out and took both Ivan's and Tamira's hands. "Of course you can stay! I would be heartbroken if you left."

Tamira cried and Ivan smiled widely. "This makes me very happy. We are still a pack, and should stay together."

"I agree," I said, grinning back at him.

"Thank you," Tamira whispered when she hugged me. "We will be like sisters—I know it."

I nodded toward the path leading to the cabin. "Horas could probably use your help."

Ivan glanced at Insepth and back at me. "Yes, of course. If I am not there, he won't make enough food."

He was beaming as he passed by, dragging a willing Tamira along with him. When they were gone, I faced Insepth. He was still staring at the dwindling flames. Enough snow had fallen to cover the grass in a thin layer. The ground sparkled in the moonlight.

"It was good of you to allow them to build their home here. You won't be alone now." Insepth stood, raising his gaze.

My heart pounded and my legs felt weak. Until that moment, I hadn't realized how much I'd miss Insepth if he left. We had shared so much since we'd met. We'd battled each other, and worked together. I'd seen the softer, less arrogant side of the former Watcher. He loved nature and animals as much as I did. And he was loyal. He had been my mentor and my enemy. We'd shared a couple of passionate kisses when we thought we were about to die. There had been our mutual connection to the earth, and even though I denied it to myself for so long, my Gaia had wanted Insepth more than anyone else, even Sawyer. But now that my elemental powers were gone, did I still have feelings for him? The way my heart was breaking at the thought that he was leaving, said yes.

"What will you do?" The words came out in a cold puff of air.

He shrugged "I don't know. I have no family, and Sir Austin is gone. I've had many acquaintances in my life, but few true friends." He looked up and away. "I count you in that small number."

I drew in a deep breath and searched for whatever strength I still had. "Is that what I am to you, just a friend?"

Insepth stood up and took a step closer—close enough that if he leaned down, he could kiss me.

He licked his lips. "Sawyer gave his life for you on more than one occasion. He was your guardian and your lover. I saw the passion you had for him. From the first moment I laid eyes on you and felt your Gaia reach out to me, I wanted you for myself. At first, it was more of an acquisition, I admit, but later it turned into so much more. But I knew in my heart that you'd never have the feelings for me that you did for Sawyer."

"So the kisses we shared didn't mean anything to you?"

"On the contrary! They meant everything to me. But you never would have let them happen if we hadn't been in near death situations. I fear that you simply felt sorry for me or needed comfort. Being near you without ever having you, especially now that we're mere humans again, would be torturous. I will not subject myself to that kind of pain."

The forest was quiet and cold, and I was filled with sadness. The world hadn't ended, but so many sacrifices had been made—Sawyer, Ila, Piper, and the magic. It was all gone. I was exhausted. But there was a tiny spark when I looked into Insepth's hurting eyes—and that feeling gave me hope.

"What would make you happy, Insepth?" I whispered. Snow fell harder and I shivered, clutching my jacket around me tightly.

"To remain by your side, if you have feelings for me." His brows lifted as he searched my eyes. "Could you grow to love me, Ember?"

My heart swelled. "I already do."

Insepth's lips parted against mine. The kiss was urgent at first, but turned sweeter as snowflakes melted on my nose and his arms wrapped around me, pulling me into his coat and against his muscled chest.

He broke from the kiss. "And you're alright with me substituting as father to the child you carry?"

His words struck my mind with the ferocity a hundred freight trains. *Child?*

I tried to pull back, but he held me firmly against him. "Surely you had some inkling."

I shook my head and stared at him.

"I felt the pregnancy a few days ago. It was very early, but it was there. Now that my connection to the earth is gone, I'm not aware of such things—but you should be—if you pay attention to your own body."

"I'm having Sawyer's baby?" I gasped.

Insepth nodded, a small smile creeping up his lips. "I think he knew—at the end. He sensed it himself."

I did it for our family. That's what Sawyer had said to me when he was dying.

"He did know—somehow he knew." My voice cracked.

"You didn't answer my question," Insepth said.

I touched my stomach through my jacket. The pregnancy was bittersweet. The love of my life was dead, but he'd left a part of himself growing inside of me. Sawyer would always be with me. A tear trickled down my cheek that he'd never meet his own child. A thick mist drifted between the trees and the corners of my mouth lifted.

Maybe he could see, and Ila, too.

I wiped my cheek and took Insepth's hand. "I think you'd be a great dad. But are you really all right raising Sawyer's child?"

"I'm proud to do so." He lowered his head and kissed me again. I sighed into his mouth.

For the first time in so very long, I knew that everything would be okay.

EPILOGUE

lifted my face to the cool breeze as a cluster of golden leaves sprinkled down from the trees into the churning foamy water, spraying the nearest moss-covered boulders. If I closed my eyes, I could picture the day I'd sat on this same boulder and kissed Sawyer for the first time. Years had passed, but butterflies still pelted my insides when I thought about him. It was a sweet-stabbing feeling, and one I wouldn't trade for anything in the world.

A laughing squeal rose above the pounding of the falls. I turned toward the noise and my heart melted. Insepth sat in a pile of leaves beside the creek. In his lap sat a plump baby with curly blond hair and rosy cheeks. Little Ilan, named after my beloved mentor, Ila, clutched two fistfuls of leaves. When the brown-haired toddler ran straight for Insepth, with arms stretched out and his own fists jammed with leaves, he'd toss them at Ilan and my baby boy would squeal with delight.

"I would think my son would have more stealth," Ivan said with a chuckle.

"At least Quintus is quiet, unlike Ilan," I replied.

"That is true," Ivan agreed.

I faked him with a punch and he ducked away, laughing.

The wind suddenly gusted, lifting the leaves into the air and scattering them through the forest. I turned my face into the strange breeze, feeling a prickling sensation along the back of my neck. Goosebumps erupted on my arms and my insides buzzed.

"Do you feel that?" I whispered, not sure why I'd dropped my voice.

"It's something I have not felt for a long time," Ivan admitted, looking around, his eyes searching until he spotted Tamira. She was gathering mushrooms at the base of a large oak tree. I followed the wide trunk into the branches with my own gaze. That's where I found Violet. She was perched on the widest branch, holding out her sketch pad in front of her. She loved drawing pictures of the trees.

She was named after Sawyer's mother, a choice I'd thought would have made him very happy. Her hair was long and dark brown, and strands blew across her face. She was always pushing those tresses back behind her ears, reminding me of her father. Her eyes were wide spaced and shiny, the color of a wintertime blue sky. She was a skinny little thing for a seven year old—not much heavier than her younger brother. And she was a fearless child, always shimmying up trees or coaxing Rhondo next to the rock wall where'd she'd climb onto his back and gallop across the meadow, alongside Cricket, who'd kick up her hooves, seemingly encouraging the child's wildness.

My smile deepened as Violet stuck out her tongue in concentration when she stared hard at the waterfall, before she began scribbling in her notepad again. The cabin was full of her artwork—pictures of animals, trees, and the mountains. She had a stubborn streak that she could have inherited from me or Sawyer, and she was special. Not very long ago when I'd tucked her in, she'd told me how she'd talked to a nice old lady and a young, dark-haired man in her dream the night before. They were part of her family she'd said and the very next morning, she'd drawn pictures of them. Sure enough, she'd captured Ila and Sawyer's appearances perfectly.

A chill had raced over me and my heart had pounded as I'd held the pictures in my hand. I'd learned anything was possible, and would never say never, but after nearly eight years since the almost-ending of the world and the loss of my powers, it was difficult to believe in magical visits from the dead in dreams. But I supposed if it were possible for anyone, it would be for my fairy-like child.

The wind gusted harder and I looked up at the tops of the tall, swaying trees. Clouds moved swiftly through the darkening sky. A jagged streak of lightning sliced the clouds and I heard a rolling rumble.

"It is a strange storm," Ivan said, jumping to his feet. He motioned for his wife to come to him, and she grabbed her basket and ran over to us.

"Violet, climb down!" Inseph called out. He pulled Quintus into his lap beside Ilan, who had his arms wrapped around his daddy's neck.

"Do I have to?" Violet whined, closing her notebook and glancing between me and Inseph.

"Yes, please come down. A storm's coming and we don't want to get caught in it," I shouted over the moaning wind.

The branches of the old oak tree bent and vibrated, pelting us with dry leaves. I scrambled to my feet and carefully stepped across the boulder, jumping to the ground.

That's when a wicked gale blew through the forest, snapping branches and bending saplings to the ground. With horror, I saw a lightning bolt strike out from the clouds, hitting the oak tree that my daughter was in with a sickening, crunching explosion.

The limb Violet was on snapped, and she tumbled into the air. I screamed and lurched forward, but I was too far away to catch her.

Maybe it was out of pure instinct or maybe Insepth sensed something. But when that tree broke apart, he thrust his arm out and curled his hand the way he used to do when he summoned the power of the Earth.

The ground trembled and a nearby poplar tree shifted, bending unnaturally at Insepth's direction. Its wide, leaf-covered branches came together, catching Violet. The tree gently rolled her onto the ground before straightening back up to return to normal again.

I covered the distance to my little girl in a few long strides and gathered her into my arms. I pressed my face to hers. "Are you alright?"

"You're squeezing me too tight," she complained.

I rocked back on my heels and snorted, giving the child a kiss on her nose before I let her go. The sky brightened and the wind died down.

"What was that?" Ivan exclaimed, picking Quintus up.

Insepth stared at me with the hint of a smile on his lips.

I held out my hand. The delicious sensation of hot fire rushed through my veins.

And then a small flame rose on my palm.

Printed in the USA
CPSIA information can be obtained
at www.ICGtesting.com
LVHW011221100324
774065LV00035B/1153